Please feel free to send me
publisher filters these emails

Violet Samuels – violet_samuels@awesomeauthors.org

Sign up for my blog for updates and freebies!
violet-samuels.awesomeauthors.org

About the Publisher

BLVNP Incorporated, A Nevada Corporation, 340 S. Lemon #6200, Walnut CA 91789, info@blvnp.com / legal@blvnp.com

DISCLAIMER

Praise for Forgotten, Saved, Loved

So I thought that I would try and make this book last for a while but it was to addictive that I read the whole thing in one sitting. I really enjoyed hearing from Comrade's point and getting to be inside his head a bit more in this book. Absolutely loved and would highly recommend.

-Niki Bryce, Goodreads

As the second book to a wonderful series, Violet has done an amazing job to capture the audience's attention and has really portrayed comrade's feelings throughout the book with his struggles within himself and with his mate. This is a must buy if you loved the first book.

-Lesley Collis, Amazon

Words cannot explain how well this book was written. It is absolutely amazing! The way Comrade's P.O.V. is stated and how he is struggling with his life and his mate's is well written. I loved the first book and I most certainly loved this book too!

-Lisa M, Amazon

This book was amazing. I couldn't put it down and finished it in half a day. Thought the first book was good but this just added to it. I was sucked into the book and really didn't want it to end. Can't wait for more of violets books.

-Tegen, Goodreads

I thought it was a great and heart-warming book, totally worth the wait. I recommend this book to anyone willing to read a werewolf paranormal story with a touch of romance.

-**Alicia Zamora**, Goodreads

If there's a third book, I'd still read it! Violet Samuels is definitely an author to look out for. I'm dying for this book. I'm absolutely in love with it just like I was so crazy about the first one. Please read this if you love werewolf-themed books!

-**Kaye Ann Rhymes**, Goodreads

Nightfall Series

Forgotten, Saved, Loved

By: Violet Samuels

BLVNP

ISBN: 978-1-68030-843-3

Table of contents

1 1

2 11

3 19

4 28

5 34

6 43

7 51

8 62

9 68

10..78

11..87

12..97

13..107

14..117

15..126

16..134

17..150

18..157

19..169

20..182

21..190

22..201

23..211

24..222

25...231

26...236

27...243

28...252

It would be my greatest honour to dedicate this book to my friends and family who pushed me to write this book when I thought I couldn't.

FREE DOWNLOAD

Get these freebies and MORE when you
sign up for the author's mailing list!

Remember the guardian who always made people laugh? Remember the guardian who always tried to help? Remember the guardian who had a backstory? Do you remember the guardian who ran into the forest and never returned? That guardian was forgotten, or so he thought.

Did he escape?

No one knew other than the ones he loved the most.

Was he loved back? Everyone knew the answer to that.

Do you?

This is a story of the guardian who was forgotten, saved, and loved...

1

In a world of war, hate, and love, I stand alone. In a world of sadness, happiness, anger, and forgiveness, I struggle alone. In a world of selfishness, honour, generosity, and empathy, I feel alone. I stand alone. I struggle alone. I feel alone.

Alone, never again will I feel complete without knowing what's going to happen to me. Never again will I feel like my life has meaning.

How do people cope with a situation like this? Three years. It's been three years since I was captured, without even a clue if they're coming for me. These three years have caused so much pain and many fallen tears. Three years have passed, and my hope is slowly slipping away. Three years... and I'm still not found. I guess you can say I'm forgotten.

Have you ever been forgotten? It's a horrible situation to be in. It makes you feel like you're not loved anymore like no one cares. Being forgotten for so long can change a person. It can change a person so much... that he can't even remember himself. He can't remember the person he used to be. He can't remember the person who used to smile and joke around. He just can't remember.

How will you feel counting the days that you've been forgotten? How will you feel counting the times you've been beaten? How will you feel counting the wishes you've made that never came true? How will that make you feel? Sad? Angry? Annoyed? For some, it may be happy. In all honesty, it makes me feel like a total and utter crap. It makes me feel like I'm not loved and that I never was.

You know, for the past three years, all I've thought about was when they're going to come for me. When are they going to magically pop-up in front of me and say 'surprise'? When are they finally going to help me escape?

Everyday, though, I wake up to the same sight. Instead of their smiling faces, I'm met with my guards' stony faces. Instead of their twinkling eyes, I'm met with the dull light of the bummed light bulb. Instead of their warm embraces, I'm met with the cold feeling that always surrounds me. I'm always met with the total opposite of what I wish, want, and need. Again, I'm all alone.

For the first year, I wished upon a star every night. I thought if all the fairy tales were true, it would work and I'd magically beam back home. Believe it or not, I even tried The Wizard of Oz trick and clicked my heels together like Dorothy, while chanting: "There's no place like home. There's no place like home. There's no place like home." It never worked.

During the second year, I stopped crying and tried to grasp a hold on things. I put up with the beatings and trained my brain to help protect me against it. I trained my wolf to stay away in the shadows of my mind. I just stopped being a baby and took hold of myself. That helped.

Finally on the third year, after holding onto hope for so long... I let go of my last grip. My fingers uncurled from the thin strand and let it broke. I let my hope go. I became numb

2

during the third year. I thought, "What the hell? No one cares anyway! What's hope gonna do, bring back my life?"

So, I became a heartless piece of nothing that rotted away in a tiny cell. My sanity, love, and happiness decayed ever so slowly. I willed my life to come to an end quicker. I just wanted this nightmare to be over. As I sit on my poor excuse of a bed, a rag on the cold cement floor, I bury my face in my hands and think. I think about what my life would've been like if I didn't end up here. I could've met my mate. I could've gotten married and had pups with her. I could've made my way up the ladder to finally become a general in training. I could've had a life. I stand up and grip my hands on the metal bars that cover the small window of my cell. It's so high up that my eyes can only see through it ever so slightly.

A beautiful sight greets me. Lush green grass is displayed on the ground, graceful butterflies are flapping their wings, wind is blowing lightly on my fingers, trees are swaying, and all I ever want is to rid myself of this confinement and get out into the world. This little window is the only way I'll know how many days have gone and passed. How many days I've been alone. I let go of the bars with a sigh and plonk back down onto the floor. Why is my life miserable? Oh yeah! Because I decided to help the ones I loved without thinking it through. I just acted on what my bloody instinct told me to do. The sound of the heavy, soundproof, metal door opening draws my attention away from my depressing thoughts. It's about five o'clock in the morning, so no guards should start their shift until at least another hour or so.

That only leaves one more person... Kate.

3

"Comrade?" I hear her faint whisper through the dim lighting. "Comrade, are you awake?" Yep, that's right. It's me, the little second choice for everything. The guardian that's forgotten, I'm Comrade Hollow.

I hurriedly scatter to the bars of my cell and stick my hand out into the darkness. "I'm here, Kate, follow my voice," I tell her in a hushed tone. The door may be soundproof, but it's still good to take precautions.

Soon, I feel a small hand grasp my own. I slowly pull her to the bars, and my eyes glimmer when I see her adorable face. Kate's a very pretty girl with waist-length dark blonde hair and hazel eyes. She's short, about 5 ft. and 2 in. That's what you expect from a 13-year-old girl, though.

"Why are you up so early? You might be caught!" I scold lightly. She giggles and rolls her eyes at my lame excuse. She's always up this early to talk to me, I should know better. "Comrade, you know I always come early on a Saturday 'coz everyone's still asleep," she tells me back as she lightly smacks me through the bars. I roll my eyes "Yeah, yeah."

Kate was only 10 when the war between the Nightfall and Moonlight packs happened. She was too young to fight, but her parents weren't. Sadly, she lost both in the battle. She's still haunted by dreams of how they could've been killed. Since her parents died when she was at such a young age, even though it wasn't meant to be, she was put up for adoption. Here's a bit of a background story...

Remember Damon? Yeah, I'm sure you all remember him.

Well, the bastard got away and survived that bloody war. He survived the war so many other wolves didn't. He took what little pack members he had left with him and set himself up deep inside the woods of his territory. At least, that's where I

4

think I am. As I chased and killed the runaway wolf, I was ambushed by his remaining pack members and got knocked out. I honestly wasn't in any condition to fight. I woke up in this cell, and I haven't been out since.

About two years ago, Damon met his mate, Phyre (pronounced fear-e). She's Spanish if you didn't get that. From what I've gathered, she's weird, funny, shy and when she first met me, she was a bit awkward. Also, for some odd reason, she wears combat boots every day. Honestly, I think she's a good mate for Damon because she can keep him in check against his harsh, cruel, and angry ways. Phyre is much smarter and more controlled.

On the other hand, that doesn't mean good news for me.

Unfortunately, they found out they couldn't produce pups. Phyre, of course, was heartbroken. Then you had Damon. He went on a total rampage. And guess who got the wrath of his fists? Yep, it was little weak me. I got all the hits and kicks and just dealt with it. That's when my hope started to slip away slowly.

Since there were many orphaned pups left from the war, Damon adopted one. That one is Kate. Kate was thrilled that she now had a family again, an alpha family at that. Phyre was also thrilled, but you could still see the sadness that lingered behind her eyes.

Overall, Damon found his mate and they adopted Kate. Since then, she's been coming to see me every single chance she gets. The stupid girl... I've never asked her why, though. I've never wondered why she's so intrigued with me.

"So, my pretty little girl," I begin, earning a small giggle from Kate. "What's been happening up above? I haven't seen you for at least four days!" I exclaim with mock outrage.

Kate breaks out into a full on laughter, and a ghost of a smile graces my face. I love her laugh. It gives me peace and makes me believe that there are still good people in this horrid and cruel world. Kate's the only one that can make me smile like this. If it wasn't for her, I don't know if I'd be coping.

"Well," she begins after her little laughing fit. "Mum has been trying to get Dad be happier and not angry all the time. You know, for certain reasons they can't help. Of course, he isn't angry around Mum and I. Um... Dad's been training all the newly shifted wolves. And apart from that, nothing much changed." For certain reasons, one of that is Damon still being angry about the baby situation.

Yes, she addresses Damon and Phyre as dad and mum. Don't ask me why 'coz I will never do that. I think it gives her closure, knowing that she has replacement parents. I know her real parents can't be replaced, though, never in a million years. No child should have to live through the pain of losing both parents in one day. I nod at her and rub my sore eyes. I sigh as I bury my face in my hands. "Has there been any word?" I whispered. Kate knows exactly what I'm talking about. I want to know if there's been any word from Celina, Axel, or even Callum. I want to know if they're coming for me.

She puts on a sad smile as her eyes fill with sympathy. I instantly know the answer. No. "I'm sorry, Comrade, but nothing's been heard. If there is, then Dad's doing really well to keep it from everyone. I'm sorry," she repeats.

I close my eyes and sigh heavily. Life just isn't fair. "You should go," I whisper, my face still in my hands. I don't want her getting caught down here, who knows what Damon will do to her. "Comrade..." she trails off with tears in her eyes. She hates it when I ask her to leave. It breaks her tiny little heart.

6

"Please, Kate. Just leave," I whisper again as I bring down my face from my hands. The truth is, I don't want her to see me like this, like the broken man I know I am. She takes one look at my eyes and her bottom lip quivers, her head nodding. "I'll be back soon," she promises, then darts out of the room. She locks the door behind her, letting me wallow in my self-pity once again.

No word from Celina. The one person who I thought I could trust. She's had three years to look for me and still, she hasn't found me. Yet, it was me who found her. I wonder how the triplets are doing. I've missed their first step, first word, first everything. I wanted to be there, to be Uncle Comrade. I guess my fantasies will never become a reality. Axel is the man who has power, strength, and courage. In all honesty, I wanted to be like him. Keyword: WANTED.

Now, all I want is to know why he hasn't found me yet. As I've said, he has power no one else in this world has. He's the Moon Goddess' son for Christ sake! He could've done something! He can do something. Then you have Callum, the first choice guardian, the first choice beta, the first choice friend, the first choice in everything. He even made Celina laugh first. He's seen the triplets' first step and heard their first word. He's the first uncle. Uncle Callum is always there to make someone laugh, always there to make Celina happy.

What did I do? I made her feel pain. I made her worry. I made her cry and cry and cry. There's one thing I did though that's good. That one little thing... was making her feel loved when   nobody   else   did. Axel abandoned her when they first met. Callum just tagged along for the ride and wanted to see where it ended. Me? I cared for her. I loved her. I made her feel safe. I helped make who she is today, the confident and kind Celina Heart.

7

Again, I hear the doors unlocking and opening. This time, though, it's not Kate. A buff man over six feet tall with greying brown hair, cold black eyes and clothes to match his whole demeanor. Everyone, I like to introduce you to Mr. Crusher. That's all I know of his name, the nickname that was given to him for a very good reason. I learned that the first day I met him. Never again, never again...

I bolt into a standing position and clench my fists. Mr. Crusher catches onto this and chuckles darkly at me. "You know what today is, boy? Workout time," he booms in his almighty voice while unlocking my cell and grabbing me around the neck.

Four times a week, I'm forced to do workouts by fighting against the most, well-trained wolves and push my limits to the max. As torturous as that sounds, I find it as a way to vent my pent-up anger, to let everything out when I feel the need to. For me, it's a way of mentally fixing myself. It's also made me a lot buffer than I was before. I have biceps, an eight pack, calf muscles, and most importantly, I have the strength to carry on. Something I needed for a very long time. Mr. Crusher drags me to the workout station that's only a few meters away from my cell. He throws me straight into the wall that's adjacent to the weights. I look at them with an emotionless expression. Here comes the pain.

"Get to work, boy!" Mr. Crusher snarls. The vein in his head starts to make an appearance and his muscles flex with annoyance. Hey, I would be annoyed too if I had to wake up at six o'clock on a Saturday to supervise a prisoner. It'll probably be better if I just do what he says and get this over with, but where's the fun in that?

I take my sweet time while getting up just to aggravate him more and make my way over to the weights. I lower myself onto the bench press and physically prepare myself for the 250 kilograms I know I have to lift. "Don't test my temper, boy. I have power over you," Mr. Crusher threatens. To add to his threat, he, of course, adds another 50 kilograms to the weights, forcing me to bench press 300 kilograms. That bloody bastard.

On top of having werewolf strength, I also have my guardian strength added to that, making me extra strong and mighty helpful in these circumstances.

"One!" Mr. Crusher booms and I lift the weights with determination, just to prove the bastard wrong. He will not overpower me! "Two!" he continues, and I lift it again. The muscles in my arms work with all their might as I strain and push them to the limit. "Three!" he booms again. I lift the weights again, and all that's going through my mind is: 'I hate that bloody son-of-a-bitch.' He continues until I've done 100 bench presses with a 300-kilogram weight. Yet, this is just the beginning. Mr. Crusher smirks at me. "Tired?" he asks curiously, his smirk still evident on his face and his eyes twinkling with hate towards me. I'm sure mine are burning with the hate I feel towards him too.

I smirk right back with a challenge in my eyes. "Not even the slightest." The smug smirk drops from his face, and a deathly glare replaces it. Bring it on, Mr. Crusher.

Hours and hours of gruesome workout and I'm just about ready to collapse. I won't though because that will mean giving in and I don't do that. I won't even mention the stuff Mr. Crusher got me to do. It's too painful to think about. "Had enough now, boy? Huh? All tired out and ready to give in?" Mr. Crusher mocks me. I shakily rise from the floor where I just had a defense and offence game with the one and only Mr. Crusher. Guess who won? Not me.

All my muscles are burning, my joints are aching, and I just want to fall to the floor and sleep. I don't answer his question, just breathe heavily. For what seems like forever, we just stare at each other and see whose stare is first to break. We do this at the end of every workout when I know I've had enough and when Mr. Crusher knows he's won. Neither of us admits it though because sometimes the outcome is different and I'm the one who wins.

His smug smirk that I've become accustomed to shows on his face. "I do believe that this workout is over." His voice smugly states and all I want to do is punch that already crooked nose   of   his.
I don't answer him. I just follow him back to my cell. He gives me a rough shove to which I growl at. He just laughs and proceeds to lock my cell then walks away.

As soon as I hear the heavy door closing, I collapse to the ground. This is what I had to live with for the last three years. This is the torture I had to go through... and it's only lunch time.

2

COMRADE

"Here ya go! Nice stale bread and a bowl of cold soup. Enjoy!" the guard says as he tosses the plate into my cell, spilling half of it, then walking out, laughing, and sealing the door behind him. Life sucks.

I eat my food in silence, no thoughts going through my head like usual, just complete and utter silence. I'm preparing myself mentally and physically. The reason? I know what's coming after this. I know what I'm gonna have to endure all over again for the sake of those I love. As much as I don't want to admit it, I still think about Celina, Axel, and Callum every day. They're the closest thing I have to a family. Had, actually had.

I finish my food and place the plate outside the cell bars. I lean on the wall and slide down so that I'm in a sitting position with my legs apart and my head against the wall, eyes closed. It's only a matter of time now...

Three.

Two.

One.

The heavy door opens and a man who's under six foot has brown hair and bluish green eyes comes into view. He's dressed in dark jeans and a black shirt. The devil himself.

Damon chuckles darkly at me once he comes to stand in front of my cell. I look at him with hatred in my eyes and growl lowly at him in warning.

Damon lets out a belly laugh upon hearing my growl. "Oh, Comrade. Dear, dear Comrade. Are you really in a position to growl at me? I don't think so!" he taunts. He unlocks my cell door and advances towards me. I stand my ground and try to fight him off when he goes to grab me. Not even a guardian is stronger than an alpha, though. He grabs me roughly and unwillingly by the shirt while dragging me out of the cell and towards the torture chamber. Yes, I said the torture chamber. I grip his hands to try to get him to let go, but he doesn't budge. The next second, I'm being thrown into a room I know all too well.

I collapse onto the concrete floor, grazing my knees and hands. I lift my head up, letting my long, overgrown, brown hair cover my eyes. All around me are torture toys, some too horrid to even mention. "So, Comrade. What shall we use today? Hmm, haven't used the whip in a while. Let's use that," Damon states with an evil glint in his eye.

Before he goes for the whip, however, he goes for me. He grabs me by the neck and leads me to the shackles that hang from the roof and the shackles that rest on the floor. He hooks my wrists and ankles so that I'm immobile, then proceeds to get the whip. He has an evil smirk on his face and a strange glint in his eyes this whole time.

He places a chair in front of me, sitting on it backwards with the whip in hand. I glare at the leather contraption while wishing I could use that very whip to whip a certain person named Damon...

"You know how this goes, don't you, Comrade? A simple question and answer session, no biggy!" he teases. My eye twitches out of major annoyance because of his stupid, bloody voice.

"Go to hell." I spit with venom dripping on every word. He isn't worth my time.

"I have every intention to... When I die, but right now, I'm happily living and breathing while torturing you." He stares smugly. I scoff at him and shake my head. You know, when Damon got a mate, I thought he would change. Become a better person. Guess I was wrong.

"So, the first question of the hour is..." Damon begins, tightening his grip on the whip. He's obviously trying to be intimidating, but it's obviously not working. "What powers do the triplets have?"

I exhale sharply and chuckle. That's all Damon wants, to know what the triplets have to offer and use it against Celina and Axel. He just wants the power like he always does.

"I told you, Damon," I spit his name like it's a curse on my tongue. "I don't know anything about the triplets. I only know their names, which I'm certainly not telling you."

An evil smirk graces Damon's face. He shakes his head while saying, "Oh, Comrade, you never learn, do you? You're still that little, pathetic wolf who ran away because he was too cowardly. You're not fit to be a guardian. You're not even worth my time! I need answers, though, and you're the only one knows them."

My anger rises every time that son-of-a-bitch opens his mouth. "You're no better! You hurt Celina for years, you've been torturing me for the last three, and now you want to use the triplets for your own little game? You make me sick," I tell him, and all I want to do is break these damn shackles and claw his face.

Oh! Another thing Damon hasn't let me do, shift. I haven't shifted for three years and what has that accomplished? It's exactly what he wanted. He wanted me to lose contact with my wolf, and now I have. He was a very happy wolf that day, going easy on the torture even. Wasn't that generous of him?

Damon growls, then quickly gets up from his chair and moves swiftly behind me. My back tenses when I feel the slight breeze of the whip getting ready to strike. I'm not letting him get to me, though, and I never have, so why start today?

"You're just power crazy, Damon. All you want is the power that comes with everything," I taunt, and that's when I feel the first crack of the whip hitting my back. I inhale sharply, but not a sound escapes my mouth. I'll admit, though, it hurts like a freaking bitch!

"Hell, I bet you only accepted your mate because she's the daughter of a beta," I continue to taunt him, but I think I hit a sensitive subject because the next thing I know, a ferocious growl fills the room, and multiple strikes are taken to my back. It's true, though, Phyre is the beta's daughter of a Spanish pack that migrated here.

I don't make a sound. Not even a peep. I won't give Damon the satisfaction of seeing me in pain.

"Never, and I mean never!" Damon booms, striking another hit to my back. I arch it in pain, but not a sound escapes

14

me. "Insult my mate! I would've accepted her if she was the lowest of the low. She's my mate!"

Another three strikes and then it suddenly all stops. I relax, letting the weight of my body be held up by the chains of the shackles. "So, you would've accepted Celina if she was your mate? Even if she was the lowest of the low? Even though you made her life a living hell, you would still accept her? Tell me that, and I'll believe you. Tell me, Damon, would you accept Celina as a mate?" I ask breathless and through gritted teeth, trying to get the point across that he really is a selfish bastard that only a mother and family can love.

He goes silent, not uttering a single word. He doesn't move, I don't think he's even breathing.

"Well, Damon, would you?" I push. I hear his footsteps slowly coming out from behind me and soon he's standing in front of me.

"No, I wouldn't," he says, emotionless. I smile in victory and dare to ask the next question because I know it will really test him if I do.

Of course, I do it anyway. "Why?" That one simple word can make anyone's brain start to get the gears turning. That one simple word can make anyone surrender and tell the truth. That one simple word... can bring any man to his knees. Even an alpha.

Instead of answering my question, Damon simply walks out of the room, leaving me hanging. No pun intended.

"What? You too cowardly to answer? Why, Damon, why! It's a simple word, with a big answer that you don't know!" I call after him as he continues to walk out on me.

I hear his footsteps stop for a brief second, but they soon continue again. They're quicker this time and in less than five seconds, the sound of the heavy door slamming shut fills my ears.

I've always wondered why Damon goes through so much shit, just to get hold of Celina. Why is she so special? Of course, I know why she's special. She's the last Shaded Wolf, with the exception of Axel.

She's one of a kind. I sigh as I let my head fall. I'm gonna be stuck here for a while...

"Comrade? Comrade, wake up" a small and frightened whispering voice tells me. I groan, but don't open my eyes. It hurts to move.

"Comrade, please wake up. It's Kate, come on. Please..." Kate whispers again. I groan while opening my eyes to see the scared look on Kate's face. I'm instantly on alert, despite my aching body.

"Kate? What are you doing down here? It's daylight! You know the rules!" I whisper harshly to her as my eyes search frantically for a guard. She can't get caught!

"I wanted to make sure you're all right. Dad came up looking pretty annoyed, and I wanted to make sure he didn't bust you up too bad," she informs me, as tears prick her eyes.

"What about the guards?" I question, and she shrugs.

"I thought that if I come down here while they're on their break, then I could get ten minutes with you. Seven now because you were asleep," she scolds me lightly in a teasing manner.

A ghost of a smile makes its way onto my face at her words. She really shouldn't be down here, though, she could get caught, and I don't want her getting in trouble.

"If I tell you what he did, will you leave? I don't want you getting in trouble with your Mum," I tell her honestly. The last time she almost got caught, her mum found out, and I didn't see her for a week. She was grounded to the confinements of her room. She wasn't even allowed to go to school for the week. Of course, Kate didn't really mind that part.

She nods her head wearily, her eyes going wide with anticipation.

I sigh. "He just gave me a few whips, that's all. Now can you please leave?" I quickly tell her. I don't want her worrying about me when there's nothing to worry about.

She gasps at me in horror. I swear, this girl moves fast. One second she's in front of my face, I blink, and she's behind me.

Her small hand touches my tender flesh that's been whipped, instantly making me flinch and for a hiss to escape my mouth.

"Sorry," she whispers as her hand withdraws. She appears in front of me again with tears in her eyes.

She opens her mouth to say something, but I shake my head. "Go, you only have a minute or so before the guards come back. I'll be fine, I promise. Just go, Kate," I whisper to her. She nods her head then dashes out of the fear-striking place.

It's times like this when I wonder what Celina, Axel, and Callum are doing if they're all laughing around or busy trying to find me. Probably not the latter...

I wonder if they'll ever find me if they even care to find me. I guess I stopped believing in them a long time ago.

3

ALEX

I run through the forest in my human form, dodging the trees and jumping over the bushes. I don't dare turn around to see if she's following me. Turning around will just slow me down and distract me from what I'm focusing on: running.

I jump over a fallen log as a flash of blonde fur catches my eye to the left. I don't stop, though, just pick up my pace. I won't let her catch me, not this time.

I quickly slip under a high branch then continue to bolt through the forest, disturbing all the peaceful forest animals.

What happens next is so fast. One moment, I'm running, giving it my all, the next... I'm being tackled to the ground by a blonde-haired wolf. She snarls at me, and I snarl right back.

I hitch kick her in the belly, and she goes flying into a tree. I swiftly jump to my feet and start to circle with the wolf. I look for her weak points. Something that will help me bring her down quicker and easier. Just as I spot one and go for a lunge, the sound of a bell going off in the distance draws my attention.

I relax my stance and smile at my friend, Taylor. She gives me a wolfy grin back, making me laugh at what it really looks like.

"Come on, we better get back to the grounds. You know how the beta gets," I joke. I smile as I remember our funny beta Callum. He always makes people smile, laugh and have a good time. He's scary when he's mad, though.

"Race ya there!" I call to her as I take off sprinting back the way I came. I laugh as I hear a playful growl behind me and see that Taylor is fast catching up.

I dodge past all the trees and bushes and slide under the same high branch as before.

"Come on, ya slow poke!" I tease her behind me as I burst through the bushes and into the grounds. I laugh while I try to catch my breath just as Taylor bursts through. She huffs in her wolf form and makes her way to the tree where her clothes are.

She walks back out fully clothed. Taylor's a very pretty girl with light blonde hair that shines in the sun, brown eyes that resemble chocolate and a body that's curvy and certainly catches the attention of most guys. Her skin is creamier than anything else, but it has that natural tan to it like every other werewolf. Plus, she's eighteen so she can do whatever she damn well pleases. Taylor's also a very smart girl; she's the brains of our little posse.

I laugh as I walk up to her, wrapping an arm around her shoulder. "You tried hard, Taylor, but it wasn't enough," I tell her in fake disappointment. She rolls her eyes at me and shoves me away while I chuckle again.

"Oh please! Everyone knows you're the fastest runner in human and wolf form in the group! It's no surprise you beat me" she admits while folding her arms across her chest. I chuckle and shake my head, searching for my other friend that completes our three-woman posse.

I catch the familiar sight of a tight bun of dark brown hair and smile brightly. That would be my other friend, Ally.

"Hey, Ally! Get over here!" I call out to her. Ally, being her tall self, easily spots us and smiles, casually making her way over to where Taylor and I stand.

Ally, as I said before, is a tall girl. I think she's the tallest girl in the pack actually, sometimes getting over the heads of some of the males. She's got afro style, dark brown hair, super dark brown eyes and her skin is like a brownish colour. In other words, she's really, really tanned. She also has a very slim figure, which is probably why she's so tall. She's flat-chested, even at eighteen, and she has a flat ass that most girls would kill for! She's a fast runner and is quick to think up plans, so she's like the getaway person that we all rely on.

Me? Well, I'm sort of the boss of the group. I have layered blonde hair, bluish-green eyes and a body that I must say has curves in all the right places. I also have a well-tanned olive skin that I absolutely adore. I'm energetic, sporty, fun, and as girly, as this may sound, I love shopping as well as travelling.

So, there ya go! Me as the boss, Taylor as the brains and Ally as the getaway. I think we make a really good team.

"Hey!" Ally greets us. We both smile at her. "So, who won this time?" she asks with a grin. Taylor and I glance at each other before grinning back at her.

"I did," we both say at the same time. I turn to look at her with wide eyes. Please! I so won that!

21

"No, I did!" we say simultaneously once again. Our eyes narrow on their own accord while Ally chuckles in the background.

"Please, you did not win that. I was so gonna pin you!" I exclaim, outraged. I so was, Taylor wouldn't even stand a chance.

Taylor raises an eyebrow at me. "Seriously? I was about to tear you apart!" she screams in my face.

This means war!

Before we can lunge at each other and finish what we started, Ally intervenes and puts a hand on both our shoulders.

She chuckles at us. "Ok, that's enough bantering you two. Callum is calling a meeting" she informs us, and when we look up, sure enough, Callum is motioning everyone to make their way over to him.

My two friends and I make our way over to him, hanging at the back of the crowd of thrity or so wolves, both male and female.

"As you know, you were specifically chosen to carry out a dangerous mission. You were informed that you may not come out of this alive, but you will be dearly remembered by everyone," Callum begins in all seriousness. I put on a blank face as he continues on.

"So, without further ado, I would like to announce that we are reducing our group of thirty to ten in the upcoming week" he informs us all while gasps and calls of disapproval are heard.

"Thirty to ten? That's like twenty of us gone!" Taylor harshly whispers in my ear. I nod with uncertainty in my eyes. How will this work...

"For this mission, only the best of the best will carry it out. You have to be fast, strategic and, most importantly, have the will to protect yourself and others." Callum makes eye contact with every single one of us, his brown eyes lingering on me for a second longer.

"Think hard about this. Work harder in training, have some practise runs with others. Let me tell you this, though, if you're chosen, there is no backing out. You are in it, and there's nothing you can do about it. Dismiss" he says after a short pause.

Everybody disperses while I turn to my friends. "Practise tomorrow at five?" I question. They both nod and start to walk off as well.

I walk in the opposite direction of everyone else, making myself comfortable against a tree.

This isn't a game anymore. This is serious, and I so badly want to be one of those ten selected few. I want to impress my dad and get him to know that he doesn't have to be the only strong one in the family. I can help just as much as he can.

"Alex?" I hear a voice ask. I stand up straight from my position on the tree and turn to look at Callum.

I bow my head in respect. "Beta," I mutter as I cast my eyes downward. He nods his head back at me.

He comes to stand next to me, leaning against the tree opposite me. I take my earlier position and lean against the same tree. "Why did you join this group three years ago?" he suddenly questions.

I direct my eyes to him and put on a blank face. "Like I said three years ago when you asked me this, I want to make my dad proud. He has to know that he isn't suffering alone." I mutter the last part as I turn my head away, letting my blonde hair cover my face.

23

"There isn't another reason?" he questions suspiciously. I shake my head. What else would there be?

"So, you're saying that you have no other reason to be in this group apart from making your dad proud when you woke up in that battlefield three years ago and saw your mum dead? You don't want to get revenge on the person who caused her death? You don't want justice for her?" he questions amazed.

I smile slightly. Everyone always thinks that I'll be mad and sad when they bring up the subject of my dead mum. Yes, she did die in that bloody war three years ago when I was only fifteen years of age. The thing is, though, I know none of this can be erased. None of this can be rewritten, and I've accepted that. I accepted that a long time ago.

"Well?" Callum pushes when I answer him with silence. I turn my head and show him my small smile and glassy eyes. He blinks after seeing my face, and he suddenly looks like he regrets asking those questions.

I sigh heavily. "The thing is, beta, what's happened can't be erased or rewritten. It can't change no matter how much I want it to. My mum's in a better place now, with the Moon Goddess. She's probably smiling down at me right now. I've accepted that she's dead, and I've moved on. She will be in my heart, though, forever and always," I tell him honestly as a single tear slips out the corner of my eye.

Callum graces me with a half smile and warm, kind eyes. "You're gonna be a very wise person when you grow up. Never let anything stop you from achieving what you want." With that said, Callum turns and walks away back to the pack house.

I stay there, leaning against the tree. I just think. I think about what happened that day, the pain, the heartache, the sadness, and most of all... the feeling of emptiness.

"Hey, you need to wake up. Come on, wake up," I hear a soft voice in my ear, as a hand shakes my shoulder lightly. I slowly open my eyes only for them to be met with a pair of brown ones.

I blink a few times before finally realising who it is. I gasp and bolt upright, wobbling a bit on my legs. The man grasps my arm, making sure I'm steady before slightly backing away, giving me space.

"Beta," I respectfully say as I bow my head, my messy blonde hair covering my face.

"What are you doing here? You should be in the safe house with all the others" he lightly scolds.

I blush. "I'm sorry, beta, but I couldn't leave my parents to die. I had to help them," I tell him as tears come to my eyes. Speaking of my mum and dad, I hope I find them soon.

"No offence, but that was a really stupid decision. You could've gotten yourself killed!" he yells at me, going into beta mode and his wolf coming to the surface.

I cower away from him. "I'm sorry, beta, but I couldn't leave them. I just couldn't." I sob as I drop to my knees.

He sighs and kneels in front of me. "How old are you? You can't be older than fourteen" he mumbles while I raise my head to look at him.

"I'm fifteen," I quietly say. At that moment, I hear a loud, painful sob. My head snaps up, me thinking the worse.

My eyes search all the battered and limp bodies, trying my hardest to ignore all the blood and stench of death. My eyes set on a man with brown hair and soft, brown eyes that are filled with pain. My dad.

Without thinking, I bolt over to where he's kneeling over a body. I look down, and the whole world seems to fall around me. A lady with blonde hair and bluish-green eyes stares lifelessly up at me. Her hair has blood going through it, tainting it to the extreme. Her body is in a weird position and three long claw marks stretch from her neck to her stomach.

This lady... is my mum.

A loud sob escapes me as I collapse over her mangled body. "Mum! No! Please, you have to wake up! Please!" I scream as I start to violently shake her. She can't be dead! She just can't be! She has to be there for my formal, help me when I get a boyfriend, put up with my tantrums, cry at my wedding! She can't miss out on all that! Another strangled sob escapes me as I realise this. She can't be dead!

My dad engulfs me in a hug as I sob into his chest. He wraps his arms around me and buries his face in my hair, trying to hide his own tears.

"Please, mum, please," I beg in a silent whisper as I continue to cry on my dad's chest. My mum is dead... and there's nothing I can do about it.

I wipe away the tears that have been falling down my cheeks. I will never forget how my mum looked when I found her. I will never forget that look in my dad's eyes as he cried. I will never forget that awful day.

This mission has given me the chance to at least bring some little justice to my mum. I know I said that I've moved on, and I have, but I want my mum to know that I helped bring an end to those who caused her and all my family pain.

I'm getting into those select ten whether I like it or not and there's nothing anyone can do about it.

4

ALEX

I storm into Taylor and Ally's room with a determined look on my face. I told them yesterday that we're doing training, and I'll be damned if they sleep through it!

I stand in the middle of their room and observe how they're sleeping soundly and peacefully. Too bad, I'm gonna ruin that for them. I think evilly.

I suck in a big breath before screaming at the top of my lungs, "Rise and shine, ladies! We have training to do! Get your asses out of bed! Come on! Chop chop! Training awaits!"

I get groans in return for my loud screaming. I roll my eyes at the two of them as they groggily lift their heads from their soft pillows.

"What the hell, Alex? It's five o'clock in the morning," Ally mumbles as she drops her face back into her pillow.

"Yeah, get stuffed. I want to sleep. Sleep is good," Taylor mutters unintelligently.

I grumble under my breath as I watch my two friends fall back asleep. "If you don't get up, I won't make your dinner tonight," I warn them in a serious tone.

Truth be told, I cook for the Alpha, Luna, Beta, and some of my friends. It's honestly an honour to be cooking for Axel, Celina, and Callum. Yet there's always an empty space at the table that nobody fills...

Both Taylor and Ally just mumble something incoherent at my warning. I sigh deeply and walk out the door. If they aren't gonna train with me, then I guess I'll just have to do it myself.

I quickly make my way to the kitchen, trying to be as quiet as possible. I open the cupboard and quickly snatch a Milo cereal bar. What? I need to eat before training!

As I happily munch on my Milo bar, I hear a loud yawn from the door. I lift my head up and stand up straight from my former position of leaning on the kitchen bench. As soon as I realize who the person is, I drop my head in respect. Why is he up so early?

"Alpha," I mumble quietly, still not wanting to be too loud. As soon as he hears my voice, his head snaps up, and his eyes widen at me.

"Alex? I didn't expect to see you up this early," he says with surprise evident in his voice. Likewise, I said in my head.

I keep my head down as I reply. "I didn't mean to disturb you, Alpha. I was just getting some break then head to the gym," I tell him as I chuck away the wrapper of the bar.

Just as I'm making my escape to the kitchen door, Axel's voice stops me. "The gym? Why are you going there at this time of the morning? On a Saturday, nonetheless," he questions suspiciously.

I lift my head and look at him. His white hair sits messily on his head like he's just woken up, and his silver eyes hold sleep. He's shirtless, so his abs and toned arms are in clear view. To any person, he would be the definition of perfect because well, he is. He's the Moon Goddess' son, he has to be.

"I'm training, Alpha. I wish to be a part of the group who's chosen to be assigned on the mission. I don't want to risk any chances of me not making it, so I'm training every morning at five. Again, I'm sorry if I disturbed you, Alpha," I say truthfully, deciding to answer his earlier question.

Without waiting for a response, I push through the kitchen door and make my way to the indoor gym the pack house has.

I go straight to the treadmill for a warm up, but I'm in a full blown run 20 minutes later. What can I say? I love my running. It lets me think and try to understand why everything around me happens because it does.

For example, I try to figure out why my dad won't let me stay with him. Not even a week after the war, my dad sent me to live in the pack house because he said he needed to mourn his dead mate. I accepted that, but that was three years ago. Since then, I've only stepped foot in my real home about seven times. Sad, I know.

I understand why dad won't let me go back though. I look exactly like her. Like my mum... I have the same blonde hair, bluish-green eyes and figure. The only thing I share with my dad is my nose. Apart from that, I'm like an exact replica of my mum and it hurts when I see the look in my dad's eyes when he sees me. I see the hurt, sadness, and guilt. I can't even look into my dad's eyes anymore, it just hurts too much.

I continue to sprint for another few minutes until I feel like my legs are about to collapse. I slow down to a leisurely walk until I catch my breath. Jumping off the treadmill, I head to the punching bag.

I strap my knuckles and breathe in and out. In and out. In and out. I keep breathing until I'm calm, then I let all my emotions bubble up and take control of me. All the anger, sadness, annoyance, disparity, everything.

You know what's annoying? When you don't know what you're training for. That's really annoying! I joined the group three years ago and I don't even know the reason why it was formed! Hell! I don't think anyone does!

I think it has something to do with a certain someone who was captured a long time ago in a certain war. In other words, Comrade. He's the one that's supposed to sit in the empty seat. He's the one that's supposed to be with Celina, along with Callum. He's the one that's supposed to make all the girls swoon. Comrade is the one who's supposed to be here and happy.

Listen to me! I don't even know the guy! I've heard about him though, and for me, that's enough. I continue to punch and kick with all my might, not caring that the wrap around my knuckles has torn. I just keep punching as I try to clear my mind. No more thinking. I just want peace and if destroying a poor punching bag is how to do it, then so be it.

Since I'm so concentrated on the punching bag, I don't notice the person sneaking up behind me before they lay a hand on my shoulder. Out of instinct, I turn around while gripping their wrist. I twist it so that the person's whole body turns, then I forcefully push them down towards the floor face first. I put my knee at the small of their back as I continue to grip their wrist in my hand. Whoever snuck up on me is a very unlucky man.

"Remind me never to sneak up on you again," he groans in a voice I know all too well. Matthew.

I chuckle as I loosen my hold and stand to my feet, offering him my hand. He takes it with a grin and hauls himself up to his full height, which is way above me and most certainly above Ally.

"Well, well, well, if it isn't my favourite person! How ya doin?" Matthew asks in a joking manner. I laugh at him and slap him slightly on his chest.

Matt and I have been best friends since high school. I met him through Callum since they're brothers. He's a year older than me, so he's 19, but he's still the first person I go to when I need to just calm down. Unless it's at five o'clock in the morning and I've already felt the wrath of Taylor and Ally. That reminds me, no dinner for them tonight.

"I'm doing good! Why are you up so early?" I question. If I know Matt, it's that he never gets up early. I'd be lucky if he gets up before eight!

"Alex, it's 8:30" he says slowly like he's talking to a mentally disabled person. I roll my eyes at him and lightly slap him on his chest. That's still pretty amazing to see Matt up before eight on a Saturday.

"Not my fault. I lost track of time," I mumble under my breath, but he obviously hears it since he's a werewolf.

He chuckles at my annoyed face before the smile on his face drops when his eyes set on my knuckles. I also look down and notice that since the wrap has torn, my knuckles are bleeding and the flesh is torn.

Matt immediately grabs my hands and runs his thumbs lightly over my knuckles. I wince as it makes contact with my skin. Damn! That burns like a bitch!

Matt sighs. "Al, you shouldn't push yourself like this," he scolds, using the nickname he gave me.

I look straight into his eyes and show him my pain and despair from everything that's happening around me. His face softens at the sight.

"I don't know what to say, Al. You know I suck at the caring thing," he tells me with a small smile. I laugh through my nose and nod my head in agreement. He really does suck at that.

Instead of using words to show me he cares, he pulls me into a bone crushing hug. I hug him back with just as much force. This is what I love about Matt, he'll have no clue what to do, but he'll still make everything better.

"Now then!" he exclaims, pulling back with a smirk. "Why don't you take on the beta and see if you win?" A challenging spark lights up his eye and I'm sure mine does the same thing.

Oh, it's so on.

5

One week later...

ALEX

We all stand out on the grounds, only twenty of us left now. Callum got rid of the ten of us just the day before, so this is our final test.

"As you all know, this will be the final test to see who shall be assigned the mission," Callum begins as he locks eye contact with each and every one of us.

"Your task is simple, don't get caught." We all look at him confused before he continues to explain. "You could say that your task is like a big game of tag. Every man or woman for themselves. If you get caught, you must return to the grounds. The last ten remaining shall be a part of the group. The last person remaining shall get a surprise."

I look towards Taylor and Ally. They're both staring up at Callum with determination and strength in their eyes. They want this just as much as me.

"You'll have five minutes to separate yourselves from each other before the taggers are set loose," Callum goes on and we all nod in understanding.

"Who are the taggers?" I suddenly ask. All eyes turn to me while Callum lets an all too familiar smirk grace his face.

"Taggers! Will you grace us with your presence?" Callum exclaims towards to the house. To my utter horror and disbelief, Axel and Celina walk out of the house with training gear on. A series of profanities are heard as we all realise that we're gonna have to outrun the Alpha and Luna.

"I will also be a tagger, so be prepared. You have the Alpha, Luna, and Beta all chasing after you. Again, if you get caught, make your way back to the grounds. You have five minutes to run and hide. Take your positions!" Callum announces, so everyone bolts to an opening in the forest.

I look to my right to see Ally; she looks back at me. I nod at her and send a silent 'good luck' her way. She smiles slightly then looks ahead of her again.

I look to my left and see Taylor cracking her knuckles. I smirk at her, and she smirks right back at me. A silent challenge is said between us -- I'm so gonna win this.

"Three!" Callum announces in all mighty voice, startling mostly everyone. Here we go...

"Two!"

I crouch down low so that I can get a good propulsion. I look around me and notice that everyone has shifted into their wolf forms except me. I look up to see Axel, Celina and Callum looking at me curiously, but I just smirk and focus my attention back to the task at hand.

"One!"

35

I take a deep breath through my nose and slowly let it through my mouth. I block out every noise around me, only listening to my racing heartbeat and even breaths.

"Go!"

Without a second thought, I launch myself in the forest. I just run forward, not making any turns or cuts, just straight ahead.

I still didn't shift into my wolf form, I run fast enough anyway. Plus, I've learnt a few things these past three years. I know that when in wolf form, your scent is more distinct and can be tracked more easily. When you're in human form, however, your scent is slightly masked and is harder to track. I'm using that fact to my advantage.

I spot a clearing coming up ahead, but didn't stop. I just bolt straight through it like lightning. If you were looking, you wouldn't want to blink.

I continue on when I hear three distant wolf howls, each belonging to the taggers. I chuckle lowly and sprint for the nearest tree. Without slowing my pace, I run up the tree horizontally, all the way to the top. I rest myself behind some branches and leaves so I can see them, but they can't see me.

I just sit there, listening and looking for any movement that could slightly distinguish a wolf. After all, I'm the only one in human form.

About 20 minutes pass and nothing happens. I decide to get down from the tree and have a little snoop around to see where everyone else is. Just as I'm about to jump from my position, a blonde coloured wolf comes barreling through the trees.

I freeze in motion and observe the wolf carefully. It's not Axel or Celina, since their wolves are black and white, and it's not Callum because his wolf has a more sandy colour to it.

The wolf looks around frantically, and that's when I notice the panicked look in their eyes. This wolf is being chased by a tagger.

To prove my point, a white wolf comes barreling through the trees and goes to tackle the blonde wolf. The wolf's eyes widen, and a startled yelp escapes it as it jumps out of the way at the last second.

I watch the scene unfold as Celina circles with the blonde wolf. The poor thing looks so scared that it actually makes me want to help. So, without thinking it through, I jump down from my tree and growl.

At the sound, Celina's wolf whips around to face me. She registers shock for a moment, and I choose that moment to lock eyes with the blonde wolf and silently tell them to run. They nod in thanks and bolt back into the cover of the trees.

Celina suddenly snaps back and turns to tag the wolf, only to realise that they're gone. She turns and growls at me while I growl right back. Luna or not, this is like a game of survival tag, and I will not lose.

She lunges for me, so I sidestep her and bolt off into the forest, still in human form. I hear her growl behind me and the heavy fall of paws. I pick up my pace as I go through twists and turns trying to lose her and small spaces that I know wolves can't get through or get passed.

As I slide under another log, I hear a huff. I turn around to see Celina looking at me with a gleam in her eyes, to which I smile. She then bolts off in the other direction, searching for another victim.

I jump up into the nearest tree and become frozen on a high branch. I stay still as I try to listen for movement again. I'm met with silence. I stay in my tree for the next three hours, not as well hidden, but still hidden enough. I wonder who's actually still out there. I'm sure Taylor and Ally will still be going strong because I've made them train every single day, two times a day. There's no way they'd be caught in the first 10.

A rustling to the left draws my attention. My head snaps in that direction as I freeze and hold my breath. I wait patiently to see who emerges, and I almost jump out of my skin when I realize it's Axel. Now remember, Axel is an alpha wolf that's midnight black with silver eyes. He can scare the living daylights out of anyone.

I gulp slightly as he stalks through the trees, looking with his striking silver eyes to see who the next victim is. I stay perfectly still as I just watch him, hoping for him to just hurry it up and move on.

Axel being an alpha, though, knows when someone's watching him. He suddenly freezes on the spot, a paw hanging in the air ready to be put down. Oh. Crap.

He looks in the direction of the tree I'm situated in, making my heart beat accelerate. Bad move.

Axel instantly hears my racing heart beat and starts looking in and around the tree I'm in. I don't want him to find me, so I close my eyes and try to control my breathing. Calm down, I mutter in my head, calm down.

My heart beat comes back down to a normal pace, which seems to throw Axel off guard because when I open my eyes, his eyes are darting around everywhere trying to spot me again.

Just to confuse him even more, I grasp a loose branch in my hand. I look for a clearing in the tree's leaves, and when I find one, I launch the branch through and wait to hear it connect with the ground. A few seconds later, the distant sound of the branch hitting the ground fills my ears. I look at Axel to see his head snap in that direction. He quickly scans the area one last time before sprinting off to where the branch landed. He's gonna be annoyed when he realises that it was only a branch that got his attention...

As soon as he's out of sight, I jump down from my tree and run in the opposite direction. So, I've been chased down by Celina and Axel, so that only leaves Callum. I wonder where's he at?

I don't have to wonder for very long, because as I'm about to race up another tree, I hear two growls, not even twenty metres away.

My eyes widen when a sandy coloured wolf and a light brown wolf come flashing passed me. I blink a couple times before getting over the shock and bolting off after them, easily catching up in my human form.

I trail behind Callum as he continues to chase the wolf. I'm so gonna pin this on him the next time I see him. I'm trailing behind him for how long while he doesn't even notice. Ha! Classic...

Callum suddenly crouches low and goes in for the tag. The light brown wolf notices and picks up their pace. Just by the looks of it, you can easily tell that the light brown wolf won't be able to get out of the tag.

Just as Callum launches himself off the ground, I take a hold of his tail and give it a good pull. Callum stops in midair, as his large wolf body collapses to the floor, just missing the light brown wolf.

I chuckle as I hear his growl, but before he can retaliate, I take off running. I laugh as I hear his heavy paws falling far behind me.

For the rest of the 'task', I run around trying to avoid Axel, Celina, and Callum, help those who are about to be tagged and keep myself high in the trees. I've had a few run-ins with other wolves, but they just nodded at me and kept on running.

The task has been running for about six hours now, I don't even know who's left. I'm pretty sure that the first ten were taken out in the first three hours, but I can't be sure. This being the reason, at this very moment, I'm heading for the grounds to check everything out.

Somehow, I've managed to dodge the taggers the past hour and arrive at the grounds without being seen or tagged. They do have to cover a lot of ground, though.

As I approach the grounds, I jump into the nearest tree. To my utter and complete surprise, everyone from the group is there. Including a very pissed off Taylor and Ally, who just looks a little shocked. I chuckle at their faces, priceless.

A black wolf, white wolf, and sandy wolf suddenly burst through the tree cover. No mistake, it's Axel, Celina, and Callum. They all head behind a different tree and shift, emerging again with clothes on.

They all make their way to the middle of the group while everyone stares at them expectantly.

Callum clears his throat. "Well, it seems like we can't find Alex. We've searched the whole territory and she's nowhere to be found. So!" he suddenly exclaims. I sit up from my relaxed position in the tree and listen intently. "Whoever finds her gets to eat her infamous 'Alex's special desert'!"

40

A round of cheers is heard as I raise an eyebrow. They expect me to cook? Please! They can cook for themselves! I ain't their bloody slave!

I jump down from my tree and strut my way into the grounds. No one notices me since they're still all cheering, so I decided to change that.

"You expect me to cook?" Everyone's head snaps towards me at the sound of my voice. I look at Taylor and Ally to see that they're sporting big grins. Probably because they know I so wouldn't cook for the person who found me. No way in hell!

I look at Callum to his shocked and slightly surprised face. I raise an eyebrow at him while putting on a look that says, 'really?' He sends me a sheepish smile and I can't help but roll my eyes at him. He's so ridiculous.

I then look to Axel and Celina. Axel's face shows one of approval and pride. My wolf howls in happiness knowing that her alpha is proud of her.

Then I look to Celina to which I realise that she's not standing where I originally thought she was. The next moment, I'm engulfed in a hug by small and dainty arms. Celina.

I stand there in shock for a moment as Celina, my Luna, my shy and kind Luna, hugs me. Why is she hugging me? Nonetheless, I hug her back with all my might. She hugs like a mother, and I haven't had a motherly hug in a very, very long time. She may be only a year older than me, but she's certainly a lot wiser than her age.

She pulls back to smile at me in relief. I stare at her confused. Relief? Why is relief showing on her face?

"Alex," she breathes. "I'm so glad you're safe! We've been looking for you for hours! Don't ever do that again! You had us worried sick!" she scolds as she pulls me into another hug.

Wha... I'm so confused...

"Celina, I think she's gonna suffocate if you keep hugging her," Axel says softly as he pries Celina's arms off me.

He pulls her into his arms as he nods his head at me. I nod back with a small smile. Axel takes Celina inside as he leaves Callum to deal with us.

I give him an expectant look as he clears his throat. He is so not getting dessert tonight.

"Right, uh... Since we have everyone here, it's time to announce who shall be assigned to the mission," he says as he looks directly at me the whole time.

I smirk at him as I make my way to stand next to Taylor and Ally. Callum continues to go on and on about how dangerous the mission is and all that stuff. To be honest, I tune out.

"Pst! Alex!" Taylor whisper yells. I tune back in and look at her. She motions to Callum with her eyes, so I turn my head to him and actually listen.

"Now to announce those who are taking part in the mission," he says as everyone's eyes transfix on him. We all hold our breaths, even though all of us know our fates.

"The following people step forward: Alex, Ally, Derek, Scott, Luke, Sam, Liam, Noah, Louie and Taylor." We all step forward, and I can't help but grin at the people who are standing beside me. "You are the people who we have chosen!" Callum says proudly and just like that, I feel like I've finally accomplished something in my life.

42

6

ALEX

After we were all announced, Callum leads us all into the pack house and to the meeting room. The meeting room is pretty much a place for the pack to meet and talk about situations, problems, etc. It's pretty boring actually.

In the middle of the meeting room is a long table, which could hold at least twenty people, with black, leather chairs surrounding it. I've never actually been in the meeting room since it's only for the high rankers and for guests who are high rankers.

"Take a seat," Callum calmly states as we all take a seat on one of the black, leather chairs. Callum then walks out of the room, leaving us to discuss what happened.

"Holy shit! I don't believe I'm in the selected ten!" Sam exclaims with a wide grin. We all grin along with him and nod our heads. We're all young adults here and most of us know each other, so it shouldn't be hard to get on.

"I know! I wouldn't be here though if Alex didn't come to my rescue. Would've been the first one out of the game," Louie suddenly states as he looks at me with a grateful look.

I stare back at him confused. "What?" I ask bluntly. Most of the guys all look at me with the same look of gratefulness while I continue to stare at them all, confused.

Derek rolls his eyes at me. "Alex, you pretty much saved all our asses by stopping the taggers from getting us."

My mouth forms an 'O' as I realise what they're talking about. Louie must've been the blonde wolf...

I shrug and lean back in my chair. "No biggie, just doing what I would've done in a real situation." The room falls silent at my words. Not an awkward silence or anything, more of a meaningful one.

At this point, Callum walks back in, but he's not alone. Accompanying him are Axel and Celina, who is also not alone. Holding Axel's hand, his eldest three-year-old boy, Jett, grips it tightly with a big grin on his face. He takes after his mother with pitch black hair. He has his father's frame though and, even at three, his infamous smirk.

Holding Celina's hand, her second born, Dylan, happily walks along with his mother with a charming smile on his slightly chubby face. He also has his mother's hair, but his father's frame.

The third little angel that is happily resting in Celina's arms is Clarissa. She has her father's snow white hair that falls gracefully down her back. She has her mother's petite and dainty figure, as well as her beautiful smile.

One thing's for sure, Jett and Dylan are going to be scaring a lot of horny werewolves away from their little sister. I chuckle at that thought.

The similarity between them all, though, is their eyes. All three triplets have silver eyes with golden swirls, making them look mysterious and magical.

Seeing Celina struggling a little with holding her excited boy's hand and holding Clarissa, I quickly jump and make my way over to her.

"Here, let me help," I offer as I get up from my chair, all eyes on me, and head towards a struggling Celina.

Celina smiles gratefully at me as I take Clarissa from her arms so that she can pick up Dylan. She lets out a big breath as she cuddles her baby boy to her chest.

"I swear, they wake up from a nap and bam! They're jumping around and almost impossible to control," Celina tells me exasperated as she takes her seat next to Axel, at the head of the long table.

I chuckle and take my seat, which happens to be next to Celina's near the head. I sigh as I look at the three highest rankers in the pack. They all look stressed and... relieved in a way.

The little girl in my arms giggles. I look down to Clarissa's beautiful little face, that reminds me so much of her mother, and raise an eyebrow.

"What are you giggling about?" I whisper in her ear. She giggles again, and I smile. Clarissa's a shy child and not very social, taking after her mother I suppose. She adores me, though because I'm always offering to help out with them when Celina and Axel have pack business to worry about.

"Nothing," Clarissa says innocently as she giggles again. I roll my eyes at her as I look to Callum, who looks like he's about to start a very important speech. I motion for Clarissa to be silent; she obediently follows.

"You were selected as the top 10 to carry out this mission because we believe you are the strongest and most capable of accomplishing it. A lot of thought has been put into this mission, and we can't afford to have a slip-up," Callum states in a serious voice. I actually blink in shock because I've never really heard Callum be this serious before.

Axel takes it over from here, saying in his naturally loud and powerful voice, "This mission is a rescue mission. You all remember the war a few years ago?" Angry growls and sad nods answer his answer, I stay quiet. "Well, one of Celina's guardians was captured that day, and we intend to get him back."

Silence. That's what follows Axel's announcement. I look around the table to see the shocked faces of my friends and shocked faces of those I still have to get to know.

Axel makes eye contact with every single one us. Stopping on me with his little girl in my arms, his eyes soften at the sight of his little angel. They instantly snap back up to me, though, hard and cold.

"Why don't you seem as shocked as the rest, Alex? Are you not feeling remorse for your lost pack mate?" he questions in an over powering voice.

I bow my head in respect as I answer. "I'm sorry if I offend you in any way when I say this, Alpha, but I figured out a long time ago that this group and mission had something to do with Celina's missing guardian," I answer with honesty, which seems to shock him for a moment.

He nods his head in approval, nonetheless, and sits back down in his seat. He puts on a thinking face as Callum and Celina look at him expectantly. He ignores them though and continues on to say what he initially intended to.

"The plan is simple, we will split into three groups. The first group will be Sam, Louie, Luke, and Taylor. Your job will be to distract those who are surrounding where Comrade is being held. We need you to lead them away so that the second group can come in." The four people who are mentioned all nod their heads and listen intently to what happens next.

"The job of the second group..." Axel continues to say, "is to infiltrate the location. You need to take out anyone who gets in the way of our mission. Don't let anything stop you or else it could change the outcome for all of us. In simple terms, the whole group is depending on you."

Everyone gulps at the warning.

"Who's in that group?" I ask when everyone's eyes fill with anticipation.

Axel clears his throat before looking at us. "Derek, Scott, Liam, Noah and Ally will be a part of this group. You five were in the top six and required the most minimal help from Alex." He spares me a look to which I look innocently back at. He rolls his eyes at me.

That's when it hits me: what group am I in?

"Uh, Alpha? If I'm not in group one or two, what group am I in?" I question confused. To my surprise, Axel grins. After seeing his face, both Callum and Celina grin as well, as relief fill their eyes.

"You Alex will be in a group with Celina, Callum, and I. We will be the ones who'll actually find Comrade and make sure he gets out safe and sound."

I stare in shock at Axel, as does everyone else.

I'm gonna be in a group with the three most high ranking wolves in the pack? Well then... Hallelujah!

A big grin takes over my face as I quickly get up, making sure Clarissa is holding on tight, and take Axel's hand in mine, shaking it vigorously.

"Thank you, Alpha, thank you so much," I say gratefully with a big grin on my face. I don't believe it! As girlish as that sounds, I honestly can't!

"You're very welcome. Now, everyone else, go rest up. You've all had a long day, and we want you well rested and ready for when training starts in two days. You're dismissed," Axel announces, so everyone makes their way out of the room, I included. I've already given Clarissa back to Celina.

"Oh! One more thing!" Everyone freezes with Taylor's hand on the door knob. We all look at him expectantly. "The group leaders will be Taylor and Ally. They were the in the top three, so you answer to them."

Curses and groans are heard as Taylor and Ally smirk at the boys. They saunter out of the meeting room with their heads held high and all the boys trailing behind them as they complain and groan.

I chuckle and go to follow them before Axel calls me back. I obediently obey as I come back inside to see what Axel wishes to tell me. Clarissa comes running back up to me, and I smile as I gather her in my arms. She giggles her adorable giggle while my smile grows bigger. She's so cute!

"So, what did you want to talk about?" I ask formally as I look to Callum. Callum looks to Celina, who looks to Axel, who then looks to me. Okay then...

"Alex, you are aware that some of the group may not come out of this alive." I nod my head in answer to Axel's stern voice. "Well, knowing your nature, you will want to help them. That is not your job. Your job is to get Comrade out of the building safely, not help those in need."

I stare at Axel in disbelief. Is he asking me to let my friends die when I can help them? Yes, yes he is.

"Alpha, I-" I start, but I'm cut off by Callum.

"Alex, the alpha's right. You need to focus on your part of the mission and not anyone else's. It could jeopardise all of us," Callum advises. I grind my teeth together to keep in a growl. They are my alpha and beta after all.

"You're okay with this?" I ask as I look to Celina. Her eyes widen at my question.

"I, uh. Well... I- you, um..." she stutters as she looks to Axel for help. Being the knight in shining armor he is, Axel steps up.

"You will not question what we have chosen, Alex. If you choose to disobey, so be it. You will be taken out of the group and stay here while we go and continue on with the mission," Axel says in a voice that leaves no room for argument.

My eye twitches in anger, but I can't do anything about it because Axel is my alpha. He's the one that tells me what I can and can't do and right now, he's telling me what I can't do.

I stiffly put down Clarissa as I ball my hands into fists. I grind my teeth together and try to take deep calming breaths. Of course, it isn't working.

The silence is the room is deafening as they all wait for my answer. Celina and Callum's eyes look panicked while Axel's eyes show he couldn't care less.

I take a deep, calming breath as I try to think of what to say. What am I supposed to say when my own alpha is telling me to let my friends die?

So, I decide to answer as honestly as I can. "Alpha, I will continue with this mission and follow your orders, but I hope you realise this comes at a price. You are asking me to

49

stand back and watch my friends die when I could potentially help them when I could potentially save their life. You are asking me to stand back and watch my own pack die? If I lose a friend that day when I could've saved them, I will promise you one thing... I will never forgive you and I will not be calling you my alpha."

With that being said, I calmly walk out of the room. I hear Axel's growl at the sound of my threat, but I don't care. What I said is true. If I lose a friend I could've kept alive, he doesn't have the right to be called my alpha.

7

COMRADE

I fight to keep my eyes ajar as I hear the heavy door open once again. Don't they see I've had enough? I've already been through six freaking beatings! I don't think I'll survive the next one...

Through my hardly open eyes, I see the usual guard bringing my dinner. I almost cry out in relief when I see he just dumps it and leaves.

With the little strength I have, I drag myself over to the food and greedily eat it. I'm not sure what the brown glop is, but it's better than a beating.

After finishing the glop, I drag myself back over to my rag. I try to make myself as comfy as possible, which isn't possible. I sigh as I slowly roll onto my back, wincing from the pain it causes me. At least tomorrow will be a better day...

Tomorrow's a Sunday, which means that I get my rest from the beatings, torture, questioning, everything including food. I've been going every Sunday without food for more than three years. I'm sure I'll survive.

Sunday's also a time for Kate to come down and spend most of the day with me. Since everyone's engrossed in whatever they're doing, Kate takes the opportunity to sneak in. I think Kate's the only one that loves me anymore. Not Celina, not Axel, and not Callum. Kate. Kate's the only one that loves me, and I'm ok with that.

With that happy thought in my mind, a really rare thought, mind you, I drift into a dreamless sleep.

"Comrade? Comrade, wake up," a soft voice says into my ear. I mumble and roll over, not ready to be woken up.

The voice giggles while a small handshakes me awake. "Come on, Comrade," the voice says again.

I groan but open my eyes anyway. I'm met with Kate's hazel eyes that are shining with happiness.

"Comrade!" she speaks as she pulls me into a hug. I wrap my arms around her as much as I can; I'm still hurting a bit.

Kate pulls back with a wide smile, that's before she sees my state. Her eyes widen in shock, and a small gasp escapes her ajar lips.

I sigh as I try to calm her. "Kate, it's ok. I'm fine. Don't start worrying," I beg her in a small voice.

Tears fall from her eyes as she slowly traces a finger around the bruise near my eye. I'm surprised I didn't have a black eye... I guess I should be thankful, though. If I had a black eye, Kate would be feeling a whole lot worse.

"Did Dad do this to you?" she questions quietly. I shake my head, and her face fills with relief. I won't mention that he caused the bruise around my eye and a few other bruises because I really don't want to worry her. She doesn't deserve to see her so-called dad as a killer; she's too sweet for that.

Kate suddenly gets all excited as her eyes light up, and a big grin spreads across her face. I raise an eyebrow at her questioningly.

"I overheard something my dad was saying a few days ago," she begins while leaning closer to me like she's telling a secret. I motion for her to continue with my hand.

"I only caught bits and pieces, but what I did hear was something important, if my dad's tone was anything to go off. He said that they're coming, that they're preparing and he needs to get the pack ready," she whispers to me, excitement lacing her voice.

I become completely still and emotionless. They're coming? Does that mean... no? No! I will not get my hopes up! It could be anyone! I will not get my hopes up believing that Celina, Axel, and Callum are coming for me. I just won't...

"It's probably nothing Kate, just let it go," I mumble as I move away from her. She frowns at me, her excitement replaced by confusion.

"Aren't you happy, Comrade? This is what you've been asking me for the past two years, and you just shut out? You're not even a little bit hopeful that your friends are coming for you? Don't you care?" Kate asks me with disappointment in her voice.

Do I care? Do I really care that my friends, on a very slim chance, may be coming to rescue me? Do I really care? The answer to that question is... no. I don't care. I stopped caring a long time ago.

I shake my head at Kate and mutter in a deadly tone, "I stopped hoping a long time ago, Kate. My supposed friends haven't even made an appearance for three years. What difference would it make now? Why would I care now?"

She stays quiet at my question, just like I thought she would. I look up into her hazel eyes, and all I see is disappointment, sadness, and pity.

"I feel sorry for you, Comrade" she whispers as she backs away from my cell and stands back up. "You deserve better than this, so much better." With that being said, Kate walks away and closes the heavy door behind her.

I sigh and bury my face in my hands. As much as I hate to say this, I know I'm right. Celina, Axel, and Callum could've come for me a long time ago, so why choose now? Why now, of all the times I've hoped they'd come? Why now?

Later that night, the same guard comes to bring me my food. I greedily eat it up as the guard stands there, waiting for me to finish. He doesn't usually do that...

"That's right, you pathetic pup. Eat up, you'll need the energy," he tells me darkly with a sinister grin on his face. I narrow my eyes at him and growl low in my throat.

He just laughs at me and walks off, leaving the door open. By this point, I'm very confused, mainly for two reasons. The first one is that guards never stay to watch me eat; they usually just leave and collect my plates the next morning. The second reason is that never, in my whole time being here, has someone left the door open. I could easily escape if I could get through these bars, but I can't sadly.

I stay perfectly still as I just watch the door with anticipation. Something has to be happening if a guard leaves the door open... It would have to be on alpha's command, meaning that Damon has a surprise in store for me. Oh, joy...

Not five minutes later, I hear the laughter of many, as a dozen or so shadows appear near the door's entrance. I stiffen as I catch the scent of alcohol. They've been drinking... a lot.

I've encountered this a few times, Damon and his buddies if you can even call them that. They get drunk every once in a while, and they find it fun to let out all their frustration on me. I spend a lot more time in the torture room when that happens...

I close my eyes to keep myself calm for a moment. Breathe Comrade, breathe. As I hear their drunken laughter come closer, I shrink away into the shadows of my cell.

Damon laughs as he approaches it and fumbles with the keys for a moment, before finally unlocking my cell.

"Here, Comrade! Come on! Time to come out and play!" he taunts as he makes his way farther into my cell. All the men behind him erupt into laughter like it's the funniest thing they've ever heard.

Damon wobbles on his feet slightly and clutches at the bars of my cell to keep him steady. How pathetic. I then make the mistake of scoffing, ever so quietly. My eyes widen when I see Damon's eyes snap directly in my direction. A sly smirk appears on his face as he advances towards me.

Oh... Shit.

"Well, well, well, Comrade, I didn't find you as the hiding type," he snarls as he grabs me by the neck and throws me towards the men's anticipating arms.

I growl as they grip my arms, legs, ankles, and neck. I try to break free, but they all just laugh and make their way towards the dreaded torture room.

At the first chance they get, they chain me up in the same place Damon did a few weeks back. I growl and snarl as I struggle against the chains, the men still laughing at me.

I stop struggling when Damon comes in, glaring a hole in his head while he just smirks evilly.

"Do you want to know a secret, Comrade?" Damon taunts as he walks towards me ever so slowly. I growl in response, to which he chuckles. "I'll take that as a yes," he mumbles as he suddenly grips my neck in a deathly manner, only leaving the most minimal space for me to breathe air into my lungs.

"All your friends, they never loved you," he continues. I struggle against his hold while he tightens his grip slightly at my movement. "Callum, he hates you. He hates you because it's his job to protect Celina, not yours. You were just a waste of space. Then Axel never wanted you near his mate. He wanted to kill you the first chance he got. You know what? He almost succeeded, but I stepped in to finish the job." He releases a chuckle at that.

His eyes snap back to my own flaming ones. I'm beyond mad. How dare he accuse them of those horrid things! He doesn't know jack shit about them! All he ever wanted to do was kill them! He still wants to, for crying out loud!

"Now, don't even get me started on Celina."

I freeze at his words as my anger bubbles to the surface. For the first time in years, I feel my wolf. He's only lingering at the surface, but he's there, all right!

"She never wanted you as a guardian!" he seethes in my ear. I suppress the growl that's trying to make its way out of my throat, he's lying. "She never even liked you, she hated you. You were a waste of space when you were with them, and they want you to be replaced."

"You're lying," I whisper in anger, but Damon continues on as his little buddies take a hold of almost every single torture toy in the room.

"You wonder why she hasn't come for you yet? It's because she doesn't love you. Never has, never will. To her, you're dead. She's never gonna come for you. Never. She's a lost cause now, and it's all because I snatched you from under her nose!" he snarls in my face.

I clench my teeth in utter fury as my body starts to shake uncontrollably. He's lying. He's lying! I may not have hope, but I know that Celina would never think that. Ever! Or would she? I shake my head. Now he's got me double guessing myself!

I growl loudly as I feel that my wolf wants me to shift, but I can't. I'm too weak, and that thought just makes my anger intensify. Damon made me like this! He brought this onto me!

I thrash around as I try and get loose of the chains. Damon and his buddies all laugh at me. I release an almighty roar at them, their laughter just becomes louder. This resulted in me becoming angrier.

"You wanna know another secret, Comrade?" Damon asks, all laughter gone from his tone, only seriousness left.

I stop thrashing to narrow my eyes into slits. He will not insult me again.

"I don't want to hear anything from you!" I snarl back at him as I spit in his face. He raises his eyebrows as he wipes the spit away. The next second, I'm being backhanded across the face.

My head snaps to the side, and I clench my jaw tighter in aggravation. I will not let him get the better of me. He gets the pleasure of torturing me three days a week; I will not give him a fourth.

"Oh no, I think you'll want to hear this one," he says with a grin. I glare at him, but his grin just grows."You're familiar with my adopted daughter, Kate."

57

I stiffen at the disgust in his voice as he says 'adopted.' What's he getting at?

"I hardly know her," I lie straight through to my teeth as I say that.

Damon lets out a dark chuckle at my confession. "Bullshit you hardly know her! You don't think I didn't know she's been coming down here to talk to you for the last two years? Do you really think I'm that stupid?" he screams in my face. By this time, all Damon's 'buddies' have left. Only leaving Damon and me alone.

I become frozen as Damon's words register in my mind. He knows. He knows about Kate coming down to see me. She was so sneaky, though, and I never said a word. I didn't even hint it!

"I told you, I hardly know the freaking girl!" I scream back at him, deciding to play dumb. He snarls and narrows his eyes at me.

"Don't play dumb with me, Comrade. I know everything that happens in this pack house and Kate coming down to see you is one of them," he says in a voice that sends goosebumps down my spine.

"I told you, I don't know the girl. Hell! She's your daughter! Why would she come to see me?" I spit in distaste, obviously lying. Damon doesn't have to know that, though... Kate's the closest thing I have to a friend. I'll be damned if Damon gets to her.

"Daughter? Daughter! She's not my freaking daughter! The only reason why I adopted her was because Phyre wanted a child! If it were up to me, I wouldn't have adopted one!" he confesses in anger. I stare at him emotionless. Honestly, his confession doesn't surprise me in the slightest.

"So, what do you say about me bringing her down here? Give her a taste of what you go through, hmm?" he asks with a smirk as he circles me.

I growl on my own accord. No one deserves what I'm going through, whether it's Kate or my guards, no one deserves this. On the other hand, Damon seems like a pretty good applicant.

"Ah, so you defend her now? What was that you were saying about not knowing her?" Damon taunts as he stops in front of my face. I snarl and bare my teeth to him.

"No one deserves what you're inflicting on me. Only you deserve this, no one else," I tell him. If possible, I swear I see a flame ignite in his eyes. He's mad. Very mad.

"Still not confessing huh? Fine!" Damon says with a new tone to his voice before practically sprinting out of the torture room.

I sigh as I let my tensed muscles relax and my head to drop forward. I'm so weak, it makes me sick.

Just as I thought I'm going to get peace, Damon storms back in. To my horror, he's not alone. With his hand clutched around her shirt, Damon throws Kate roughly to the floor.

I swallow hard as I see her eyes fill with tears. I will not break. Kate looks up at me as a single tear slips down her cheek. I silently send her a look with my eyes to keep quiet. She nods slightly, telling me she understands.

"So, Comrade, still don't know her?" Damon asks with a certain look on his face. I look away from Kate to see Damon looking straight at me.

"No!" I growl. His eyes twitch in anger, and then, he does something I never thought he would do.

"Maybe I'll just have to... force it out of you." A sadistic grin forms on his face as I prepare myself for whatever he's gonna throw at me.

Then, to my horror, Damon turns to Kate and backhands her right across the face. I stare shocked as tears fall from Kate's eyes while Damon keeps the same sadistic grin on his face.

I growl loud, causing Damon to smirk at me. That's low, even for him. Never would I have thought that Damon would hit Kate like he did. That's just... cowardly.

"Just admit it already! This bitch had been coming down here to talk to you! The pathetic little pup that she sees as a weakling. You make me sick."

I snarl at Damon's words. Damn him! Damn him to the bloody ends of the earth!

The next few hours are unmentionable. The torture he inflicts upon me is nothing compared to the torture he inflicts upon Kate. When he finally gets the decency to leave, me being out of my chains, I rush to Kate and cradle her head in my lap.

Silent tears fall down her face, as she struggles to keep her eyes open. I grind my teeth and ball my hands into fists to stop myself from running after that bastard. Does he have no shame? Does he even have a heart?

"I'm sorry, Comrade. I'm so sorry," Kate whispers as more tears fall. I wipe them away, being careful of the bruising all over her face.

"Don't be sorry, Kate. You don't have to be. I'm sorry I got you in this mess. I promise, if what you say is true, about Celina, Axel, and Callum coming, I promise to take you with me. I promise," I whisper to her as she closes her eyes and falls into a motionless sleep.

I will get my revenge on Damon, for everything he's ever done. This isn't just about me now. He's hurt every single person ever close to me, and now it's my turn.

8

COMRADE

The next few days are miserable. Instead of picking on me, Damon starts picking on Kate. I don't know how much longer she'll survive. She doesn't know how to cope with this. The worst part is that I don't even know what he's doing to her! She just comes back to the cell battered, bruised, and she won't tell me anything. Most of the time, she falls asleep from exhaustion.

Damon's given up questioning me about Celina since he believes I know nothing. I haven't seen the torture room since that night. I shudder at the thought of it. I feel sorry for Kate, though; she's seen it a lot lately.

"Get in there, girly! You're done for the day!" Mr. Crusher, yes Mr. Crusher, says while he throws Kate back into the cell. I quickly rush to her side and cradle her head in my lap. I growl at Mr. Crusher as he walks out. I hear his laugh before the door is slammed shut.

Kate lets out a painful groan. She's gripping her left wrist in her hand, so I softly peel her fingers away and inspect it.

"It's not broken, just badly bruised. I'm so sorry, Kate," I whisper. She just smiles timidly at me and closes her eyes, falling asleep.

I sigh as I stroke her hair. She can't keep going through this, she just can't. She won't last, she hasn't even shifted yet! Just another reason for me to kill that son of a bitch, Damon. He better watch his back.

After hours of just sitting there with a sleeping Kate in my arms, the door opens to reveal the usual guard who brings food. I look up to glare at him, but I'm met with a sight that actually shocks me. Instead of food and a stone face, he's holding handcuffs, and his face is filled with fear. Why? I have no clue.

He yanks open the cell door, clasping the cuffs on our wrists before I can even retaliate. He throws Kate over his shoulder, causing me to growl. He doesn't pay me any mind, as he grips my shirt and starts dragging me along with him.

I look at Kate to check if she's all right, but she hasn't even opened her eyes. I panic. She has to be okay. Maybe she's just in a deep sleep, yeah... that's all. She's just sleeping.

I shake my head, even I know that's a stupid thought. Kate's not waking up because something's wrong. Something's not right, and I don't know if she's gonna make it.

"Hurry up!" the guard seethes. I use all my strength to try and hold him back, trying to get him to slow down. In my weak state, though, it doesn't really work.

"Why should I, you son of a bitch?" I growl back in challenge. In response, he growls.

"Don't test me! I can knock you out cold," he warns. I ignore his warning and send a harsh kick on the back of his leg.

He stops in his tracks and slowly turns around to face me with a menacing face. We're literally less than a metre away from the door, less than a metre away to the outside world.

"I said don't test me!" the guard roars then, true to his warning, he punches me square in the face, knocking me out cold.

I feel myself weakening as a headache hits me like a brick wall. I hold in my groan by gritting my teeth and slowly peeling my eyes open. I'm met with the shirt covered back of the guard who knocked me out. This time, I have to hold back my growl. He better watch his back too.

I turn my head to the left and still see an unconscious Kate. Her head keeps knocking against the guard's back, making me worry about her even more. I feel myself bobbing a bit too, so I'm guessing we're running. What's the rush?

"Damn it!" I hear the guy growl before he dumps Kate and me on the forest floor. I look up to the sky to see it pitch black, a full moon with no stars.

I look at Kate and wriggle my way over to her. I press my ear to her chest to see if her heart's still beating. It still is... thankfully.

"Seems like the boss can't do what he intended to do, so I'll just have to do it for him," the guard mutters before flipping out a pocket knife.

My eyes widen, and I growl. He pauses his movements before smirking and advancing to me.

I jump to my feet and snarl at the guard. He snarls right back and lunges for me. I jump into the air as he dives under me and I kick him square in the back.

He groans as he collapses to the floor, dropping the knife. He went to grab for it, but I quickly kick it out of his reach.

He stands wearily, eyeing me. I growl at him from low in my chest, it even surprises me a bit. His eyes widen as he stumbles to get away from me. I watch him run away like a coward, wishing that I could go after him. I can't though because that would mean leaving Kate alone. At night. I can't and won't do that.

I strain my ears to hear something, anything, as I cradle Kate's head in my lap. Well, as much as I can with my hands bound behind my back.

"It's all gonna be okay, Kate! It's all gonna be ok," I mumble in her ear as my eyes start to droop, the sudden coldness of the night hitting me hard.

Kate's small figure starts to shake from the cold, my body mimicking her. I need to keep her warm... I don't care what I'm feeling right now, all that matters is Kate.

As softly as I can, I remove Kate's head from my lap and lightly place it on the grass covered ground. Taking a deep breath, I close my eyes and jump, tucking my knees to my chest. When I open my eyes, my hands are still bound, but they're at the front instead of the back.

I quickly hug Kate's body to mine to try and keep her warm. Despite my efforts, her body continues to shake violently from the cold. I sigh as I come to the conclusion, that I may not be able to help her...

Hearing a howl in the distance makes my head snap up, and my eyes widen. Someone's here. I don't know if they're good or bad, but someone's here, and they can help.

I scoop Kate up bridal style the best way I can and take off running. Please be someone good who can help us. Be someone who can help Kate and I. Please, I'm begging you Moon Goddess, please.

I don't know how long I've run for, maybe twenty minutes, but I almost cry out in joy when I hear the sound of wolves. I burst out from the cover of the trees and enter what could be the description... of hell on earth.

I shrink back away into the cover of the trees and lightly set down Kate near a tree. I make sure she's comfy leaning against the tree before I slyly move through the cover again.

All different colours of wolves are battling it out what seems to be a broken down pack house outside. That must be where Damon was holding me. I growl at the thought. I will get that bastard one of these days.

A light brown wolf seems to hear my growl because the next thing I know, I'm being tackled to the ground. I growl at the wolf and buck her off me. She growls back but moves on to her next opponent.

The door of the pack house suddenly bursts off its hinges, revealing a sight I never thought I would see again. My breath catches in my throat at the sight of them. They came. They really came.

Time just seems to slow down as I look at them. There, standing just outside the door, are Celina and Axel in their wolf forms. Celina's beautiful snow white wolf looks as graceful and elegant as ever, next to Axel's pitch black wolf that looks as dominating and powerful as I remember.

66

I look to the left and see a sandy coloured wolf, the same sandy colour as Callum. A big grin makes its way onto my face at the sight of him. They came. They all came.

Axel lets out a howl that causes me to block my ears. All the wolves look at him, the only ones left are his pack. There's about ten of them all up.

They all shift back into human form and make their way to Axel. He starts speaking, but I don't hear a word he's saying. I just stand there with a big goofy grin on my face, one thought on my mind: I'm being rescued.

He continues talking as I look to Celina. She looks sad and defeated, but a little hope still shines in her eyes. All I want is for her to look up and see me; that's all I want. To see Celina's shining golden eyes locked with my dark ones. That would make my day, my cold, sad, and miserable day.

As if sensing me, Celina looks up. She freezes for a moment, her mouth ajar as she just looks at me. My grin becomes even wider at the sight of her tears of joy. She missed me. She actually missed me.

Her eyes suddenly fill with fear as she averts her eyes behind me. I give her a confused look and start to turn around. Before I can do that, though, a sharp pain goes through my lower abdomen. I look down to see the tip of a knife just peeking through my skin.

"You can run, but you can't hide forever, Comrade. I'll find you and get you if it's the last thing I do," a menacing voice, I can only recognise as Damon's, whispers harshly in my ear.

My vision starts to get blurry, and my world starts to spin. I collapse to the ground, but not before I see Celina push everyone out of her path and scream, "Comrade!"

9

ALEX

"Damn it!" I scream as I kick the wall beside me, leaving a nice dent in on the middle of it. We failed! We freaking failed! Damon is nowhere to be found, Comrade is nowhere to be found, and Damon's supposed daughter is nowhere to be found! This is ridiculous! The only bright side to this whole thing is that no one from the group is hurt.

Celina, Axel, and Callum have already gone to break the news to them. I can't bear going down there knowing we've failed; it's like a punch to the ego.

I sigh as I slowly start to make my way down. I have to show up sooner or later. I lift my hanging head to see the backs of Celina and Axel standing just outside the door. Axel's going on about how we didn't find Comrade, and we need to go back to work something out and *yadda yadda yadda*. Honestly, I could care less.

Just as I'm about to make my way through the door, I hear Celina scream. I don't understand what she says, but I'm on full alert. Her voice is full of pain and regret, which worries me. I quickly burst through everyone to see Celina collapse to the floor next to a man.

I quickly rush to her, since everyone else seems to be in shock, and place a hand on her shoulder. She looks at me with teary eyes, her bottom lip trembling. Sometimes you can forget that, although Celina is very strong, she's still only nineteen and can break down just like anyone else.

"Celina, you need to back away. I can help," I say cautiously to her. She draws in a shaky breath but nods her head. Axel gathers her in his arms as they both watch me.

I inspect the man lying unconscious before me. He's got dark brown hair and a slight stubble covering his jawline. Muscles can clearly be seen everywhere on him, but he still looks weak in a way. Overall, this man is beautiful.

I gently cup his cheek with my hand and feel sparks shoot through me. I gasp and draw it back, looking at this man in shock. He... He can't be. Can he?

'Mate!' I hear my wolf scream in my head, itching to get out and see her mate. I stay frozen, though, not believing my eyes or my feelings. This can't be happening... not now.

"Alex!" I hear Axel suddenly scream. I shake my head to get rid of those thoughts and quickly get to work. I can't let the fact that this man being my mate get in the way of me saving his life. I may not end up with a mate at all.

I turn him on his side, looking for the handle of the dagger. I saw the tip poking through, so I'm guessing it's a dagger. Easily finding it near the lower abdomen, I slowly draw it out.

I don't bother looking at it as I throw it away. This man is my main priority, and that's all I'm gonna think about right now. I quickly do a brief look over of the wound. Blood quickly escape him, and since it's cut straight through him, it may have hit a major organ. I can't tell, though, he needs proper medical attention to see if it's true. I hope with all my heart it isn't.

"Please help him, please help Comrade stay alive," I hear Celina whisper, causing me to freeze. Comrade? This is Comrade?

"This is Comrade?" I voice my thoughts. I look to Celina for confirmation; she only nods her head in sadness. For the love of the Moon Goddess, my mate is the long lost Comrade? This can't be happening to me...

I quickly shake my head and get back to work. Without really thinking it through, I rip off the whole bottom part of my shirt, right up under my bra line. I didn't shift for this mission, so I'm fully clothed.

I turn to Taylor, Ally, and Celina, since they seem to be wearing shirts also. "Rip your shirts! I'm using it as a bandage," I order, to which they immediately comply.

Once I have the four ripped fabrics, I tie them together to make a really dodgy bandage. I hope this works...

"Hang in there a little bit longer Comrade," I whisper in his ear as I start to wrap the bandage around his wound. Blood instantly stains the fabric, but the bandage luckily gets around him at least three times. At least the blood has to get through a few layers. Plus, I tied the pretty tight so that pressure is being applied.

"Ok, that's all I can do. The best thing for him now is to seek proper medical attention. I can't do anything more," I tell them strongly, though, on the inside, I'm slowly breaking down. This is my mate we're talking about, and he's dying. The thing that angers me the most is that I can't do anything more for him.

"Group One! You will escort Comrade back to the pack house as fast as possible! Taylor!" Axel bellows. Taylor stands to attention immediately. If we weren't in this situation, I would laugh at her face. "Carry Comrade and for the love of the Moon Goddess, don't drop him."

Taylor nods and quickly leads her group away. I go to follow them, but Celina's hand on my shoulder stops me. I look at her with pleading eyes.

"Please, Luna, I'm begging you. Just let me stay with him," I plead with her. Axel's telling Group Two what to do, so he isn't paying attention right now. This gives Celina the opportunity to put her stupid observing skills to the test and catch me red handed.

"He's your mate, isn't he?" she questions softly. I direct my eyes downward and nod. No point hiding it from my Luna. What will she say, though? Will she accept me as Comrade's mate? I mean, he's her guardian and friend. What will she think of it?

"Hey, stop looking so down. You've found your mate, that's something to celebrate," Celina tells me with a small smile. I look into her beautiful golden eyes that seem to shine with constant happiness. She's ok with this?

"You accept me then?" I question quietly. Celina looks confused for a moment before it dawns on her about what I mean.

"Of course, I do! Why wouldn't I? You're perfect for Comrade. You'll keep him in line and stop him from running off into the woods," Celina mutters with a shake of her head. I chuckle at her. I guess she's right.

"Anyway, I couldn't have asked for a better mate for Comrade. I promise he'll make you very happy and vice versa," Celina wraps up with a big smile. I smile back and wrap my arms around her, pulling her into a hug.

"Thank you, Luna," I whisper in her ear. She hugs me back with a big squeeze as I close my eyes in content. I guess something good has come out of today then.

"Alpha! Luna!" I hear a frantic voice, sounding a lot like Ally's, suddenly yell. I rip myself from Celina's grasp and quickly run over to her. I grip her shoulders and look into her shocked eyes.

"Ally? Ally, what's wrong?" I question her calmly. All she does is raise a shaky hand and point. I follow her hand and the vision that my eyes are seeing shocks me.

I quickly rush over to the unconscious, battered, and bruised girl. She can't be older than thirteen. I inspect the purple bruises that seem to be all over her body and check to see if there are any broken bones.

"Alex? Is she ok?" Celina's worried voice asks me. My brows furrow as I inspect the girl more closely. These bruises are fresh.

"These bruises are fresh," I voice my thoughts to everyone as I lightly touch one on her cheek. "They could have done this not more than two hours ago," I continue to say.

Damon must have done this, that bastard. Does he have no heart? No remorse for beating an innocent child? When I get my hands on him, I'm gonna-

"Any broken bones?" Axel's question brings me out of my raging thoughts. I blink a few times to come back to the present.

I clear my throat before answering. "Uh...no. There doesn't seem to be any, but her wrist is pretty much on the

72

verge of being broken. It's already swelling up!" I tell him as I observe her wrist more closely.

I squint my eyes as I look at the marks on her. They're... whip marks? Not massive ones like you see in movies and such, but just small ones that seem to cover her whole wrist. Then there's the imprint of a person's fingers in the shape of a bruise. Whoever did this certainly knew what they were doing. I don't have any doubt in my mind that it was Damon.

"I think we need to get this girl to doctor Aileen. This isn't a normal wrist injury," I mumble as I continue to inspect it. It's so strange...

"What do you mean it's not normal? Like someone beat her wrist?" Ally questions with a scoff.

I draw my eyes away from the girl's wrist to look Ally in the eye. "Precisely," I tell her, no room for thinking on her part.

Her eyes widen as she rushes to the girl's side. She lightly brushes away the hairs on her forehead, before looking at me, then to Axel.

"Please, Alpha, may I take her to doctor Aileen? I want to do it myself since I found her," Ally questions while standing up.

Axel nods and tells her to take the rest of her group. She nods and gently scoops the girl up into her arms. She directs her attention to the woods and takes off running with her group.

I watch her go, wishing that the girl will be alright. She seems pretty beaten up for someone her age.

"We better be heading back too, the pack will be feeling antsy," I hear Axel say as he directs Celina towards the forest. They both shift and take off running. I stay where I am.

I walk to stand in front of the pack house, the place that held Comrade for so long. The place that held my mate for so long.

I can't even begin to imagine what must have gone on inside this house, but one thing's for sure... Comrade is one strong guy to have lived through it. The strength he must have used to stay alive in this hell hole is just unthinkable. He's truly brave to be able to put up with it, to put up with Damon.

"Alex?"

I jump at the unexpected voice. I thought everyone has gone. I turn around to see Callum standing there, looking at me. I turn back to the house, knowing he's not a threat.

"Are you alright?" he questions as he comes to stand next to me and stares up at the run-down house. The paint on the walls is peeling off. The place looks like it's about to collapse and you don't even want to see inside.

"Just peachy," I mutter, causing Callum to chuckle at me. I sigh. Peachy is definitely not the best word to describe what I'm feeling right now.

"You know, Alex, when you first joined the group, I thought: what's a girl like you doing in a group like this? That's honestly what I thought. Well, I was certainly proven wrong. You're one of the strongest wolves I've ever trained, and that's saying a lot since I train the pack's warriors," he tells me jokingly. I chuckle when he nudges my shoulder playfully.

"I learnt something about you, though," he continues on. "I learnt, that no matter what you were doing, you always had this look in your eye that said 'don't give up.' You showed that today, so don't beat yourself up over the fact that we didn't accomplish every single detail we intended to."

I look at Callum to see him smiling slightly. He's right, though; I shouldn't dwell on what's already happened. It's happened, and that's that, nothing can change it.

"I'll kill him, you know?" I say after a few moments silence. I look at Callum in the eye as he stares back at me.

"I know," he says before shifting into his wolf. That's the good thing about Callum; he just accepts the inevitable. I will kill Damon, and no one will stop me.

He nudges his head towards the forest, asking me if I'm coming. I nod with a half-smile then take off running in my human form next to him.

So many things have happened in such a short time span. We found Comrade and saved him, but now he's lying on his death bed because we couldn't find Damon to stop him. We found that girl battered and bruised. If we came earlier, could we have prevented that? On top of all this, we lost Damon. We lost the reason why all of this is happening. We lost our missing link.

Callum and I arrive back at the pack house in a few hours. As soon as I step through the door, I go to my room for a shower. A nice hot one at that. I quickly get my clothes and head into the bathroom.

Twenty minutes later and I'm stepping out of my room with one destination in mind: Comrade.

Truth be told, ever since Taylor ran into the forest with him on her back, I've been missing him. I know, weird right? I don't even know the guy, and I'm missing him! Although my mate is on his death bed right at this second, all I want to do is hold him in my arms. So, that's exactly what I'm going to do.

I walk fast to the medic room, where I know Comrade is being held. Doctor Aileen will take good care of him, though, she's the best doctor I know.

I come to an abrupt stop at the front of the medic room door. Do I really want to go in and see my almost dead mate? Yes. Do I want to come off as an obsessed, crazy person who looks like she's about to kill something? No.

I take a deep breath and calm my racing heart. It'll be no good if I walk in there looking like a crazy person, so I may as well be calm about it.

Here goes nothing...

I gingerly push the door open and walk inside. Doctor Aileen looks up to me surprised. I smile nervously at her. I didn't think that I'd have to go through Doctor Aileen to get to Comrade.

"Alex? What are you doing here?" Doctor Aileen questions with a hint of suspicion. I probably should've come up with an excuse before walking in here.

Me being me, though, I just come up with an excuse on the tip of my tongue. "The Alpha actually sent me to check up on Comrade. He wants me to stay with him to monitor his progress," I tell her with a straight face. I must say, I'm pretty proud of that excuse.

She raises her eyebrows at me. "The Alpha, huh? I'm pretty sure he would inform me if he were sending someone to monitor one of my patients," she says while walking closer to me.

I lift my chin high and answer her back, "Well, I was the one who tended to him on sight, so the Alpha thought it was appropriate. Accept my apologies if he didn't inform you."

Doctor Aileen searches my eyes for a few minutes, before nodding and directing me to Comrade. That was a lot easier than I thought it would be. Maybe she knows... nah! She doesn't know. How could she?

"This is his room, stay as long as you wish," she tells me then walks away. I stay frozen on the spot, not answering her back.

Right behind this door is my mate, the person I'm supposed to spend the rest of my life with. I'm pretty sure I'm gonna walk in and see his motionless body just hanging on for dear life, so I take a deep breath and push the door open before I can second guess myself.

The sight I'm greeted with is something I never expect to see. Something that shocks me to the point that I'm frozen with my mouth ajar, my eyes wide as saucers, and my hand still on the doorknob.

10

COMRADE

I turn my head to the side as I hear the door open. My eyes are half open, my body limp and most of my injuries are on full view, except for the knife wound. That doesn't stop the warm feeling that envelopes me when I see the most beautiful girl standing at the door.

Her perfectly layered blonde hair falls down past her shoulders, framing her glowing face. Her shining bluish-green eyes remind me so much of an ocean during a storm. So many emotions are running through them: love, adoration, happiness, but there's also hurt and pain, and that makes me sad. This beautiful girl shouldn't feel hurt; her pink lips should be smiling instead of frowning.

I weakly lift my hand the slightest bit - it's sad how much effort this takes me. The girl looks hesitantly at my hand, her stormy eyes looking like she's having an internal battle with herself.

"Come here," I mutter weakly. The girl's face breaks just like that. Tears fill her eyes, her bottom lip starts to tremble, and she just launches for my hand.

As soon as her tight grip locks on my hand, sparks ignite. I lay my head back with a small smile on my face, suddenly content. Mate. I've found my mate. This beautiful girl is my mate. The only thing that doesn't make sense is why my wolf didn't tell me when I first saw her.

She suddenly burst out crying, burying her head in my shoulder as she sobs uncontrollably. My heart breaks at the sound. My heart breaks ever more at the realisation that I'm the cause of her tears.

"Shh, it's ok. Everything's ok," I coo into her ear, softly kissing her temple. I lift my hand to stroke her hair as she cries even harder, the sobs racking her body.

"E-everything's not o-ok!" she wails, pulling back from my shoulder to look at me. Her eyes are bloodshot and puffy, her lips trembling and tears are still running down her flushed cheeks. All I want to do is wipe them away, tell her everything's okay, and take her in my arms.

"Y-you almost died! D-don't you see! I expect to c-come in here and s-see you half d-dead! Half dead! Do y-you know how m-much that r-reality hurts me? I don't k-know what I would've d-done if I came in h-here and saw that, I just d-don't." Her voice dies down to a whisper near the end.

I grip her hand again, but I don't think she notices. She just stares into space like she's remembering a memory.

"I can't lose you, I can't lose anyone else. I just want you to be safe," she says with a whimper. She closes her eyes and takes a deep breath, trying to compose herself.

I gingerly lift my hand, straining my muscles to do so and gently cup her face. She leans into my touch and places her hand over mine.

"You won't lose me, ever. I promise. There's no getting rid of me," I lightly joke, wanting to see her smile. To my relief, a small smile breaks out on her face.

"Promise?" she whispers, her eyes still closed.

"Promise," I confirm.

We sit there in silence for what seems like an eternity. I don't mind, though, it's nice to be able to hold my mate's hand.

Mate. This is a word I never thought I would say, let alone actually have! I actually have a mate... A beautiful, strong, and caring mate. I wonder what her name is...

My eyes snap open at the realisation. I don't know my own mate's name? I don't believe I haven't asked yet!

"Hey, you awake?" I ask quietly, lightly patting her cheek. She stirs and her beautiful eyes open, then she graces me with a tired smile.

"Yeah," she breathes out.

I smile slightly before asking quietly, "Sorry, but what's your name?"

Her eyes widen, and her cheeks flush a cute pink. Her eyes widen even more as she covers her cheeks with her hands. She groans and drops her head onto the bed. I laugh at her but wince as pain courses my body.

I feel a hand on my shoulder, making me look up and into the worried eyes of my mate. I give her a reassuring smile, causing her to frown.

"Alex. My name is Alex," she tells me as she sits back on the chair she pulled over a while ago. Alex?

"Alex," I test out on my tongue; it comes out of my mouth with ease. I see Alex shiver out of the corner of my eye and grin. I'm glad I have an effect on her, it'll come in handy.

"Well, I'm Comrade," I tell her with a smile, holding out my hand. She chuckles and shakes her head, but clutches my large hand in her smaller one.

"Nice to meet you, Comrade," she says in a joking manner. I chuckle as well, thankfully not causing myself pain.

A soft knock is heard before Doctor Aileen pops her head through the door. Alex looks at her with a sad expression, already knowing what she's going to say.

"I'm sorry to disturb, but the Alpha and Luna wish to see Comrade. Alex, you're going to have to leave," she says in a soft voice then closes the door with a click.

Alex sighs while getting up and taking the chair back to where she got it from. She comes back to me and places a kiss on my cheek. I close my eyes as sparks travel through me. She pulls back too soon, smiling sadly.

I realise something at this moment: I'm falling in love with this girl I just met... and I'm ok with it. This thought brings a smile to my face, a very small smile.

"You'll come back?" I question. Alex smiles again and nods.

"I'll always come back," she whispers. With that, she exits the room with her shoulders slumped.

I close my eyes as I watch her leave, as I watch my mate leave. My mate. I still can't get over the fact that I've actually found my mate. The one I will cherish forever and love to the ends of the earth, is finally with me. Finally.

I relax into the bed with a smile on my face. When I get out of this bed, the first thing I'm gonna do is spend time with my mate. Every single second of every single day, I will be with my mate.

"Comrade?"

My eyes snap open at the voice. The voice I've been dying to hear for three years. The voice that really brought me hope all those years ago when I met her. Celina.

"Celina?" I whisper as I turn my head. She's as beautiful as ever. Her pitch black hair longer than the last time I saw her, but still the same. Her golden eyes gleam with happiness and adoration as she stares at me, just like they always have.

She takes cautious steps forward, slowly making her way to the bed I'm laying helplessly on. I stretch out my hand to her, edging her to come to me. She does immediately.

Celina engulfs me in a hug, being careful not to agitate any of my wounds. I hug her back with one arm since I can't find the strength to use two at once.

"I missed you," she whispers into my neck. I stroke her hair with my hand and smile.

"I missed you too, Celina. You can't even begin to imagine how much," I whisper in reply.

She pulls back after a long while, wiping away some tears that have leaked through. I always wondered how Celina was coping with me being taken. I thought she gave up looking for me and moved on. I honestly did. How wrong can I be? Just by her reaction here, you can tell she missed me, and I doubt she rested for a day while searching for me.

A clearing of a throat draws my attention to the door. I look to the door, only to see Axel lazily leaning against it with a half-smile.

He makes his way over to me, wrapping his arms around Celina's waist, just like the happy couple I remember.

82

I hold out my hand to Axel and say, "Hey, long time no see."

Axel grips my hand in a firm grip, making me wince slightly.

He loosens his grip while answering, "A very long time. Sorry about that."

I chuckle a bit and shake my head, telling him it's all ok now.

Celina's eyes fall to my abdomen where a bandage covers the stab wound. She runs her delicate hands over it, feeling the bumps of the bandage as she goes.

"Does it hurt?" she whispers with tears in her eyes. Axel quickly takes her in his arms while trying to soothe her. I wish I could've done that with Alex, but I can't. Not yet anyway.

"A little, but not too much," I answer back with a reassuring smile. Axel nods at me, probably thanking me for lying to Celina. In all honestly, it hurts like a bitch. It's constantly throbbing, and it still feels like the knife is lodged in my skin.

A soft knock sounds at the door before it seems to magically open. I stare at it confused while Axel groans and Celina gasps in what seems like... outrage?

"What did I tell you three? Uncle Comrade isn't well enough to see you yet," Celina scolds while staring down at the floor.

"Mummy, we just wanna say hi," a small voice says from the floor. I'm beyond confused at this point.

Axel takes Celina in her arms while staring her in the eyes. They're mind linking each other over something, that much is noticeable. Finally, Celina sighs and nods her head.

Both Celina and Axel crouch down to the floor where two excited cheers are heard and a faint giggle. The next moment, they both stand back up to reveal three children who can't be older than three.

Celina's holding a girl in her arms. She has Axel's white hair and Celina's small, petite frame. She has beautiful eyes that are mainly silver with swirls of gold. I smile at her while she buries her head in Celina's shoulder. I see she has her mother's shyness.

I then look to Axel to see him holding two boys, one a little smaller than the other. They both have pitch black hair, just like Celina's. They both have the builds of an alpha, though. They have silver eyes swirling with gold, the perfect mix of Celina and Axel's unique eyes.

"Who are these little guys?" I question with a smile. Celina and Axel look at each other before smiling.

"The youngest is my little angel, Clarissa Rosemary Knight. She has Axel wrapped around her little finger," Celina tells me with a giggle. Axel groans.

"You haven't seen her puppy dog face, you can't say no to her! Anyway, I'd rather her be a daddy's girl than have her go chasing boys," he grumbles the last part, making me chuckle. Axel sure has his hands full with her.

"Our second born is Dylan Ronald Knight. He's turned out to be the real charmer. Somehow, he always manages to be at the wrong place at the wrong time. Yet, he never gets a scratch, splash, nothing on him. That child is a mystery," Celina mumbles the last part while Axel nods along.

I look towards the smaller of the two boys. He also looks at me, and I see the same spark I usually see in Callum's eyes. I shake my head with a small grin. Good luck, Celina...

"Then, um, our first born."Celina awkwardly clears her throat before saying, "Jett Comrade Knight."

I blink. They named their first born after me? I blink again. Did they think I wasn't coming back? Did they not think they'd be able to save me? Why? Why would they think that?

"Comrade?" Celina questions softly. I lock eyes with her and feel a swell of emotions. I can't keep track of them, they're all polar opposites. I feel happy that they named their son after me, but heartbroken because they thought they wouldn't find me.

"Uh, it was great seeing you guys. I'm a bit tired, though, so yeah..." I mumble as I look away. I honestly don't mean to hurt them, but I really need to get my emotions in check and having Celina and all of them around isn't going to help.

"Oh, ok. Come on, Uncle Comrade isn't feeling well. Let's go play outside," Celina says in fake cheerfulness to her children.

"Yay!" the two boys cheer while Clarissa releases a giggle. They all trail out, Celina sparing me a sad glance before leaving.

I sigh and close my eyes. Why does all the bad stuff happen to me? I was shunned by my pack because I was accused of my parents' death. I was a loner pretty much all through my schooling days. I had to watch Celina go through so much pain. I had to go to war. I got kidnapped. I was beaten and broken, then on top of that, I feel all of Celina's pain! I haven't felt it for the last three years, though... Probably because it wasn't as worse as what Damon was doing to me. Again, why does all the bad stuff happen to me? Why?

I feel anger course through me at the thought, raw anger. Everything that happens to me is somehow bad in its own special way. The only thing I can think of that isn't bad... is Alex.

Alex is the one thing that hasn't brought pain into my life. She's the only person who will ever truly love me for who I am now.

I'm not the same person I was three years ago. I'm different and tainted. No one, not even Celina, will understand that. Axel and Callum were once good friends of mine, but I'm changed. The only person who will understand me and help me be who I really am is Alex. She may even bring back the old me. With the way I acted with her, it's like I was never beaten, never bashed, never kidnapped.

What Damon's done to me is something no one can forget, no matter how hard they try. It's something that no one will understand because they haven't lived through it.

I hear the door open and close, but I don't bother to open my eyes to see who it is. It's probably just doctor Aileen coming to do a checkup.

I feel myself drifting off, but not before I feel sparks on my hand. Alex, she's come back. Just like she said she would.

11

COMRADE

"What! Chocolate is way better than strawberry! How can you even say that?" Alex yells at me. I laugh at her face, wide eyes, open mouth, and flushed cheeks. She's never looked more beautiful, though.

"No, strawberry for the win," I tell her with a grin. She shakes her head while mumbling on about how everyone loves chocolate.

It's been three weeks since I was rescued and I'm still in the bloody medic room. It gets boring just staring at bleach white walls that aren't decorated in any way. I can't wait to get out of this place.

It hasn't been that bad, though. Alex has been here 24/7 without complaint, and she's been helping me get back on my feet. Literally. Doctor Aileen has been getting me to go through physical therapy.

Celina and Axel come to visit often, sometimes just Celina. We talk about random things, but it just doesn't seem the same as it used to be. It's like... we don't even know each other. We're both older now, though. We've got our own things to worry about, and I'm sure Celina has a lot on her plate since she's the Luna of the most powerful pack.

Celina hasn't brought the triplets back. I think she got the idea the last time. I still don't understand why she would name her first born after me, it doesn't make sense. It's like she knew I was never coming back and lost all hope the day I disappeared.

"Comrade? Comrade, you ok?" Alex asks, waving her hand in front of my face.

"Hmm? Oh, yeah, I'm fine. I just can't wait to get out of here," I say exhausted. It's true; a white room with no excitement in it can get annoying. I just wanna be free like I've been wanting to be for the past three years.

"Well, Doctor Aileen says that you're improving with your physical abilities and that you should be out of here soon," Alex says with a soft smile, making me smile in return.

As if on cue, Doctor Aileen walks in through the door, scribbling something down on her clipboard. She looks up and smiles at us both before heading over to me.

"How are you feeling today, Comrade? Any pains, headaches, newly discovered injuries?" she questions. I shake my head. I actually feel perfectly fine; the only thing I don't feel is my wolf.

"Ok then, I'll just do some tests and then we'll see what happens," she tells me with a smile.

Alex excuses herself from the room, silently walking out the door. She hates seeing tests be done on me, it seems to get under her skin.

Doctor Aileen wraps the tests up within an hour, quickly scribbling down on her clipboard what she recorded.

She excuses herself from the room, but before she closes the door, I see her turn to Alex with a serious face.

I wait patiently, knowing the news can't be that bad. If anything, it'll be good news. I don't really know what can be worse than being cooped up in a tiny room with no form of entertainment. I honestly don't...

A few long minutes later, Alex walks back into the room. I stare at her face, easily reading her emotions. By the way her wide eyes, mouth slightly ajar, and the way her movements are stiff, she's in shock.

As soon as she's within arm's length from me, I grip her hand, sending sparks shooting through the both of us. She looks down at me, her stormy eyes looking like they can't believe what they just heard. "Alex, what did Doctor Aileen say?" I ask softly, drawing small circles on the back of her hand with my thumb.

"She- I- you- I mean..." she mumbles before taking a deep breath and looking at me in the eye. "You're being released."

I blink at her, released? Does that mean... A full blown smile comes to my face, and I feel a new hope starting to grow within me. Seeing my reaction, Alex smiles hesitantly and grips my hand.

"This is great news! When can I leave?" I ask eagerly. Alex chuckles and shakes her head at my reaction.

"You can leave right now if you want. Doctor Aileen says that your health is in tip-top shape, your muscles may need a bit more working and that everything seems to be in order. You're free to go," Alex says while beaming at me with a toothy smile.

Not even twenty minutes later, I'm finally walking out of the medic room. Doctor Aileen smiles at me, I smile back. She's helped me a lot over the past three weeks, and I can't be more grateful than I am now, in this moment.

Alex grips my hand in hers, looking nervous herself. I gently lift my hand to her cheek and turn her to face me. I place a soft kiss on her forehead, telling her everything's gonna be alright.

I grip the handle and take a deep breath. Finally... I push the door open, and the first thing to grace my eyes is sunlight. I grin and pull Alex along with me, heading straight to the backyard. I feel like a little kid at Christmas, I'm that excited.

"Comrade! Slow down! I don't want you to hurt yourself," Alex scolds me. I stop and turn to her, wrapping my arms around her waist for the very first time. Sparks go straight through me, and I can tell by her face that Alex can feel the same thing.

"It sounds like you're scolding your child than talking to your mate. Have you forgotten that I'm the older one in this equation?" I whisper in her ear, sending shivers down her spine.

I grin, pulling my head away to look at her face. Her eyes are closed, and she seems to be taking deep breaths through her nose and letting them out through her mouth, letting her mesmerizing scent wash over me.

"Sorry," she mutters, still in a daze. I grin wider as her stormy eyes open, revealing the submission she felt the need to show me.

Not wasting another second, I drag her the rest of the way to the backyard, bursting through the door. Birds are chirping, the wind is blowing, the pack children are running around playing, and the sun's light is raining down.

I let go of Alex's hand and make my way to the middle of the backyard. I lay down on the grass, my face up to the sun. I close my eyes and sigh contently. This is what I've missed. Just being able to lay in the sun with no worries in my mind... is the best thing.

Alex comes to sit next to me, placing my head in her lap. She runs her fingers through my hair, making a shiver run down my spine from the feeling it gives me.

"Comrade, I-" Alex begins, but is cut off as a child launches herself at her. She falls sideways, causing my head to fall from her lap and to the ground.

I hear Alex groan and quickly look up to see what caused her pain. On top of her, is a little girl that I can never forget. White hair and a small frame are all I can see from here, but it's all I need to see in order to know that it's Clarissa.

"Geez, Clarissa, can you launch yourself any harder?" Alex grumbles as she pushes herself up, Clarissa sliding into her lap.

Clarissa giggles and shakes her head, her long white hair dangling with the movement. I sigh and stand up, walking to stand behind Alex and place my hands on her shoulders.

Clarissa looks up at me, and her little cheeks flush bright red. I chuckle at her; she's so much like Celina. How did I not see this when Celina brought the triplets to see me?

"Clarissa!" a voice booms, traveling through the yard and making Clarissa's giggles cease. She looks up to Alex with wide eyes and quickly scurries off her lap, she goes to hide behind my legs.

91

I look up to see Axel storming across the yard, not looking very happy. I keep my face neutral when his eyes lock onto me.

"Comrade?" he questions confused, walking up to me. "I didn't know you got released."

"That's because I only got released about fifteen minutes ago," I reply with a halfhearted smile. He nods at me. He looks down at Alex and grunts. She rolls her eyes at him. I look between the two, sensing some tension. I wonder what Alex did to get under Axel's skin?

"Um, am I missing something?" I mutter to them but get no response. Alex glares up at Axel, her eyes like knives. Axel growls at the challenge, sticking his chest out and showing his dominance over her.

"Stand down, Alex! You can't beat me," he growls lowly at her. I feel a growl bubbling up in my chest. No one threatens my mate. Before I can retaliate, though, Alex beats me to it with a new determination in her voice."I know I can't beat you, but I know someone who can break you."

Axel growls at the threat while Alex just stands up and walks behind me. I'm frozen in shock over what's occurring. She's threatening her alpha and seems to be taking her chance at a fight with him. Is she crazy? I haven't even done that since I've met Axel.

A giggle soon fills the air as Alex emerges with Clarissa sitting effortlessly on her hip. I feel my heart melt at the sight. Alex will make an amazing mother when we have pups. Hopefully, that will be soon.

Axel looks down at his youngest and only daughter, his eyes softening. I feel my own eyes soften as I stare down at her. She's certainly a gem to behold, making everyone who sees her fall in love with her instantly.

"Daddy!" Clarissa exclaims, jumping from Alex's arms to Axel's. I stare at the little girl in shock, that's the first word I've ever heard her say, she only giggles or stays silent around me.

"Clarissa, were you hiding from me?" Axel asks cheekily. Clarissa giggles in his arms and shakes her head. "Told ya she'd break ya," Alex says with a triumphant grin while Axel just grumbles something about females. Alex laughs at him as he walks away, leaving us alone once again.

I turn to her in slight disbelief and awe. This girl, this beautiful and amazing girl, just stood up to her alpha and used his own daughter against him. She's certainly something... It's gonna keep me busy to make sure she stays in line.

"What was that?" I question with wide eyes. She just shrugs and grins at me. I roll my eyes at her and wrap an arm around her waist.

"I want you to meet some people," she tells me then starts dragging me back inside the pack house. I grin at our connected hands, feeling sparks all over my body. I can get used to this.

She stops outside a door on the second floor. She smiles a bit nervously at me before knocking and screaming, "Oi! Open this door, you crazy people!"

Before I can fathom, the door opens, and she's dragged inside, the door being shut and locked instantly after. I just stand there, slightly confused, looking at the door that my mate just disappeared into.

Two excited squeals are suddenly heard, and the door is quickly unlocked as a firm hand locks around my wrist and hauls me inside. I stumble slightly but quickly regain my balance.

"Careful! I don't want him to break," a voice mutters that I can only describe as my mate's. I turn my head to glare playfully at her as she attaches herself to my arm.

"Please! Look at these arms! We couldn't break him no matter how hard we tried!" a foreign voice exclaims. I look up to see two girls, one blonde haired and one brown haired. They both have brown eyes, just different shades, and the one with the brown hair is definitely taller than the other one.

"Comrade, I would like you to meet Ally and Taylor. Ally and Taylor, meet Comrade," Alex quickly says, getting the introductions over and done with. I quickly discover that Taylor's the blonde one, and Ally's the other one since Alex points them out.

Ally and Taylor's eyes widen, looking between Alex and myself. I stare back at them with a blank face, making Alex slap my arm lightly. "You mean the Comrade that..." Taylor trails off after getting a look from Alex. An awkward silence suddenly fills the room, making Alex's two friends shuffle on their feet.

"So, uh..." Ally starts but never finishes. She looks at Alex unsurely while Alex just shrugs and looks down.

"I'm leaving," I grunt, my mood quickly changing because of the atmosphere. I don't bother to see how the three girls react. I just push the door open and shut it with a little too much force.

I head to the room I once inhabited before the war, needing some me time. As soon as I walk in, I notice that nothing's changed. My bed is still unmade, some lone clothes are still on the floor, and my desk is still piled with work I never completed from school.

I sigh as I go and collapse on my bed, feeling a sense of familiarity wash over me. It's nice to be back in my own bed.

I flip over and look up at my plain white ceiling, thinking of nothing. I don't want to think of anything really. Thinking means pain, pain means hurt, and hurt means more pain. I don't want to go down that road for the hundredth time. That's exactly what will happen if I think about what just happened back with Alex.

A soft knock at the door makes me slightly lift my head from the pillows. I don't answer, not really wanting to see anyone. The person knocks again, then a third time, then a fourth.

"Oh for the love of the Goddess, go away!" I snap at the door. The knocking stops, the room going silent. I sigh and lay back down, happy to finally be alone.

The faint sound of someone leaning against the door and sliding down to the floor makes a heavy sigh leave my lips. I don't let that distract me, though, so I close my eyes and just listen to the nothingness.

"I'm sorry," a gentle voice says. My eyes snap open when I realise it's my mate. I slowly stand up and lean against the door, sliding down to the floor just like she did.

"I didn't think they'd react to you like that, I just... I don't know. They were part of the group that came and rescued you, you know? They helped, and I just thought they'd be happy to meet you, but then they reacted like that, and I didn't know what to say or do, and my mind just went blank, and I'm so sorry," she rambles on.

I stay silent, not really knowing what to say. How her friends reacted, it really got to me. They seemed so unsure and didn't know what to say like they were walking on eggshells. Is that how everyone's gonna react to me now, knowing that I've gone through something no one wants to experience? I don't think I can handle that.

"Well, dinner's in an hour or two. You're having dinner with the Alpha, Luna, and their kids, so be nice," she says jokingly. I laugh through my nose at that, a small smile appearing on my face.

I hear her get up and walk away, leaving me alone. I drop my head into my hands and run them through my hair. My life is different, and I hate it. I want things to go back to normal, the way they were before I was taken. That's not possible though, because it has happened, and there's no changing the past.

12

COMRADE

I drag myself out of my room, really not wanting to go to this dinner. I've seen Celina, Axel, and the triplets, so why do I need to have dinner with them? Geez, I sound like a whiny teenage girl. I grimace at the thought.

I make my way to the dining room, right on time. Celina sees me walk in and smiles, her eyes shining with happiness. Her smile takes away some of my reluctance, but not all.

Axel notices Celina smiling at me and sends me a curt nod. Now that he knows I'm fine and dandy, that's probably the best I'll get out of him. Axel and I were on good terms three years ago, we got along. I guess that's changed now.

"Comrade, take a seat. Dinner should be ready in a second," Celina tells me, her smile still in place. I turn to her confused. Doesn't she usually cook?

"Don't you usually cook?" I question, deciding to voice my thoughts. Celina always cooks, no matter what the occasion.

"I didn't want to be traveling between the kitchen and here because I want to spend time with you. So, I got one of our best cooks to cook us her famous lasagna," Celina says with a grin.

I blink. If Celina claims that this person is one of their best cooks, I'll take her word for it. Celina doesn't give out compliments for cooking very often.

The smell of lasagna suddenly wafts through my nose. I close my eyes at the smell of real food. Yes, I got real food in the medic room, but nothing to this extent.

"Alpha, Luna," a voice I instantly recognise says, as she places down two plates of lasagna in front of Celina and Axel.

"Thank you, Alex," Celina says with a smile. I stare at Alex as she places a plate down in front of me, hoping to catch her eye.

She looks into my eyes for a split second, sending me a wink. I chuckle as she leaves, catching the attention of Celina. She gives me a knowing look as a half-smile graces her face.

Alex walks back in with three more plates of lasagna, these of a smaller portion.

"Now then, which one of you is my knight in shining armor? Always ready to save the day?" Alex asks with a grin. Celina giggles while Axel just rolls his eyes.

I look to the three triplets to see Dylan shoot his hand up at the same time as Jett. The two boys look at each other and glare. Alex chuckles while putting a plate down in front of Dylan.

"Told ya so!" Dylan yells playfully at his older brother, sticking his tongue out. I let a ghost of a smile appear on my face, watching as Jett grumbles under his breath.

"Don't worry, Jett, you're the charmer. You'll have girls swooning at your feet in a few years," Alex says with a wink, causing Jett to puff out his chest. He's so much like Axel, always taking the glory and power.

She places the plate in front of Jett. He gets ready to tuck in before Celina sends him a look. He pouts and crosses his arms over his chest. For a moment, I forget that he's named after me and just stare at the three-year-old boy. The moment is short lived when I remember that they only named him after me because they thought I was dead.

"Last, but definitely not least, the princess that everyone loves," Alex says, placing a plate down in front of Clarissa. She looks up at Alex with a smile and giggles. The funny thing is, Clarissa is a Princess.

Alex bends down to whisper something in her ear, causing a wide smile to appear on Clarissa's face and for her to erupt into a fit of giggles.

"Enjoy your dinner, everyone," Alex says with a large grin before walking out of the room, leaving us to ourselves.

"I swear, I worry about that girl sometimes," Celina mutters under her breath. I chuckle, totally agreeing with her.

"Mummy? Can we start now?" Clarissa asks in her sweet and innocent voice I've heard only twice.

Celina smiles and nods, gazing at her daughter with adoration. I'm gonna have that one day, with Alex. We're going to have the most wonderful pups, and nothing's gonna keep us from it.

"So, Comrade. You doing ok?" Axel asks, shoving a forkful of lasagna into his mouth. I copy his movement, almost

99

moaning as the taste explodes in my mouth. Goddess, this is good.

"Yeah, why wouldn't I be?" I question after swallowing. Axel shakes his head, his lips rolling into his mouth.

"He's worried about you, Comrade," Celina informs me with a sad smile. "Although, he won't admit it. I'm worried about you too, so are you really ok?"

I grip my fork tighter, trying to control the anger that's bubbling to the surface. They're looking at me differently like I'm a totally different person. That may be true, but they don't have to rub it in.

"I'm fine," I grit out through clenched teeth. I quickly take another bite of the food, not wanting to answer any more questions.

Silence falls over the table after that, no one willing to break it. Celina has a frown on her face, looking like she's thinking something over. Axel just sits back on his chair, already finished his food.

I look at the triplets only to see that Jett and Dylan are having an eating contest, stuffing as much food into their mouths as possible. Clarissa just continues to eat her food in peace, eating just like her mother.

I look back to Jett, something on my mind. With Jett being the next alpha, he should have a name that represents strength and power. The name 'Jett' certainly catches your attention, the same with Knight. Comrade, though? Not so much.

"Why'd you name him after me?" I suddenly question. Celina blinks, escaping her thoughts while Axel stiffens next to me.

"Why don't you kids go and play for a bit, we'll call you when dessert's ready," Axel mutters to the triplets. In less than five seconds, all three triplets are out the door, even Clarissa.

"Why'd you name him after me?" I ask again, not changing my expressionless tone.

"Comrade..." Celina starts but trails off. She doesn't know what to say to me, and that just makes this even harder.

I look at Axel. "What about you? Are you gonna tell me why?" I ask again, a bit more aggressively. Axel growls at me in warning, reminding me he's still my alpha.

"I think this is Celina's story to tell. She decided to name Jett after you," Axel grumbles, looking pissed off at my disrespect. I look at Celina expectantly.

"After the battle, when you went to chase after that wolf, Axel called for you," Celina starts with a far off look in her eye. "When you didn't come the first time, he called again. You still didn't come. I panicked and ran, I ran to go find you, but you were already gone. I-I found the wolf you killed, but I couldn't find you."

She takes a deep breath, tears brimming her eyes. I don't know what I'm feeling at the moment, I feel... empty. I just want to know why they felt the need to name their eldest son after me. It just doesn't make sense to me.

"When we gave the triplets names, we didn't give Jett a middle name because I'd already given my parents' names to Dylan and Clarissa. We just left it at Jett Knight," Celina continues on but stops.

"You still haven't answered my question," I push. Axel growls at me, but Celina places a hand on his chest to reassure him.

"Comrade, when you disappeared, I couldn't bear to not have you in my life. You were my first friend here, you led me to Axel, you opened up your life to me, you became my guardian, and you gained my trust. We named Jett after you because we didn't want to forget you, we didn't want you to be out of our lives forever. It was a way of holding onto you without really losing you," Celina says sincerely with tears falling down her cheeks. Axel brings her to his chest, stroking her hair and muttering words in her ear to help calm her down.

A way of not losing me? Did they think they were gonna lose me? Forever? I close my eyes at the thought; they will never lose me.

"You won't lose me, Snow. Not in a million years," I whisper, using the old nickname I gave her. Celina's head snaps up, her eyes wide.

"I'm so sorry, Comrade," she blabbers, throat hoarse from the crying. She launches herself out of her chair and brings me into a bone-crushing hug. I chuckle and hug her back, more gently, though.

Celina pulls back and goes back to Axel, being engulfed in his arms. He spares me a look that says, 'you finally understand,' to which I nod at.

"I have more questions, but I think that's for another day," I tell them with a sigh. Celina wipes the tears away while Axel nods.

Alex chooses to walk back in at that moment with desserts set on her arms. She takes one look at Celina though and forgets about the desserts, putting them on the table, and rushes to her side.

"Luna, are you ok?" she asks in a gentle voice, placing a hand on her shoulder.

Celina looks at Alex with a wobbly smile and nods, telling her she's alright. Alex smiles back, going back to handing out the deserts.

"Alex, do you mind getting the triplets?" Axel asks, eyeing the chocolate mud cake in front of him.

"Of course, Alpha," Alex says with a fake enthusiastic smile. Axel rolls his eyes, ignoring the disrespect he seems to always get from her.

"Triplets! Dessert!" Alex yells, not moving from her spot as her voice travels through the pack house.

Axel growls while Celina giggles. I just roll my eyes at her. She's so weird; she never ceases to surprise me. I'm guessing that Axel actually meant for Alex to go and get them, not yell for them to come.

"I could've done that," Axel grumbles to her. Alex just shrugs innocently with a wide smile.

The triplets come rushing in, not bothering to wait before they tuck in. Alex chuckles before walking out of the room, my eyes unashamedly watching her hips sway if you know what I mean.

For the rest of the dinner, the triplets babble on and on about their day. I smile at them, finally getting used to them and accepting what Celina's told me.

I still have questions, though, like why it took so long to come and get me. What was so important that they had to wait three years before they came to rescue me? It may sound like I'm being selfish, but I just want to know. I just want to know why!

Axel starts to get more comfortable around me throughout the dinner like it used to be. It can never be the same, though. In the back of my head, I will always remember what's happened to me, and nothing can change that.

After I helped Alex wash up the dishes, splashing water on her every now and again, I start to make my way up to my room with Alex's hand in mine.

We walk in silence, not really wanting or needing to discuss anything. It's just nice to walk through these halls without a worry, my mate's hand in mine and a smile on my face.

Alex suddenly stops outside a door, looking like she really doesn't want to go. I guess this is her room... Well, not anymore.

"This is my stop," she mumbles, looking at the door with annoyance. I don't say anything as I continue pulling her along until we're outside the door of my room.

"No, this is your stop. You sleep with me now," I say with a grin. A full blown smile overtakes Alex's face, her eyes shining with mischief.

I open the door, revealing my plain room. I tug on Alex's hand as I pull her towards the bed. I sit down on the edge and pull Alex to me, making her straddle me.

"You know what I've wanted to do ever since I saw you?" I mutter, looking into her stormy eyes. She bites her lip, my eyes zeroing in on the movement.

"What do you want?" she breathes, leaning her face closer to mine. I feel my jeans getting tighter and internally groan. Damn this girl and her effect on me!

Not answering her, I plant my lips on hers. She instantly reacts, melting herself into the kiss. Her lips are soft and delicate, making the kiss sweet and pleasurable.

She moans softly when I lick her bottom lip, asking for entrance. I keep my hands firmly planted on Alex's hips as I dive my tongue in her mouth, groaning at the feel of it.

The kiss doesn't escalate from there. It's full of the love we don't know we have for each other, the passion we want to share and the trust we both have given. It's slow and soft, the perfect first kiss to share between mates.

I pull back after a while, opening my eyes to look at Alex. Her mouth's still slightly open, and her eyes are still closed. I cup her cheek with my hand, gently stroking my thumb over her lips. She opens her eyes to stare at me, a new sparkle in them.

"A kiss, that's what I've wanted," I tell her quietly with a smile. She smiles back at me, the sparkle in her eye twinkling.

"So, what now?" she questions, leaning her head on my chest. I weave my hand into her hair and lightly massage her scalp. She groans in satisfaction, making me grin slightly.

"Now, we sleep," I mutter as I pull her down with me onto the bed. I tuck her under the covers as her eyes start to droop.

"G'night, Alex," I whisper in her ear, placing a kiss on her temple. She mumbles something unintelligible before her light snoring is heard throughout the room.

I sigh as I slowly get out of bed and head to my wardrobe. I strip down and pull on some boxers. I grab one of my shirts and head back out to where Alex is sleeping.

I gingerly peel the covers off her and slip her top off. Honest to Goddess I try not to look, but they're just there! I sneak a peek when the shirt's about to cover them and almost groan.

Ignoring what I just saw, I let the shirt drop down to mid-thigh before taking her jeans off. I don't think Alex will appreciate this in the morning, but at least she's comfy for now.

I quietly get back into bed with her, pulling her back up against my chest. I lazily rest my arm over her waist and kiss the back of her neck. She hums a little, making me smirk. Oh Alex, what am I going to do with you?

13

COMRADE

I wake up and instantly bring Alex's body closer to mine. She mumbles in her sleep, turning over so her head is against my chest. I chuckle the slightest bit at her sleeping form. She looks like a baby, sweet and peaceful.

I brush some of her blonde hair away from her face and place a light kiss on her forehead. She stirs a bit before opening her beautiful stormy eyes and gazing up at me. She smiles slightly, her eyes still filled with sleep.

"Morning," she mumbles, burying her head closer to my chest. I smile slightly while softly stroking her hair.

"Good morning, my little mate," I whisper in her ear. She shivers and releases a shaky breath. I smirk at the power I have over her, but who can blame me? After not having power over anything for three years, having a little can make a guy happy.

"Why do you call me that? Can't you just call me Alex?" she questions, her cool breath hitting my chest. I close my eyes and massage her scalp, earning myself a groan.

"Where's the fun in that?" I question in a cheeky voice. I hear her chuckle, the sound being muffled by my chest.

We stay like that for a few minutes, just enjoying the peace and quiet. It's nice just being able to relax and not worry about anything. For three years, that's all I've done -- worry. I was worried about when Celina was coming for me, I was worried about when I would get my next meal, I was worried about Kate and what would happen if she was found out, I worried about-

My thought cuts off at the mention of Kate, my whole body stiffening. Kate... Did she get out? Is she safe? Where is she? Is she even alive? I need to find her.

No longer paying attention to Alex, I quickly get out of the bed and pull on a loose pair of jeans and the first shirt I can find. I quickly dress and head for the door, but a hand on my shoulder stops me.

"Comrade, listen to me. What's wrong? What's going through that thick skull of yours?" Alex questions me, coming into my line of sight.

I stare at her emotionlessly, making her slightly cringe. She places a hand on my cheek, but I step out of her embrace. I don't pay attention to the hurt that crosses her face. If I weren't so focused on Alex, maybe I would've been worrying about Kate a lot sooner. How could I just let her fly over my head? She's the only thing that kept me sane while I was with Damon, and I forgot about her. How stupid can I be?

"No, Alex," I say in a tone that says to not mess with me. Alex looks at me, studying me for a moment. I look into her stormy eyes and see them harden, her lips forming a straight line.

"Fine!" she says before walking out of my room and slamming the door behind her.

I sigh and rub my face, getting rid of the sleep that still sits there. I can't deal with this right now. I need to know about Kate.

I exit the room and make my way to the kitchen. I don't know what's happened to Kate or if she's even alive, but the one person who will know is Axel. So, I intend to ask him.

Entering the kitchen, I see him sitting with Callum, just chatting quietly. As soon as Callum catches sight of me, though, his body becomes rigid. I don't pay any mind to him as I approach Axel.

"Axel, was there a girl when you found me?" I ask, getting straight to the point. Axel growls lowly at me.

"You may be Celina's friend, Comrade, but I am still your alpha, and I want respect," he growls at me. I clench my teeth, not really caring at this moment in time. Kate's the only thing on my mind.

"That's nice, Axel, but I'm asking a question. Was there a girl when you rescued me? She's got dark brown hair and looks to be about 13. Was she there?" I question in a rush, my voice coming out slightly panicked.

Axel stares at me in anger and curiosity while Callum's eyes go distant. I stare at the two of them, silently hoping that Kate is safe and alive. She needs to be, she has to be.

"Was she the girl that Ally found? The one slumped on a tree?" Callum suddenly questions, recognition dawning on his face.

Axel ponders for a moment as I anxiously watch him come to a conclusion. He nods while mumbling something about how bruised she was.

"Kate!" I whisper and bolt out of the room, ignoring a confused Axel and Callum. If they found her, that means that she'll be in the medic station. Kate, please be alright, please.

I burst through the door, startling Doctor Aileen and the patient she's attending to. She sets her eyes on me and frowns, the teenager she's attending to squirms in her seat.

"Comrade? What are you doing here?" she questions with a confused look on her face. I don't answer her question as I stalk up to her.

"That girl that Ally found, where is she?" I seethe, not really wanting to deal with anything other than seeing Kate safe and sound.

"Comrade, you're not allowed to-" Doctor Aileen begins, but I cut her off with a growl.

"Don't you give me that crap. Let me see that girl or so help me, I will find her myself," I tell her menacingly, my breathing labored.

Doctor Aileen looks at me for a moment before excusing herself from the patient she's attending to. She starts walking down a hall to the right, and I instantly follow her. She stops outside a door and jerks her head to it, before going back to her patient.

I stand outside the door, guilt eating away at me. I should've come sooner, I should've asked about her the very moment I woke up. She should've been the first thing on my mind, but she wasn't. I will never forgive myself for that.

I firmly grip the doorknob and twist it, opening the plain white door. The room's dark, the windows closed and the lights off. I hesitantly close the door behind me, letting my eyes adjust to the darkness. Once they do, the shape of a bed enters my vision.

I hold my breath as I move over to it and take a seat in the chair next to the bed. The shape of a body lying still on the bed is as clear as day to my eyes.

My eyes become glassy as the familiar sight of waist length dark brown hair enters my vision. Kate.

I slowly get up from the chair and walk over to the window. I gingerly open the blinds the tiniest bit, to let some light in. I turn back around and look at Kate, really look at her.

Her face is covered in bruises, along with her arms, legs, and chest. I always found it cruel how Damon could make a bruise last for weeks on end before it slowly disappearing. Apparently, he liked to use that method on Kate.

I slowly walk towards the bed and brush away some of her hair, revealing more bruises on her forehead.

I sigh and drop back into the chair, leaning my elbows on my knees and burying my face in my hands. Why Kate? Why did this have to happen to Kate? She's so pure, innocent, and she's been through so much. She's lost her parents, and now, the parents she thought loved her. Why Kate?

"I'm so sorry, Kate," I whisper, a single tear escaping my eye. "I'm so sorry."

I sit there for hours just staring at her, willing her to wake up and beam her beautiful smile at me. Hoping that she'll crack some joke or even scold me. I'll even deal with seeing tears in her eyes for me snapping at her if I can just see her hazel eyes again. I just want her to wake up.

My head snaps up at the sound of the door opening. I don't recognise the person for a moment before I place her as one of Alex's friends, Ally I think.

She closes the door behind her, obviously not noticing me. As soon as she lifts her head up, though, she jumps in fright and draws in a sharp intake of breath.

"Holy shit! Do not do that to a girl!" she exclaims, placing a hand on her heart. I just stare at her for a moment longer before looking back at Kate.

"Um, are you supposed to be in here?" Ally questions nervously, fidgeting a bit with the pen in her hands. I don't answer her. I just keep staring at Kate. She has to wake up...

"Do you know her?" she suddenly asks, taking fast steps towards the bed. I growl at her when she gets too close for comfort. She immediately freezes and looks at me cautiously.

"Yes, I know her," I grunt, looking back down to Kate's still body. Ally takes the last few steps to the bed cautiously and places a hand on Kate's forehead.

"Why isn't she awake yet?" I question quietly, my voice hardly having any sound to it. Ally looks at me for a moment, her head tilting to the side.

"She was beaten pretty bad," she mutters, looking down at Kate. "I'm surprised she even survived. If I hadn't found her, though, I don't think she would've."

She smiles slightly down at Kate, adoration glowing in her eyes. I also look down at her and close my eyes, imagining what she looked like before Damon got a hold of her.

"Kate, her name's Kate," I tell Ally, not opening my eyes. Kate's smile, laugh, and purity shines in my mind, reminding me of what she used to be like.

Ally stays silent at my confession. I open my eyes to see her gazing down at Kate with a confused expression.

"Why would anyone ever do this to an innocent child?" she asks, letting the question linger.

"Cause he has a sick mind!" I say with venom, before walking out of the room and medic station, heading straight for the living room.

It's empty when I enter, so I plop down onto the single seat and let my mind wonder. Damon's a sick man with a sick mind and has a sick way of doing things. He's a monster, and he needs to be rid of.

He's hurt so many people in his lifetime. He's hurt Celina, his pack, me, and now Kate. He's hurt all the people he killed during the war, and he hasn't even batted an eyelash. He acts on impulse, never thinking of the right way to handle things. Damon is a bastard, and he will die in my hands. No one else will be ripped apart because of him, I swear on my life.

"Comrade?" a voice asks from the doorway, sounding a little hesitant. I blink, coming out of my thoughts. I look to the doorway of the living room to see Celina standing there with a tired looking Clarissa in her arms.

"Celina," I say, standing to my feet. She shakes her head at me, so I sit back down on the single seat.

She sets Clarissa down on the floor, giving her a small hug.

"Why don't you go ask daddy to put you to bed? Mummy needs to talk to Uncle Comrade," Celina murmurs to her daughter. Clarissa yawns nods her head and walks away. I smile slightly at the sight of her rubbing her eyes.

Celina takes a seat on the couch adjacent to me and looks down at her hands. She's come such a long way since I've been gone. She's had a family, a beautiful one at that. She's run this pack alongside Axel, and she's only 19. Above all, she came to rescue me when I thought all hope was lost. She truly is unique in every aspect of the word. The only thing is, I missed everything.

"So, how have you been?" I mutter, looking anywhere but Celina. It just doesn't feel right to meet her eyes after what I've thought about her.

"Comrade, I-" she starts, but doesn't finish. I glance at her curiously, my dark eyes lifting to meet her gold ones.

"I hate this," she finally admits, looking at me with sad eyes. "I hate not being able to talk to you like I used to. I hate not being able to hear you call me Snow like you used to. I hate what Damon's done to you and I hate that I couldn't help you. I hate it, I hate it so much."

Tears fill her eyes, but they don't fall down her cheeks. I clench my fists, but not in anger. I clench them to restrain myself from running over to Celina and giving her a hug. I miss her, I miss her so much. I don't deserve her, though.

"Things have changed, Celina. It will never be the same," I tell her, looking straight into her eyes. Her bottom lip trembles, but she keeps it together. She's grown stronger too...

"It can be the same again, though, Comrade. I healed from what Damon did to me! Axel helped me through it. You can heal too! Alex will help you, she already has. Even Chloe has healed from what's happened to her." She says the last bit in a murmur, but I hear it loud and clear.

Chloe? Is she dead? Is she alive? I haven't asked. Another person I've forgotten. Chloe was a good friend of mine. She always made me smile and always had this way of lifting the mood. I don't know why I haven't asked about her sooner.

"What happened to Chloe? Did she, um... you know?" I question uncomfortably. My eyes cast downward as I try to look anywhere but at Celina's face.

"No, she didn't. I honestly thought she would, but she didn't. We opened the box a little after you disappeared to see Chloe as healthy as ever. She changed, though. She's still the same person, but something inside her has changed. Her mindset, I guess. She couldn't stay with us anymore, so she left. The last time I heard, she's in Portugal having the time of her life. She's happy now, even though her life has never been perfect," Celina tells me with a smile.

At least she's happy. I would rather know she was happy than dead any day. I'll have to get in touch with her, let her know I'm ok. I'm sure she'll be happy to know I'm not dead...

"At least she's happy. I wouldn't have it any other way," I mutter to myself. Celina nods, her smile still in place.

"You know what the first thing she said was as she left that box?" Celina asks, her eyes shining with pride. I shake my head. "I'm happy, I'm truly happy. That's what she said, and I believed her with all my heart."

We stay silent after that. Celina seems absorbed in her thoughts, but I just stare out the window. The sun's shining and there seems to be a slight breeze. It's a beautiful day, but there's nothing happy about it.

"You know you can talk to me, right?" Celina suddenly asks, looking at me. I don't avert my eyes from the window as I answer her.

"Course," I mutter, but I don't know if it's a lie or not. My heart is telling me to believe it, but my brain is telling me not to.

In my heart, I know that I still love Celina the same way I loved her three years ago. I also know that what's happened to me has changed me for the worst.

My brain is still shouting at me to not trust anyone, though. It's like my mind is stuck and won't tell me to think anything else. It's shouting at me to ignore Celina, Axel, this pack, everyone, and run. Run as fast as I can, but I can't.

I want answers to my questions. I want Kate to wake up. I want to stay with Alex. I want to have a life. I want to forget everything that happened to me. First things first, though. I want Damon dead.

14

COMRADE

A few weeks ago, I would've been trapped and most likely being beaten. I would be scolding Kate for sneaking down to my cell in the middle of the day. I would be aching and wishing to be rescued. That wish has come true. Now I'm free, and all that my mind's set on is Damon. I want to know where he is, what he's doing, how many breaths he's taking. I want him.

As soon as this realisation came to me a few days ago, I went straight to Axel. I asked him to help me, to bring down Damon. I must admit, he did look a little hesitant at first, but he agreed once I brought up the safety of Celina and the pups. Bribery can be very helpful when used correctly...

"This is hopeless!" I growl as I swipe my arm across the desk, papers going everywhere. We've been trying to locate Damon for a whole week, and we still haven't even found a glimpse of him. It's infuriating!

"Calm down, Comrade. If we approach this out of pure rage, then we will fail. We need a plan, and we need patience," Axel tells me as his eyes skim over the paper he's holding.

The door suddenly opens, causing both our heads to snap up. Axel growls when Alex comes into our line of sight, but I just smirk. Oh Alex, always the disrespectable one.

"I thought I told you to knock when you enter my office!" Axel growls, his jaw ticking. I very quickly discovered that Alex really doesn't care for Axel's authority. I asked her about it, but all she said was that he betrayed her in a way. I didn't question her after that.

"Well, I'm here now, so no point getting worked up about it," she bites back while making her way over to me.

As soon as she's at arm's length, I grab her around the waist and bury my head in her neck, inhaling her sweet and luring scent. My anger instantly bubbles down, and all that's left is a never ending want.

Alex runs her hands through my hair and softly asks, "What's wrong?"

I sigh and softly kiss where I'll soon mark her, earning myself a shiver. I smirk against her neck, loving the control I have over her. After being out of control for over three years, it has really changed me. I feel the need to have my little mate submit to me and let me have control. So, by the way, she's reacting now, I've definitely got at least some control.

"We can't find him, I can't find him. It's like he's disappeared off the face of the earth and it's quite stressful," I murmur, still lightly kissing her neck.

"Maybe you should take a break, have a breather?" she suggests, also looking to Axel. He shrugs, looking back at the papers in his hands. I sigh. Axel may not need a break, but I do.

"Axel, I'm gonna take a break. My brain needs to relax," I say, standing up. Alex falls off my lap and lands lightly on her feet. Axel just grunts and waves a dismissing hand.

Alex grips my hand tightly and leads me out the door, heading straight to the backyard. It seems to be my safe haven whenever I'm stressed, angry, sad, or when I'm just feeling any strong emotion.

Alex takes a seat up against a tree and motions me to lie down in front of her. I do as I'm told and lay my head in her lap.

"You work too much. You need to spend more time with me," she mutters as she starts to massage my temples. I groan in approval.

Alex and I quickly made up after I pretty much pushed her away from me. She gave me the silent treatment for a while, reminding me of when Celina gave Axel and Callum the silent treatment and only spoke to me. Good times...

Anyway, after a little... persuasion from my part, Alex easily gave in. I must say, it felt good to please my mate in certain ways. I don't mean in 'that' way, just making her happy and smile. It really is a nice feeling.

"You know, I can always help in trying to find him. I mean, I helped find you. Kinda..." she trails off as her hands travel down to massage my shoulders.

Letting out a groan, I mutter, "I don't want you getting hurt. Having you rescue me was enough of a risk. I don't want you doing it again."

I hear her sigh before she rests her forehead on mine. I run a hand through her hair and lightly massage her scalp.

"Why does this have to be so difficult? This should've ended with that bloody war. So many lives could've been saved, but no. You just had to run off, didn't you?" she jokes in a teasing manner. I chuckle at her and open my eyes.

"That I did," I admit. I slowly lift my head from her lap and switch our places, so that I'm the one leaning against the tree while Alex is straddling me.

"You naughty boy," Alex mumbles, her eyes going down to my lips. I smirk, knowing I'm having an effect on her.

"That I am," I admit once again, bringing my lips softly down onto hers. She sighs into the kiss, resting her hands on my chest.

I pull back after a while and gaze at her. Her eyes are still closed, and a small smile is gracing her face. The way her blonde hair shines in the sun and falls over her shoulders, it makes me wonder how I ever got so lucky.

"You're truly something, Alex. Truly something," I mutter, softly kissing her forehead. I pull her closer to me, causing her to rest her head on my chest. I sigh and run my fingers through her soft hair, lightly taking out the knots that have formed.

"Alex!" a voice suddenly screeches, pulling me out of the moment. I groan as I see one of her friends, Taylor, stomping up to us. Alex chuckles and pecks my lips.

"Be right back," she whispers, jumping off my lap and turning again. Seeing the sight of her friend seems to put her into shock, though.

"What the hell happened to your hair?" she yells, running up to her fuming friend. Now being able to actually get a good look at Taylor, I notice that her usual brown hair is neon green. It doesn't suit her.

"Why don't you ask Ally?" Taylor seethes, pointing behind her to a laughing Ally, who is trying to catch up to her. I just watch on in amusement as the scene unfolds.

"Oh my god! Y-you should've s-seen her face! It was hilarious!" Ally laughs, falling to the ground and clutching her stomach. I see Alex's shoulders start to shake slightly at the sight of her friends.

"Don't you dare start laughing!" Taylor warns as a bark of laughter escapes Alex's lips.

"I-I'm sorry! It's just that... you look ridiculous!" she exclaims then bursts out laughing all over again. She falls to the ground next to Ally as Taylor looks down at them with a glare.

"Stop laughing!" she screams again, her glare looks like it could kill someone. She looks around the backyard, searching for something. Her eyes suddenly land on me, and she stomps over. I raise an eyebrow at her.

"You! Get your freaking mate to stop laughing at me!" she yells in my face, her neon green hair going everywhere as the wind blows."Now!" she screeches when I don't move.

I chuckle but get up anyway and make my way to an 'out-of-control' Alex. I wrap my arms around her waist and haul her up against my chest. Her laughter doesn't cease as she throws her head into my shoulder.

"Oh my god, Comrade! Look at her! Her hair is green!" Alex laughs as she grips my arms that are around her waist.

"Neon green, actually," I correct her with a grin. Alex laughs even harder, laughing so hard that she starts laughing silently. You know, when your mouth is hanging open, and you look like a seal?

"Not helping," I hear Taylor mumble. I chuckle, feeling sorry for her. Having dealt with Matthew, I have been on the receiving end of a prank that involved hair dye.

After Alex and Ally finally start to settle down somewhat, I release her and make my way to Taylor. I motion her to follow me while Alex and Ally are still distracted with their laughing.

"What?" she asks, clearly annoyed I didn't help her. I chuckle and shake my head. Her hair does look pretty ridiculous.

"Stop staring at my hair!" she suddenly snaps, sending me a glare that could bury me six feet under.

"Ok ok, sorry," I say with a chuckle, holding my hands up in a surrender position. She huffs, crossing her arms over her chest.

"Is there a reason I'm here?" she questions, clearly irritated with me.

"Actually yes. I've been on the receiving end of many pranks, so I know how this stuff works. My offer to you is to get back at Ally," I offer, raising my eyebrows mischievously.

"I'm listening..." she trails off, stepping closer to me. I smirk. This should be fun. Alex will kill me, but it'll be fun.

The next day, I'm happily sitting out in the backyard with Alex nicely tucked under my arm and Taylor lounging on another chair to my right.

I glance at her, sending a sneaky wink her way. She sends me one back before going back to her drawing. The Funny thing is, this is only the second time I've actually spent time with Taylor. The first time was weeks ago, and she seemed so awkward around me. I think Alex yelled some sense into both Taylor and Ally though because they seem a lot more comfortable around me. They're not walking on eggshells around me like the rest of the pack.

"So, are you spending the day in Axel's office again?" Alex asks while gazing out into the forest.

"I don't know, probably," I mumble absently as my mind wonders to my wolf. I haven't really felt him much, but I know he's there. He's got to be...

A sudden yell brings a smirk to my face.

"Oh my freaking god! Taylor!"

Ally comes bursting out the back door with her afro like hair standing up in all directions. Literally. Taylor takes one look at her and burst out laughing, dropping her drawing pad and falling to the floor.

It was actually Taylor's idea. She had some spare glue for some reason, so we decided to pour the glue in Ally's hairbrush, shampoo, conditioner and anything else to do with her hair. In result, her hair is coated with so much glue, it's literally as stiff as a board. It doesn't look like an afro anymore...

Alex gasps and turns to look at her laughing friend. She just glares then looks at me, narrowing her eyes at my smirk. My smirk instantly drops off my face as Alex directs a murderous glare my way.

"You had something to do with this," she growls as she pokes my chest. "Do you know what you've started? You've started a prank war that will go on for years!"

I chuckle at her, knowing she's just exaggerating. Alex growls at me and pinches the bridge of her nose.

"This is gonna be just like the great year of '05," she suddenly mumbles, falling back into my chest. I rest my head on her shoulder, about to ask what happened in 2005, before Ally beats me to it.

"Ah yes, '05, the great pranking year," Ally says proudly, momentarily forgetting about her hair. Suddenly

123

remembering her situation, Ally goes back to glaring at a still laughing Taylor. I must admit, I've never seen Ally's hair so tamed. Even if it is with glue.

"What happened in 2005?" I question, totally confused. Alex huffs and stands up, turning around to face me and putting a hand on her cocked out hip.

"One day, I decided to play a prank on Ally and Taylor because I was bored. I put super glue on their hairbrush handles, so when they picked them up, they couldn't let go. That triggered a whole year worth of pranks, ranging from hair to clothes to childish school pranks. Eventually, our parents had to break it off. That's what happened in the great year of 2005, and now Ally has started another round. Thanks, Ally," Alex bites sarcastically, causing Ally to grin innocently.

"Hey, I only started it. It could've been stopped if Taylor didn't prank me back," she defends.

"What!" Taylor suddenly exclaims. "I only got you back because Comrade offered to help me!"

All eyes snap to me, Ally's looking shocked and Alex's looking pissed as hell. Oh dear...

"What?" Alex seethes, walking up to me. "You helped her? You helped her start a bloody prank war!"

I flinch at the sound of her tone and quickly bring her to my chest. I stroke her hair to calm her down, but she pushes me back.

"You know what? You can deal with your fate now. As of this moment, a prank war has begun. Contestants including Taylor, Ally, Comrade, and myself." She puts emphasis on my name, making sure we all heard it loud and clear.

Alex smirks at me as she walks away, leaving a grinning Taylor and Ally. I look between the two, instantly knowing they're forming an alliance.

"No alliances!" I hear Alex shout in the pack house, making Taylor groan. Ally rolls her eyes and makes her way inside, her eyes look calculating.

"Better suit up, Comrade! A war has officially begun," Taylor says with a smirk before also walking into the pack house.

What have I gotten myself into?

15

ALEX

"Dammit!" I yell rather loudly as the bandage around my hand rips again from the strain. I've been punching this bloody punching bag for the last hour because a certain alpha has pissed me off. Seriously, though! Who the hell does Axel think he is? The alpha? Well he is, but he doesn't have to make that known every single minute of every single hour of the day. I mean, come on!

I don't see why he got so annoyed anyway. All I did was accidently splash flour on his face. It was actually really funny... I was just happily baking a cake, keeping an eye out for Ally, Taylor, and Comrade since the prank war is still on when Axel appears out of nowhere and scares me half to death. So, technically, it was his fault he got flour all over his face, not mine! I tell ya what, though, he gave me an earful and now I'm pissed off about it because it wasn't even my fault!

"Stupid alpha, stupid rules, stupid him, stupid, stupid, stupid..." I mutter to myself while wrapping my hands again and wiping the sweat off my face. I angrily walk back to the punching bag and go for a swing, but before my hand can come in contact with the bag, another person's hand stops me. My eyes snap to a familiar pair of almost black eyes. Comrade.

My breathing comes out in short pants as I slowly pull my hand out of his grip. His black eyes study me for a moment like he's searching for something. I stare back at him, but more emotionless and blank.

"Don't give me that look," he tells me in a soft voice as he slowly steps up to me. I sigh as his hand lands comfortably on my cheek, stroking it with his thumb. Why can he always seem to do this to me? He can always make me calm down and breathe with a single touch. Do I also have that effect on him?

"What do you expect, Comrade? I'm annoyed at a certain alpha," I grumble, my bad mood surfacing again. It quickly sizzles down, however, when I hear Comrade's chuckle. I look at him with a raised eyebrow, silently asking him what's so funny?

"You and Axel seem to have some background, may I ask what?" he asks mischievously with both eyebrows raised. I sigh and take a seat on the mats that cover the whole floor of the gym. Not many people know that the pack house has a gym; it's tucked away in a hidden door. Only a few pack members know that it's here, including me. Apparently Comrade too.

"Well, when we were planning to come and rescue you, Axel had assigned everyone jobs and groups. I was to go with Axel, Celina, and Callum because they needed a fourth person for a lookout. Then Axel announced that no one was to help other pack mates in different groups, to stay focused on your job. Obviously, I didn't agree with this, so I told him that if any of my friends died, he would no longer be my alpha. That's it, that's the only background we've had really. I hadn't even formally met him until we made up a group to come and rescue you," I sum up in a neat little package. I look at Comrade to see what his reaction is, but all I receive is a nod and a pucker of the lips.

"I get where you're coming from, but you shouldn't have said that to Axel. Axel is someone who needs to be respected in this pack and on top of that, he's a good guy in general. You'd be surprised by the amount of things he's done to just be able to keep this pack and Celina safe," Comrade tells me, wrapping an arm around my waist so that I can rest my head on his shoulder.

"Plus, if you're going to hang around with me, you'll have to learn to deal with him," he jokes, sending a wink on my way. I breathe a laugh as I roll my eyes. Whatever...

Comrade and I just sit there after that, consumed by our own thoughts. I don't really know much about Comrade, but I know enough to know that he respects Axel and that he'll trust him with his life. Me, on the other hand, not so much.

I would love to know Comrade's backstory, though, like where did he come from? Why is he in this pack? Most importantly, what happened to him? All I ever heard about Comrade was his fun and cheerful attitude, all the time. I've never heard him as the type to be serious, sad, broken, or angry. From what Celina's told me, he was even joking only minutes before he was captured. Why isn't he like that now? He's like that around me, most of the time that is. I know for a fact, though that he's hardly like that anymore around all his old friends. For goodness sake, he hasn't even spoken to Callum more than three times! I need to know, or he needs to talk to someone about it.

"Comrade?" I ask, gaining his attention. "Why don't you meet me in our room in about ten? I wanna talk about some stuff."

Not waiting for an answer or a remark, I bolt up and hightail it up to our room. I quickly get some leggings and one of Comrade's shirts before having a quick shower. By the time I'm out, Comrade is patiently sitting on the bed waiting for me. His eyes don't look focused, though like he's having a memory. Usually, a bad one.

"Comrade!" I yell loudly to snap him out of it. He jumps in fright and falls off the bed, much to my amusement and liking. I release a laugh, covering my mouth with my hand to hide it, not that it does.

"Alex! What the hell?" Comrade screams at me from the floor. I drop to the floor next to him, gripping my stomach as my shoulders shake from laughter. Oh god, this is funny! Comrade glares at me, getting up from the floor to look down at me disapprovingly. I just laugh harder at his face. After my laughing dies down a bit, I get up with an innocent smile.

"Yes?" I ask innocently. Comrade just shakes his head at me, a grin slipping onto his face. This is what I mean. Why is he like this with me and not with anybody else?

"Oh, Alex, what am I going to do with you?" Comrade asks as he wraps his arms around my waist. I shrug my shoulders with the same smile until I remember why I asked him to come up here. If he doesn't talk to me, though, I will force him to walk down those bloody stairs and go find Celina so that they can have a heart to heart talk.

"What happened?" I ask quietly, placing my hand on his cheek and stroking slightly, my fingers running over his two days' worth of not shaving. Comrade looks at me confused, gripping my hand in his own, as he brings it away from his face.

"What do you mean? What happened where?" he asks confused, as his eyebrows draw together, and a frown overtakes his face. I sigh as I sit on the bed, Comrade still standing.

"What happened there? What did Damon do to you?" I question, my only emotion is one of worry. All I want is to know, know what happened to him in that horrible place. Is that so much to ask?

Comrade's face drops, but it quickly becomes hard and emotionless. He stares at me blankly then says in a dead tone, "Nothing, Alex! Absolutely nothing."

I blink a few times as I wait for more, wait for him to tell me everything, but he says nothing more. He just continues to stare at me. I stand up slowly, tilt my head and narrow my eyes just that little bit.

"Something happened in there, Comrade. I know it did. I saw everything. I saw the basement, I saw that dreadful torture room that I wish I could erase from my mind, I saw the weapons everywhere, I saw everything. Why can't you tell me what happened? Why?" I desperately reason, trying to convince him that whatever he'll say is nothing to me. It doesn't work. He just stares at me, but this time with anger.

"You think because you saw a few rooms and weapons that you think you know what I've gone through? Do you really think that, Alex?" he asks in that tone again. I gulp, not really expecting him to react like that.

"Of course not. I just want to help you-" I try to say, but Comrade cuts me off.

"Help me? You want to help me? Ok then, here's what you can do: don't ask me about it, don't talk about it, don't do anything mildly related to it because you have next to no clue of what I've been through. Not one clue," he says with a fire in his eyes before he storms off, not looking back.

I sink to the floor, wrapping my arms around myself. Don't do anything? Not one thing? Fat chance there, but that's what Comrade wants... Isn't that what mates do? Follow the other's every command without complaint? It's times like these where I wish that my mum was still here. My dad won't help me; he won't even look at me. Who do I go to for this?

Having one person in mind, I slowly get up and walk out of the room like nothing's happened, even though everything's happened. I gingerly make my way towards Axel's office, knowing that Celina will probably be in there. I knock on the door, for the first time in my life, and wait for an answer. All I get is a grunt as an approval, but I take it anyway.

I push the door open, and sure enough, Celina is sitting on Axel's desk while curiously looking at me. I glance at Axel to see him in mild shock, but with a smirk. Well, I don't normally knock on his door. I just walk in unannounced. This must be a pleasant surprise for him. He better not get used to it.

"Alex, what can I do for you?" Axel asks in a smug voice. I glare slightly at him. Just because I'm in a weird mood doesn't mean he can get my respect. He has a long way to go before he can get that back.

"You? Nothing," I bite back, averting my eyes to Celina. Out the corner of my eye, I see Axel frown and shake his head. Whatever...

"May I talk to you, Celina? It's kinda important," I tell her, waiting for an answer. If she doesn't want to talk, I'll be sulking for the rest of the week. If she does, maybe I can get this Comrade problem off my mind and help him focus on getting Damon.

"Actually, she's busy-" Axel starts to say before Celina cuts in.

"Of course, I can. Anything for my amazing babysitter," she says with a small smile, sending Axel a look that says not to argue. He grumbles for a bit but nods his head as I smile smugly at him. Ha! The irony...

Celina gives Axel a kiss on the cheek before jumping down from the desk and heading over to me. I throw a quick smile at her before hurriedly walking away. Celina easily follows me, but I don't have the heart to look at her face.

Once we reach the backyard, I stop and take a seat on the grass, the sun hitting my face. Celina sits down next to me, staying silent as she waits for me to say something. What do I say, though? I can't just come out with it. It might bring up some unwanted memories.

"This is about Comrade," Celina suddenly states, breaking the silence. I sigh as I nod, not really knowing what else to do.

"It's about how he's not his old self," she states again like this is a big guessing game that she already knows the answers to. I turn my head to lock my eyes with hers.

"What do I do? He won't tell me anything, not one thing. I tried to ask him just before, and he went blank on me. How do you deal with that?" I ask as I lay back on the grass with a sigh.

"Comrade just needs to get used to it, that's all. He needs to adjust to normal life again. He's been tucked away for three years," Celina tells me with a sad smile.

"You were tucked away for sixteen years, and you're fine," I grumble, then realise what I just said. My eyes widen as I look away, not wanting to see the sadness in my beloved Luna's eyes. To my surprise, though, a giggle travels through the air. I turn my head back to Celina to see her with a smile on her face.

"Yes, I was. That was all I knew, though, I grew up with it. Comrade, on the other hand, has already experienced a normal life and wasn't ready for the onslaught that he got. He just needs to adjust again," Celina says as she joins me to lie down on the grass.

"How long will that take, though?" I ask, already knowing that I won't like the answer I'm about to get. Celina sighs and rolls on her side, propping herself up on her elbow. I copy her movement, asking the question silently through my eyes.

"My guess is that Comrade will go back to normal after Damon has been killed and he has to be the one to do it. If he doesn't... Well, then he'll always have this nagging voice at the back of his mind telling him that Damon's coming to get him. You just have to be patient and help him find Damon, then you'll get your happiness," Celina says wisely and in a quiet voice.

Patient? I'll be honest and say I don't have a lot of patience to work with.

16

ALEX

"Ally! You get down here right now, you bloody bitch!" I scream at the top of my lungs as I stay glued on the same spot. Literally.

Ally had this amazing idea to pour a bucket of superglue all over the kitchen floor, and me being me sometimes, didn't notice the thick lake of glue. So, I'm now stuck in a lake of glue with my favourite yellow socks now drenched in the wretched stuff.

"Ally! Get your skinny ass down here!" I scream again. She finally comes sauntering into the kitchen, stopping just before the door.

"Yes?" she asks innocently, but you can see the laughter hiding behind her eyes.

"I'm gonna kill you!" I seethe, twisting my body around and reaching my arms out for her. She shamelessly erupts into a fit of laughter and falls to the floor. Unfortunately though, she doesn't fall onto the glue that I have so conveniently stepped in.

"What's all the racket?" a very powerful voice suddenly booms. I smirk as Ally's laugh dies down completely and is replaced by fear. She knows the kitchen is Celina's safe haven, so what happens when her mate finds out what she's done?

I put on the best sad face, slump my shoulders and make my eyes glassy. This'll be fun...

Axel comes storming into the kitchen with a fire in his eyes. He takes one look at Ally on the floor, one look at my near crying self and then looks at the kitchen floor.

"I'll ask once and once only... What happened to the kitchen floor?" he asks, emphasising each word after 'only'.

"Well, you see, Alpha-" I begin, but he cuts me off. I blink and narrow my eyes, the sad facade disappearing in an instant.

"Is this a prank?" he asks, calm as the ocean. Why is he calm? He should be furious! I mean, come on! Look at this place! It's a lake of glue! Does this man have no sanity?

"Yes, it is," I bite back, crossing my arms and turning around towards the direction my body is forcing me to face. "A stupid prank, too," I grumble quietly to myself. I had hoped no one would hear me, but from Ally's snicker, I know she did.

"I'm guessing this is Ally's prank to you. Ally, you'll be cleaning this up. Alex, you'll try to figure out a way of getting out of that mess you're in. Have fun," is the last thing he says before he walks off down the hall, his footsteps echoing behind him. Bloody alpha...

"Uh... that went better than expected," Ally chirps, stands up, and gets a mop. I scoff. She thinks a mop will clean this up. Ally looks at me with a raised eyebrow while I shake my head.

135

"You seriously think a mop will clean this up? Girl, you have to get a cleaning crew in here!" I exclaim, throwing my arms in the air dramatically.

Ally rolls her eyes at me then says, "Please, I so got this."

An hour later and I'm still stuck in the bloody glue, along with three mops, two brooms, ten sponges, and a broken vase. Ally has a bit of a moment and lashes out at a poor vase.

"Are you done trying to do this yourself?" I ask tiredly. I've been standing here for over an hour. I'm hungry and all I really want to do is go and hug Comrade. I haven't seen him all day and he wasn't there when I woke up this morning. I'm almost positive he's locked up in Axel's office searching for Damon again.

"Friggin' super glue! I'm never touching that shit again!" she exclaims, running a hand through her hair. I run a hand over my face. She thinks she's staying away from that stuff? Oh no... I'm going to get her back for this and it's gonna be with super glue.

I stay silent as she reaches into her back pocket and brings out her mobile. She quickly dials a number and the cleaning crew is here in less than 15 minutes.

"Finally," I huff. I see Ally's lips form a smile before she starts walking away. I gape at her for a second then clear my throat. She stops in her tracks and turns around. She sees the look in my eyes and sighs.

"Give me one of those scrubs," she grumbles as she snatches a scrubber from one of the cleaning crew. I smile smugly at her.

An hour and a half later, I'm finally out of the bloody glue. My favourite yellow socks are in the rubbish, my legs are aching from standing still for too long and my eyelids are heavy. Damn you, Ally. Damn you.

"Thank you! See you when we have another mishap!" Ally yells after the cleaning crew walk out the door. I cock my hip to the side and face her, running my tongue along my teeth. Ally turns around slowly, feeling my eyes on her back. She takes in my stance and gives me a cheeky smile.

"Now, before you go off at me-" she starts, but I hold up a hand. I slowly walk towards her, my legs feeling stiff and sore.

I get right up to her face before saying very lowly, "I would guard your hair brushes if I were you."

I then leave the kitchen calmly, making my way to Axel's office. The scent of Comrade quickly fills my senses and it's like my whole body relaxes. I didn't even know I was tense.

I softly knock on the door, not really wanting to deal with Axel's glare on me walking into his office unannounced. I hear Axel grunt and decide to take that as a 'come in'. I slowly open the door and peep my head in. Sure enough, Comrade is standing in front of Axel's desk and leaning over what seems to be a map.

"Comrade?" I ask with a small voice. I feel so tired right now, all I want to do is collapse into his arms.

Comrade whips around, takes one look at me and wraps me in his arms. I bury my face in his shirt and grip it with my hands.

"You ok?" he asks sweetly. I badly want to shake my head, but I nod and pull away. I offer him a smile to which he returns, a bit concerned.

"You sure?" he asks again, to which I nod once again. He takes that as my answer and shuts the door behind me, leading me into Axel's office. Axel glances at me, but quickly looks back down to his files.

"Found him yet?" I ask as I lean against him. Comrade shakes his head and runs a hand through his hair, his muscles flexing as he does it. The way his hair sits on his head now looks messy, but man does it look hot. I blink and shake my head. Where did that come from?

'You're nearing heat, that's where that came from,' I hear my wolf whisper then disappear into the corners of my mind again.

Heat? Seriously! Ugh! The one bad thing about finding your mate is that you go into heat within the first three months of meeting them. It's different for everyone. Some may go into heat in a week, others a month and some lucky few go into heat after the three-month period. I think Celina did, but I'm not too sure about that one... The only way a girl can get out of heat is if her mate has already marked her, which isn't my case.

"Alex?" I hear Comrade ask as his face suddenly appears before my eyes.

"Hmm?" I hum, silently asking him to repeat what he just said. He rolls his eyes at me in a playful manner and kisses me on the cheek. Sparks shoot through me and it's hard not to shudder. Geez, I won't be surprised if I'm in heat by tomorrow.

"I said do you have any ideas of where Damon might be hiding?" he repeats as he wraps an arm around my waist. I purse my lips and look at the map to distract me from the shocks. Damn it!

"Well, when we found you, he seemed to be hiding in plain sight, but also hidden at the same time," I explain, looking at the map once again. "If I had to make a hunch, I would say a few kilometers from the border or in the same place as he was the first time."

138

Comrade stays silent as Axel looks up at me. I look at both men and sigh at the dumb looks on their faces. They obviously didn't think of that then.

"I'll have a team of my best warriors go tomorrow and search around the pack border and the place where we found you," Axel tells Comrade, looking at him dead in the eye.

"Alex?" Axel asks, to which I look at him with a raised eyebrow. "You're by far one of my best warriors, so be ready tomorrow."

"Will do, Alpha," I say respectfully. I've decided to treat him a little less hostilely. Comrade seems to be good friends with him even if it doesn't show, so I'm gonna put in the effort to do so.

Both Comrade and I exit Axel's office after that. I lean heavily into Comrade's side as we make our way up to our room. He wraps an arm around my shoulders and draws small circles into my arm. It feels nice.

When we make it to our room, Comrade silently shuts the door as I collapse onto the bed head first. I hear Comrade sigh before I feel his weight on my ass.

"Comrade," I groan, turning my head to the side to glare at him. He leans his head down and lightly kisses me under my ear. I shudder at the feeling. I blame it on my upcoming heat.

"What's wrong, Alex? You're tired and you're being respectful to Axel. What's wrong?" he asks as he starts to lightly massage my back. I groan at the feeling of my unknown tense muscles fully relaxing.

"Well, first of all, I've been stuck in super glue for three hours. Second of all, I woke up with no mate in my bed to start my day off good. Third of all, the only thing I've eaten is some cereal. Lastly, I'm worried sick about you," I conclude, feeling Comrade's hands travel further down my back, just above my butt.

"Why are you worried about me? You have nothing to be worried about," he tells me as he somehow gets my shirt off so he has full access to my back. I gasp softly as his hands make contact with my skin, sending shocks to my very core.

"You're just so caught up on Damon, it's seems like all you do is look for him," I say distractedly as his hands continue to work my back.

"No worrying, Alex. Can you do that for me? No worrying," Comrade tells me, to which I can just groan and nod my head. How did he learn to massage like this?

I lay there with Comrade straddling me from behind as he massages my tense back, letting all the muscles loose. It feels nice, both the massage and Comrade on top of me.

We stay like that for who knows how long, before I finally say, "I should probably shower."

Comrade chuckles at my suggestion, but doesn't stop. I sigh and somehow flip my body over so that he's now straddling my torso.

"I really need to shower," I complain as I put my hands on his chest and give a light push. Sparks ignite from his chest and into his hands, traveling all the way down my arms and into my hands. I try to mask the feeling that erupts in me, but I think Comrade sees it anyway.

Comrade's eyes shine with an unknown emotion as he grips my hands and brings them up to his mouth for a kiss. Something's different about him, he's sweeter. In this moment, I feel like I could ask him anything or do anything and he would be fine with it.

"You're going into heat," he states as my eyes widen and my cheeks become scarlet. Crap! How did he know? Way to ruin the moment...

"How did you know?" I ask bewildered, voicing my thoughts. He can't have just known!

"Mainly because you've been shuddering at my touch a lot lately and I don't want to keep my hands off you," he tells me in a low whisper right in my ear. I close my eyes as his hot breath fans over me, causing a shiver to travel down my spine.

"What are you going to do now?" I whisper, not knowing if I dread the answer or not. Comrade plants a light kiss under my ear lobe then pushes back off me, but still straddling me.

"I'm not gonna do anything unless you say it's ok. However, I'm still gonna do this..." he says as he places another kiss on my neck.

"...and this..." Another kiss. "...and this..." Another kiss.

"...and also this." His hands travel up my stomach, tracing the hem of my bra. A small moan slips through my lips as my eyes close on their own accord. My eyes suddenly snap open and connect with Comrade's lust-filled ones when I feel his fingers lightly trace my breasts.

Never breaking eye contact, his lips connect with my lower abdomen, causing my stomach to knot and my core to tighten. This boy, I swear...

He kisses his way up my stomach, stopping to dip his tongue into my navel. He eventually comes to my bra, but it doesn't stop him. He kisses along the bottom of my bra before planting a kiss in the valley of my breasts. I moan as he starts to suck lightly, soon giving me a love bite.

141

Comrade doesn't make any move to take off my bra or go any further. He just continues to cover my exposed stomach and breasts in light kisses, giving me love bites here and there.

He finally makes his way up to my neck and sucks hard just under my ear. The sudden action shocks me and I let out a loud gasp before a moan quickly follows. It just feels so flipping good!

Comrade finally pulls back and gets off me, offering me a hand. I place my hand in his, letting him help me get up.

"Now you can go shower," he whispers in my ear before he walks out of the room, shutting the door behind him. I stare after the door, longing him to walk back in with a cheeky grin and sweep me away to the shower with him joining me. As I wait for a few minutes in fantasy land though, the door doesn't open again. I sigh as I head to the bathroom and shut the door softly behind me. Tomorrow's going to be a long day...

I wake up the next morning covered in sweat and with the sheets feeling like sand paper. The arm wrapped around my waist seems like the only thing that's bearable to me at the moment. I take a glance behind me, my eyes meeting the sleeping body of Comrade's. He looks so hot just lying there.

Heat. Crap.

I tear myself out of Comrade's hold, bolting to the bathroom and locking the door behind me. I instantly feel even hotter now that Comrade isn't touching me, but man do I hate heat! It doesn't only affect me, but it also affects Comrade's wolf because all he'll want to do is mark me as his. In more ways than one.

I lean against the door and groan out in pain. Everything aches and burns and there's nothing I can do about it. I decide to take a cold shower, so I strip out of my nightgown and jump in the shower.

The cold water doesn't help. It feels like I'm trapped in my own skin. My wolf is restless and all I want to do is go die in a hole. Why do girls have to go through heat? I mean, don't we go through enough? We have to go through pregnancy, the pain of losing our virginity, getting our hearts broken, the mood swings of periods and now we have to go through heat! It's so unfair! To add to that, we have heat once a month now! That means only two weeks out of four that we get to be normal! Ugh!

I huff as I get out of the shower, now in a bad mood. I get a towel and try to ignore the pain it brings me as I dry off my body. By the time I'm done, I'm back into sweating and my hormones are sky rocketing. Can this get any worse?

I open the bathroom door, still wrapped in my towel, and quietly sneak past the bed where Comrade is still fast asleep. Thank the Moon Goddess.

I quickly change into some sweats and a thin sports bra. Even these don't feel comfortable, but it's all I have that's the most comfortable.

I suddenly remember that I'm supposed to be helping Axel and Comrade try and find Damon today. I curse quietly as I take a sneak peak at the time, 5:56am. I didn't know it was that early.

I walk back into the room and head to the door when I suddenly hear Comrade take a deep breath. He moves around a bit before his eyes snap open, instantly locking on my sweating and heated form.

His eyes fill with heated lust as he slowly lifts himself off the bed, revealing him in his boxers. I push myself into the door as far as I possibly can, my breathing accelerates in an instant.

Comrade continues to take slow steps towards me, his eyes never leaving my shaking form. He finally comes to stop in front of me and I think I'm gonna hyperventilate from how labored my breathing is.

With Comrade's proximity, I can't help but drink every little detail of him in. The way his now black eyes shine with lust, the way his dark hair is a mess on top of his head, how his arm muscles are still evident even though he's not flexing them. This man is truly a price of work.

"C-Comrade..." I warn as he takes another step closer to me. "You know I'm in h-heat. Don't do anything rash."

"Rash?" he questions, his voice low and husky. I shudder at the sound of him, feeling like my knees are about to collapse. Comrade notices this and uses it to his advantage. Sneaky boy...

He steps even closer to me so that he's less than an inch away, our breaths mingling. My breath catches in my throat as my heart stops.

"Does that mean I can't do this?" he asks as he grips my waist and brings our lower halves together. Fireworks erupt all throughout my body and it's like the hotness I'm feeling is suddenly swept away and replaced by want. What is this boy doing to me?

"I-I-" I try to say, but the words seem to catch in my throat as I stare into those gorgeous black eyes. They seem to captivate me as everything else around me melts away.

144

Comrade starts to slowly lean down, his eyes flicking to my lips. Just as his lips are about to come in contact with mine, he turns his head and kisses the side of my lips. I whimper as he continues to kiss me, but across my cheek and down my neck. I want him to kiss my lips.

"Comrade!" I whine, putting my hands over his that are still on my hips. He chuckles before finally granting my wish and crashing his lips to mine. I moan into his mouth, savoring his taste for as long as I can.

He licks my bottom lip, asking for entrance which I gladly grant him. His hands leave my waist and travel to my lower back, then down to my butt. I squeal when he suddenly squeezes it. I jump and wrap my legs around his waist. I feel his member poking my entrance and almost die. I want him inside me and I want him now.

"Comrade? Comrade, the bed!" I scream, desperately wanting this to hurry up. Why won't this hurry up!

"A little eager, are we? Well then, I better make this as slow as possible," I hear Comrade's muffled voice from where his face is attacking my neck.

"Comrade, please!" I cry, just wanting to get this over with. I hear Comrade chuckle again before he throws me roughly on the bed. I bounce a bit from the force as I see Comrade's eye lock onto my chest.

"Geez, you're beautiful," he murmurs before climbing onto the bed and giving me a grin. I bite my lip in return.

"I hope you're ready for this. I'm not gonna go easy," he whispers in my ear before biting it roughly. I gasp and squirm a bit at the feeling.

Comrade kisses down my body, his hand trailing behind him. I shiver every time his lips come in contact with my skin. I take back what I said about heat. I love it! I love everything about it!

Without warning, my sweats are off my legs and Comrade's hands are massaging my thighs. I groan as he slowly starts to spread them. We haven't even started yet and I think I'm going to explode.

Comrade's teeth suddenly graze my lower stomach and a sound between a scream and a moan escapes me. His teeth latch onto my underwear as his eyes lock with mine. The only thing that is held in their depth is an evil look that says, 'I warned you'.

Comrade pulls my underwear all the way down with his teeth, never breaking eye contact. He bites, yes bites, his way back up my legs, stopping right before my core to nibble on my thigh.

I scream out in frustration as I grip his hair and force his face to my core, his hot breath fanning over it. My legs lock around his shoulders to keep him in place as he takes a deep breath, taking in my smell. Let me tell you, it's the sexiest thing I have ever seen in my entire life. The way his eyes become animalistic, the feral growl that leaves his mouth and the want that is burning in his eyes all make this moment one to remember.

Without wasting another second, Comrade attacks my core with his mouth. A loud moan escapes me as he sucks, licks, bites, everything. I don't think I can hold on much longer.

"C-Comrade?" I try, but I don't think he hears me.

"Comrade?" I try again, but he just sucks harder, pulling me closer and closer to the edge.

"Comrade!" I finally yell, getting his eyes to snap up to me, but his mouth never stops its onslaught.

146

"I-I can't hold on much longer," I say, throwing my head backward and arching my back. Comrade's hands trail up my hips to my sports bra, ripping it to shreds. His hands cup my breasts as I release yet another moan.

"Comrade, Comrade, please!" I beg, tightening my legs around him. Instead of answering my pleas, his mouth becomes agonisingly slower. I scream or cry, I don't really know which one.

"Comrade!" I growl ferociously. His hot breath is suddenly blown straight to the centre of my core and I nearly lose it.

He blows again as my core clenches, but Comrade spreads my thighs wider with his hands. He gives it one last, long blow and everything around me comes tumbling down.

I spasm on the bed and release moan after moan after moan. Comrade's hands pin me down, but all I can do is shake until the wonderful feeling of my orgasm is gone.

"I did warn you," Comrade's teasing voice suddenly fills through my ears. I growl at him as I suddenly flip us over. Not letting him have a second to think about it, I rip his boxers apart and lock my hands around his long, hard, and rough shaft.

I get a groan as my encouragement and start to slowly pump him up and down. A smug smile slowly forms on my face as I watch Comrade's face contort into one between pain and pleasure. Oh, he's so gonna pay for what he just did.

I switch my hands with my mouth, hearing Comrade's breath get caught in his throat. I take his head first then gradually swallow the whole thing and for the love of the Moon Goddess does he taste good.

"Alex!" Comrade groans, gripping my hair with one hand. I intended to go slow, but Comrade has other ideas.

147

Using the grip he has on my hair, he starts to rapidly pump my head up and down, over and over again.

His other hand reaches down in between us to roughly squeeze one of my breasts, playing with the nipple. I moan around his member as his pace starts to slow down. I graze my teeth from top to bottom before my mouth is suddenly sprayed.

I try to quickly pull my head away, but Comrade keeps it firmly planted there, forcing me to take all of him. I run my nails down his chest at the amazing taste of him. He tastes spicy and sweet at the same time, but it's oh so good.

Comrade flips us back over as I try to get some air back into my lungs. His blazing black eyes stare at my chest as I take breath after breath. Comrade's own breathing is pretty erratic, but not as much as mine.

"Do you want to keep going?" he suddenly asks, looking terrified that I might say no. Not having the strength to talk or even hum, I give him a nod.

I close my eyes as I feel Comrade line up with my entrance. I take a deep breath and hold it, but nothing happens. I open my eyes to see Comrade looking at me dead serious before he asks, "Are you a virgin?"

I feel like slapping him across the face right now. Of course I'm a bloody virgin! Why the hell wouldn't I be? Just to play with him though, I'm not gonna tell him. The question I wanna know is if this is his first time.

"Why don't you find out?" I ask with a cheeky half smile, my voice coming out breathless.

Comrade's feral growl bounces off the room's walls before he thrusts into me with one hard push. I cry out in pain as he breaks my barrier. Holy crap this hurts!

"Shh, shh. I promise it won't last long. Come on, shh," he whispers, peppering kisses all over my face. I take a deep breath, telling him I'm ok. He looks at me unsurely, but I nod.

He starts to slowly pump in and out of me, being sure to be careful. Honestly though, I don't want careful.

"Comrade, faster, please!" I beg in a whisper, trailing my nails down his back. He instantly complies, pounding into me harder and harder, faster and faster.

"Oh my god..." I groan, never wanting this moment to end. After all the fun we've already had though, it's a bit hard for the end to come quickly.

Not even five minutes after, Comrade has finally entered me, my core clenches and my heart rate picks up.

"Come for me, my little mate," Comrade whispers in my ear. I quickly comply, releasing a loud scream from the amount of pleasure that has just engulfed me. Comrade soon follows after.

I take ragged breaths as I close my eyes, just wanting to fall asleep. Before I have the chance though, I feel Comrade's lips graze just under my ear. My hips suddenly buck at the now intensified feeling.

His teeth suddenly sink down into my flesh and all I can do is gasp like a fish out of water. During all that time, he forgot to mark me. The bloody idiot.

Comrade retracts his canines, leaving a lingering kiss on the fresh mark.

"That should keep your heat at bay for the rest of the day," he teases with a charming smile. I let out a breathy laugh before my eyelids droop and I'm engulfed in darkness.

17

COMRADE

The first thing I see when I wake up is my beautiful mate sleeping and her steady breathing filling up the room. I smile as Alex snuggles closer beside me, burying her head in my shoulder. I lift my hand and gently brush away the strands of hair on her face. She's the definition of an angel – a very feisty angel.

I don't believe it... I legitimately don't believe it. I don't believe I've fully mated with this beautiful girl lying here with me – this beautiful creation.

Alex stirs a little in her sleep before a big yawn escapes her mouth. Her eyelids flutter open to reveal those amazing stormy eyes of hers. She instantly locks her eyes on me and smiles before asking, "Did last night really happen?"

I smirk at her and peek under the sheet. Alex laughs and whacks me across my arm, her cheeks flushing red.

"I do believe so," I reply, lightly kissing my mark that's below her ear. She shivers, her eyes fluttering close again. I chuckle at the reaction I have on her as she opens her eyes once again to set a glare at me.

"What's the time?" she questions, changing the subject. I chuckle again as I sit up and let the sheets drop down to my waist. I see Alex's eyes go a shade darker as she looks at my chest. I love it when she looks at me like that. It also helps that she's in heat.

"It's 8:30 at night. You slept the whole day; I must've worn you out," I whisper as I maneuver myself on top of her. Alex watches me with a smirk as she lifts her arms up and wraps them around my neck.

"Comrade..." she suddenly says. I look at her as I feel my wolf coming closer to the surface.

"Yes?" I ask, slowly leaning down so that my lips are centimeters away from hers.

"I'm hungry," she says with a grin, pushing me off her. I fall next to her with an 'oomph' and a shocked look.

Alex laughs at my face before getting out of bed, pulling the covers with her. I growl as she walks away from me, but I only get a sneaky wink in return before she bolts into the wardrobe.

I sigh as I lie back on the bed, running my hands over my face. This morning was pure heaven, and it's certainly something I'm never gonna forget. The way her body moved and the amount of pleasure she can give me is unbelievable... and it's all mine. Nobody else's.

Alex walks back out wearing a strapless, sea green dress. She throws her hair up in a low ponytail and smiles at me. I smile back at her and slowly get up. Alex squeals and covers her eyes, a bright blush coming forth to her cheeks.

"What?" I question, already knowing the answer. Alex uncovers her eyes but looks anywhere but me as she points

151

down. I smile deviously at her and quickly wrap my arm around her waist. It's actually quite funny. This morning she didn't have a problem with me being bare, but now that her heat has subsided for the moment, she got this adorable blush on her face.

"What was that, my little mate?" I purr in her ear as I hear her gulp hard. She clears her throat before answering in a whisper, "You're naked."

I smirk. "You didn't have a problem with it a few hours ago," I breathe in her ear. She just pushes me away and points to the wardrobe. I laugh as I pull on some shorts and walk back out. I look at Alex for approval.

"Much better," she says with a cheeky grin as she runs her nails down my bare chest. I growl lowly at the feeling.

"Let's go get some food," I mumble as I pull her laughing self along with me. I roll my eyes at her, but can't help feeling happy at the sound coming from her lips.

Ever since we fully mated, it's like everything is a hundred times better. Her laugh, her smile, her voice, her growl, her walk, everything is so much better. I love it. I love her. I've loved her for so long now, and I've never had the chance to say it. Maybe tonight I can.

As we enter the kitchen, Alex lets go of my hand and takes a seat on a stool.

"What are we having?" she asks, drumming her fingers on the bench. I let my eyes follow from her fingers to her hand, to her arm, to her bare shoulders, and finally, to her gorgeous face.

"Whatever your little heart desires," I tell her with a smile. She beams back and instantly says pancakes. I chuckle.

"Pancakes? For dinner?" I question incredulously. She eagerly nods her head, so I just shrug and get out the pancake batter.

"You cook?" she suddenly asks, getting up from the stool and walking around the counter to wrap her arms around my waist. The sparks that fly through me are so intense that I realise her heat is going to be back in the next hour or so.

"Nope, but I'm gonna attempt to," I joke, causing a smile to split her face. That beautiful smile will always make my day, no matter the circumstances.

"I'll help you. The easy part is done, so all we have to do is flip the pancakes," she tells me as she gets a frying pan and puts it on the cook top.

Flip them? A piece of cake. Not.

I watch Alex pour a small amount of batter in, the gooey stuff expanding into a small circle.

"You wait for the bubbles to start forming and popping, then you flip!" she exclaims with a grin. I smile. She actually gets a thrill out of this. Cute.

I wrap my arms around her waist and rest my chin on her shoulder. She sighs as she leans her head on mine, patiently waiting for the pancake to start bubbling. Well, at least she's patient for food.

"I'm sorry," she suddenly whispers. I lift my head up to examine her side, shocked from what she just said. Sorry? Why in the world would she be sorry?

"What are you sorry for? There's nothing for you to be sorry for," I tell her, putting my finger under her chin to get her to look at me. She does so without a fight.

"It's just that you wanted so badly to capture Damon, and you were going to do that today, but my stupid heat stopped you. I know I'm being really selfish right now, but I

153

can't help it because I've finally gotten to fully mate with you, and I've loved every second of it. I really hate my emotions right now because they are going haywire and I would really appreciate it if you kiss me," she rants out in one breath.

I smirk at her as I place a soft kiss on her lips, not going any further than that. Alex obviously has other ideas, though because she wraps her arms around my neck and pulls me closer, forcing the kiss to go deeper than I intended.

"Alex!" I growl, wrapping an arm around her waist. Well, I was right. Her heat's come back full force and it hasn't even hit the hour yet.

A foul smell suddenly hits my nose, and I cringe away. Alex whimpers, trying to pull me closer again. I shake my head and furrow my eyebrows.

"Can you smell something burning?" I ask. Alex's eyes go wide as she looks at the frying pan.

"Crap!" she curses. She rushes to turn down the heat and throws the frying pan in the sink with a loud 'clunk!' That's sure to wake everyone up.

I chuckle at her overreaction while she glares daggers at me.

"Don't you laugh, lover boy. You don't get pancakes now," she shoots back with a huff.

"Me? You were the one that was hungry. If I had my way, I would be eating something else right now," I say lowly, letting the lust seep into my eyes. Alex shivers before looking at me evilly.

"Well, lover boy, you're gonna have to catch your dinner first," she teases before sprinting out of the kitchen. I growl. She wants a chase? She'll get a chase. You better run, my little mate.

154

ALEX

Finally! For the love of the Moon Goddess, finally! My heat is officially over for a whole month! Be happy for me! You cannot feel the relief and happiness I'm feeling right now! It's beyond anything!

"Geez, Alex, why are you so excited so early in the morning?" I hear Comrade's muffled voice from the bed. I laugh as I go and jump on top of him. He groans at the sudden weight, but it doesn't wipe the smile from my face.

"Comrade! I'm not in heat anymore! I can be free and go dancing in the rain!" I exclaim, falling onto his chest and beaming at him like the mad hatter.

Comrade rolls his eyes at me and smiles. With the new and improved bond between us, I can feel his emotions and all I'm feeling right now is adoration. Aww, he adores me.

"Well then, the fun is over, huh?" he asks as he gives a fake disappointed look. I chuckle at him and shake my head, leaving a lingering kiss on his lips.

"Of course not! Think of my heat as a kick start!" I tell him with another million watt smile. He releases a laugh at my words and I can't help it when my smile gets bigger. I love that sound, the sound of his laugh. I love his eyes, the mysterious darkness. I love his lips, the roughness, and softness of them. I love everything about this man. Not boy. Man.

I love Comrade. I love this man with all my heart.

Coming to this realisation, my smile drops and my mouth becomes ajar. I love this man. This mysterious and dark man that has gone through so much is the man that I love and forever will.

"Comrade?" I whisper. His eyes open slowly. He takes one look at my face and instantly sits up with me slipping into his lap, the only worry reflects in his eyes.

"What's wrong, Alex?" he asks in a hurry, cupping my face with his hands.

I take a deep breath and say the three words I'm never going to take back with so much emotion, that it even shocks me, "I love you."

The expression that takes over Comrade's face is so worth the sound of those three words leaving my mouth. His eyes widen, and a grin splits his face, reaching from ear to ear. I've never seen him smile so much in the past week, but this smile beats them all. By far.

"I love you, too," he whispers.

His lips crash against mine as we pour out all our emotions into this one kiss. Pain for what we've both been through, anxiety for what's coming for us, devotion for knowing that we're never going to leave each other's side, and finally, our love for each other that will never break.

"I love you. I love you. I love you!" Comrade keeps saying over and over, planting kiss after kiss on my lips as I just laugh at him. He seems so much lighter now like he doesn't have the weight of his past on his shoulders. We both share each other's burdens now, each other's secrets, and that's the way it's supposed to be. Now and forever more.

18

ALEX

I chuckle evilly to myself as I watch Ally check every single one of her five hairbrushes. Oh, Ally, you're in for a big surprise...

Once she's satisfied that her hairbrushes are free of super glue, she picks one up and starts to brush her hair. Nothing happens. Perfect. Now she thinks that nothing's going to happen to her.

I glance above me, on the top of the door - a full bucket of coloured glue sits there. I get my phone and camera ready. This is gonna be good.

It takes Ally another three or so minutes before she starts walking towards the door. Her afro-like hair is up in a frizzy ponytail, and she doesn't suspect a thing.

I quietly and slowly back away from the door, holding my phone up. Three. Two. One.

Ally opens the door to see me. Her eyes go wide as she hears the bucket tip and looks up at the very last second to see the coloured glue come pouring down on her.

"Ahh!" she screams, her hands up near her face, picturing of utter shock. I snap the picture and a few others as the glue drip down her face and onto the tiled floor of the bathroom. I try so hard not to laugh, but I can't help it! She looks hilarious!

"Alex! You- you-" she tries to say, but it seems like she can't get her words out. I think it's mainly because she has glue in her mouth.

"Yes, Ally? What can I do for you?" I ask sweetly, my shoulders still shaking with silent laughter. This is gold! I wish there were someone else to see it!

As if my wish was heard, Taylor comes running into the room. She takes one look at Ally and bursts out laughing, which makes me start laughing again. Gold I tell you, gold! I should report this to funniest home videos! Ha! Best prank. Ever!

Ally tries to say something but keeps her mouth shut so that the glue doesn't get in her mouth again. I laugh harder at that, and it seems like Taylor does, too.

Ally just screams, her mouth still closed, and stomps off out of the room. Taylor and I keep on laughing until we look like dying seals. You know when you laugh so much no sound comes out? Yeah, that's what we're doing now.

"Oh my gosh, that was brilliant!" I yell, my grin and laughter never leaving me. Taylor can only nod in agreement.

A good ten minutes later and we're ready to go back downstairs to everyone else. Taylor and I make our way down the stairs, still chuckling under our breaths.

I appear in the kitchen and my eyes instantly lock on Comrade's. He smiles at me, to which I return in a full beam. I jump over to him and wrap my arms around his neck, giving him a light kiss on the lips.

"Morning, my little mate," he whispers in my ear as he places a kiss on my mark. I shiver and mumble a morning back. He chuckles at me while wrapping an arm around my waist and pulling me closer.

"Yeah, yeah, that's enough now. Keep it PG, people!" Callum exclaims, walking into the kitchen with a big grin.

I pull away from Comrade to grin at Callum. I've missed him! He hasn't been around for a while.

"Comrade! How ya doin?" Callum asks with the same grin. Comrade chuckles and nods while giving him a normal answer. They continue to have a semi-conversation while I stand there gob-smacked. When did these two become good friends?

"Whoa, whoa, whoa!" I exclaim, holding my fingers up between the two men. They look at me questioningly while I look at them dumbly.

"When did you two becomes best friends? And where did you disappear to?" I accuse them both. I really shouldn't be questioning my beta, but Comrade seems to be good friends with him, so I may as well be.

Comrade looks at me with a small smile and wraps his arms around me again while saying, "Alex, Callum's been helping us try to find Damon. He went away for a week because he went searching for his mate."

I stare at Callum shocked. He was looking for his mate? Did he find her? What's she like? Is she pretty? Maybe we could be friends. That is if he found her.

"Did you find her?" I question eagerly, getting excited to try and make a new friend. Callum offers me a sad smile and a shrug. I instantly know the answer.

"I'm sorry," I mumble, getting out of Comrade's arms and engulfing Callum in a hug. He stays still for a moment, probably because I'm hugging him and I shouldn't be. He hugs me back, although it just takes him a moment before he does.

"Ok, that's enough hugging," I hear Comrade say before I'm pulled away and into his arms once again. I chuckle at him while shaking my head. He's so overprotective.

"Well, I'm gonna head back to Axel's office, and you'll be there soon?" Callum states, but it's more of a question. Comrade nods his head and kisses me on the cheek.

"See you soon," he tells me before following Callum out of the kitchen. I sigh as I watch his retreating back. He turns around and gives me a sneaky wink to which I just chuckle lightly at. I know I won't see him anytime soon. I'll probably see him in the morning, though.

I decide that I'm not gonna sit around the house and wait for the next prank to attack its victim, so I decide on something that I don't normally do. I'm gonna go see my dad.

I sit there awkwardly as dad tries to avoid looking at me at all costs. This is nothing really. You should've seen him when I knocked on the door. The first thing I noticed was that his face dropped, and his eyes became heavy. I am the spitting image of my mum, so I can't really blame him. I can blame him, however, for being a bad dad ever since my mum died.

"So, huh... What's been happening lately? Gone for a run?" I ask him, hoping to get something out of him. His eyes snap to my blue ones, and they instantly fill with pain. I quickly look away, not wanting to see that stupid emotion in his eyes. It's the only emotion he seems to feel now.

"Yeah, uh... I haven't gone for a run in a while," he tells me, clearing his throat.

It falls silent after that, it's almost suffocating. I look around the walls and notice that he's taken all the photos of us down. There used to be photos of Mum and me, all three of us, just me, just Mum and Dad, and now it's bare. All except for one lone photo. I smile as I get up and walk towards it. I feel my dad's eyes on me as I observe it.

It's actually one of my favourite photos of us. It's when I was younger. wW're in the park. Mum was laughing and cuddling me in her arms while Dad was sneaking up behind her to scare us. He got us good that day, and Mum was so annoyed that she gave him the silent treatment until that night. Nevertheless, Mum made him beg before she muttered a single word to him.

"Do you remember this?" I whisper, turning to face my dad to see him already standing behind me. He rests his hands on my shoulders with a small smile.

"I do. Your mother gave me the silent treatment for the rest of the day. I had to beg on my hands and knees for a good hour," he says with a chuckle.

"Yeah," I say breathlessly with a nod. "She sure did."

Dad and I continue to just stare at the picture, remembering all the good times that we used to have.

Mum was always the fun one out of us. She always lit up the room. Dad was always the one to help her see the responsible side of things, but he never ruined her fun, no matter how irresponsible it was. As for me, I was just the one that always tried to make them smile and have a good time.

Dad clears his throat and paces back to his seat. I quickly follow suit, hoping to strike up another conversation.

"So, uh... I met my mate. It's Comrade, the guy who was missing for three years," I tell him quietly, not wanting to meet his eyes. I don't expect him to blow up or anything, but he could at least acknowledge that I've found my life long partner.

"That's good," he answers back, not doing anything to show that he's happy for me. He just stays in the same tense pose since I've gotten here. Seriously, though, 'that's good'? That's all he has to say to me? I met my freaking mate!

I take a deep breath and unclench my teeth, not remembering when I clenched them in the first place. If he wants to be this way, then fine.

"So, I'm going for a run later, wanna come?" I ask him, sticking a thumb behind me as a gesture. I actually wasn't planning to go for a run, and I don't want to go for a run with him, but he is my dad whether I like it or not.

Dad looks up to my eyes, and I instantly know the answer. He's given me the same one a million times, what would make this time any different?

"No," is all he says before getting up and opening the front door for me to exit his house that also used to be ours. I sigh but accept the rejection anyway. It's normal.

"I'll see you around, Dad," I mutter before walking out and hearing the door slam behind me. The thing with Dad now is that he's happy for one tiny second, then he's a coldhearted man who doesn't care if I live or die, or if I've met my mate. Gotta love daddy!

I really don't want to go back to the pack house right now, so I think I'm gonna take that run. I detour on my way

162

back to the pack house and head towards the forest. It's about time I let off some steam. I haven't gone for a run since Callum had us do that game thing for choosing who gets to rescue Comrade. That was like, two or three months ago! I really need to let my wolf go...

Once I'm far enough into the tree cover, I strip my clothes and shift into my wolf. I take it slow as I feel all my bones break and morph, my muscles contract and flex. It's a nice, yet slightly painful feeling.

'Glad you finally let me out,' I hear my wolf mutter to me, but I don't bother replying. I just pull back and let her take over, enjoying the feeling of not being in control of my body for once. I can finally relax for once in my life.

I watch through my wolf's eyes as trees pass by and everything blurs around me. I'm surprised I haven't run into anything in the few years that I've been able to shift.

I run until the sun goes down and finally reel my wolf in so that I have control. I lead her back to where the pack house is, but I can hear her constant whining about not being able to run some more. I just ignore her because she always ignores me.

I make it to the pack house and drop the clothes I have in my mouth behind a tree. I slowly shift back again, feeling my body change back into its original anatomy. I sigh as I pull my clothes on when I suddenly hear a crash from inside. I quickly pull on my shirt, bolting into the pack house.

"Oh my god!" I whisper-yell to myself as I see the place. As soon as you walk through the front door, it's like a cyclone has been through! Everything that isn't heavy or tied down is everywhere. Literally. Things are broken, glass is shattered, furniture is turned over, nearly everything is ruined!

That's when I notice something. It's quiet. Too quiet...

163

I gingerly make my way through the broken glass and furniture, trying really hard not to step on anything. Where is everybody? They couldn't have trashed the place and left! They're more decent than that! I hope...

I make my way to the kitchen and see the dinner half-cooked, the knife still sitting on the counter and the oven fan still running. This is ridiculous!

I go to the stairs next. Placing my foot on the first one and hearing it groan under the pressure is not very helpful. I shoot up the steps, just to see if it keeps the steps from groaning, which it certainly does. Luck was on my side for that.

I peer left and right before checking all the rooms. They're all empty. The only room I haven't checked is the third level and Axel's office. The third level is a no-go zone, so I'm gonna go with Axel's office.

The weird thing is, there's been no danger so far. I half expected someone to jump out and knock me out or something! Honestly, this just seems like one big setup. Where is everyone though if it is a setup? This makes no sense to me...

I come to Axel's door to see it slightly ajar. Should I? Yeah, I should. I slowly and carefully open the door to be met with pitch blackness. I think I'm blind for a second! I almost slap myself though when I realise it's just that the lights are turned off.

I flick the lights on with the switch and get ready for something I don't even know is coming.

The second the lights turn on, I see that Axel's office is untouched. The next few seconds is absolute shock and seem to go in slow mo.

Comrade, Ally, Taylor, and Celina all jump out at me, all doing scary faces that will put all three-year-olds to shame. I turn around out of pure shock and come face to face with

Matthew, Jasper, Declan, Callum, and can you believe it, Axel. This time, I scream, and I scream loud. Everyone blocks their ears as I grip my hand to my heart.

"What the actual hell! Is this some kind of a sick joke! I almost died of fright, my heart is going a million miles an hour and-" I start to scream until it all finally hits me like a ton of bricks.

This is a prank. A bloody prank.

"You just got pranked!" they all scream at me together before bursting into laughter and falling to the floor. Oh. My. Flipping. Bloody. God.

Let's just say, I am fuming.

My hands ball into fists as I feel my face turn red from anger. Did they seriously just do that to me! Oh hell no!

"You have no idea how much I hate you all right now!" I seethe as I start to walk away, never looking back. How can you top that? This prank has officially ended the prank way of 2014, and I didn't even get to prank Comrade.

"Come on, Alex! It was just a joke!" I hear Callum's brother, Matthew, yell after me. I stop in my tracks, still hearing their out of control laughter.

I turn slowly on my heels, just at the top of the stairs, before saying to them in a low and cold voice, "Well then, have fun cleaning up without me."

That certainly stops their laughter because they all groan and bang their head against something. All except Celina, that is.

"Well then, have fun cleaning up without me also," she announces, walking towards me with a smile. I raise an eyebrow at her as everyone starts to yell.

"What!"

"That's so not fair!"

165

"I don't wanna clean up!"

"Why'd we have to do this?"

"You were a part of this too!"

"Celina! Sweetheart! Come on!"

Ok, that last one was definitely Axel.

Celina just giggles at them all and turns around with a hand on her hip and says, "I was not a part of this because I was suddenly hauled into Axel's office about five minutes before Alex showed up. Also, I need to look after the triplets who are still out in the backyard and Alex here is going to help me. Isn't that right, Alex?"

I nod eagerly, a smile gracing my face. I haven't seen the triplets in ages! I miss my knight in shining armor, my charmer, and most of all, my little princess.

Everybody groans again, but that's before Callum reminds everyone why they're on the floor, "Gotta admit, though, her face was so worth it!"

The laughter starts again while I just huff and start to walk down the stairs, trying really hard to block their laughter from my ears. At least I can get one of them back. Comrade. I have power over him, and I intend to use it. An evil smile creeps its way onto my face as a plan starts to form in my head. Oh, this will be good.

"So, ready to tackle the task of babysitting again?" Celina asks me as we walk out the house and into the backyard. I laugh and nod my head.

"Of course, I am!" I exclaim just as a small pair of arms wrap around my legs.

"Alex!" Dylan screams with a big grin on his face. I laugh at him and poke his cheek. He giggles at me and holds my legs tighter.

"Hey, my little charmer! Whatcha doing?" I ask as another pair of arms wrap around my legs from the back. I look behind me and see Jett, his black hair going everywhere.

"We're tackling you!" Dylan exclaims, hugging my legs tighter again. I laugh silently to myself as Jett also hugs my legs tighter. You can already tell that Jett is that little bit stronger than Dylan, but not enough to bring me down.

"Nice try, boys, but I'm too strong for you," I tease as I hear Celina muffle a laugh. I look at her and wink.

I suddenly see Clarissa running at full power towards me. My eyes widen as I start to panic. Last time she did that, I fell down with her on top of me.

"Clarissa... Don't you dare!" I threaten, but her laugh just filters through the air as she jumps at me and causes me to tumble down.

I squeal and put my hands out to avoid face planting, also making sure that I don't land on any of the triplets.

I land with a thud, Clarissa on top of me, Dylan still holding onto my legs and Jett standing by my head with a triumphant grin on his face. Little bastard...

"Ha ha! We're stronger than you!" Jett tells me loudly, pointing a finger at me and sticking his tongue out. I raise an eyebrow at him and think to myself, this kid is going to be the next alpha?

"Jett, you don't point fingers at people or poke your tongue out at them," Celina scolds with her hands on her hips. I chuckle and lift Clarissa off my lap, somehow also getting Dylan to let go of my legs.

You know, for a 19-year-old, Celina is a damn good mum.

Dylan instantly runs towards Celina, who picks him up without thinking. She smiles at him and kisses his forehead. He grips her shirt and holds onto her tighter as I smile at the adorable sight. Dylan is so gonna be a mummy's boy.

"Sorry, Mummy!" I hear Jett mutter, hanging his head low. I bend down to his level and tap his head to get him to look up. He does so, and all I have to do is wink before a big grin splits his face.

"Wanna tackle Mummy?" I ask him in a cheeky and quiet voice, but loud enough for Celina to hear. Her eyes widen as Jett nods his head fast.

"Now, now, remember who feeds you, Jett," Celina tries to bribe, but Jett's got his mission, and he's sticking to it.

"Charge!" I yell, and both Jett and I start charging at Celina. I make sure I'm a bit behind Jett, just to make sure I don't damage his ego. What? He's three; he needs to build up a big ego to be an alpha. Not really, but if he did, he would be a lot like his dad.

"I wanna play!" a small voice suddenly announces. Soon enough, Clarissa comes running up next to me. I laugh as I pick her up and place her on my back, still running.

"Run, Mummy! Run!" Dylan yells as Celina takes off running with him still holding onto her. So a mummy's boy...

Celina laughs, and we spend the rest of the afternoon chasing Celina and Dylan while the rest of the people who scared me clean up.

I want this one day. I want a family. A family would be nice.

19

COMRADE

"They wouldn't be hiding in plain sight, they couldn't!" I snap at Axel for the millionth time this morning. I'm just so frustrated! It's been two weeks since Alex gave us the idea that Damon might be hiding in the same place they found me or near the border and we've still got nothing. Nada. Zilch. It's infuriating!

"I swear on the Moon Goddess if you don't stop snapping at me, I'll snap you!" Axel threatens. I groan and fall back into my chair, the sleepless night I had, catching up to me. After that little stunt we pulled on Alex, she decided she was going to camp it out somewhere. Much to my displeasure, I had no mate to sleep with and knowing she was out there by herself wasn't the greatest feeling either.

"No sleep?" Axel asks, taking a seat next to me on the couch. I sigh, close my eye,s and nod.

"The worst sleep," I mumble. I hear his chuckle which makes me crack a smile. He hasn't chuckled for a while, and I'm sure he's feeling the pressure of having his pack, Celina, and now his three pups in danger.

"How's Celina?" I ask quietly, opening my eyes to look over at him. He sighs and rubs his eyes with his fingers.

"Honestly, not too good. After a whole day of having to deal with the triplets and then having them in bed by six, she's exhausted. She literally just showers and goes straight to bed. I don't think she's eaten dinner for the past week," he admits, a new kind of pain in his eyes.

"Maybe you guys should go out, have a break. I'm sure Alex will be happy to take care of the triplets," I suggest. Axel is the best alpha and friend you could ever ask for, but he doesn't know when to catch a break and relax. He's stubborn in a way really.

"Maybe... I really need to focus on this now, though," he states, standing from his position and walking back over to the maps. I sigh and shake my head. He needs to stop.

"Where's Celina?" I ask, also standing.

"In our room," he mumbles distractedly, too focused on the maps to really let his brain wander anywhere else.

Without him noticing, I sneak out of his office and up the stairs to the third floor where I know Celina is. I softly knock on the door and call out a soft, "Celina?"

I get no reply, but I open the door anyway. I'm met with the sight of a peaceful Celina sleeping soundly in the king-sized bed that makes her frame look as small as a pea. I chuckle at the sight, remembering the first time I ever saw her in this bed. She was cuddled up into a ball, crying her eyes out like there was no tomorrow. She's come such a long way since then.

I timidly walk into the room, not wanting to make a sound that will awaken her. I sneak into the wardrobe and take out the first dress I see, which happens to be some blue one, then a pair of white flats. I lay them on the edge of the bed with a little note saying, 'Meet me outside.'

I go back into the wardrobe again and take out a white v neck and light blue jeans for Axel, slinging them over my arm as I glance at Celina one last time. I feel like I haven't had a conversation with her in so long. It's like we don't even know each other. I was so happy when they finally found me, but now... I don't know. It just feels like everything's changed.

I quietly walk out the room and shut the door behind me with a soft click. I hope she wakes up soon...

Making my way back down the stairs, my eyes catch some movement. I turn my head just in time to catch a wisp of blonde hair heading to the kitchen. I grin in excitement. Alex.

I quickly move back to the office, throwing the clothes at Axel and saying, "Get dressed and outside. You have until Celina wakes up."

Before he can even react, I'm out of the office again and into the kitchen. I burst through the doorway with a massive grin on my face, but freeze when the frame standing in front of me registers. This is not Alex...

"Comrade?" The voice I haven't heard for so long travels through the air to my ears. I stare at her with my mouth wide open. Her dark blonde hair falls down her back with its usual shine, her hazel eyes shine bright, and her small face is in perfect condition, no bruises or anything. How could I have forgotten about Kate? Little, innocent Kate?

"Kate?" I whisper, stepping further into the kitchen. I gently put a finger on her cheek, as if checking it's her. I haven't seen her in so long.

171

"Kate, I..." I honestly don't know what to say. This girl, this beautiful girl that I haven't seen, or even thought about for weeks, is standing in front of me with a small smile on her face.

"I know, Comrade, I know," she whispers before wrapping her arms around my shoulders. I stay in the same position, not believing this girl.

I quickly snap out of my amazement and bend down to her height to hug her around the waist.

"Oh my Goddess, Kate! I'm so sorry, I'm so, so sorry," I whisper into her hair. I hold her closer to me, tightening my arms around her.

"Hey," she starts as she pulls back to look at my face, "there's nothing you could've done. That's all in the past now. I've moved on and now it's time for you to move on too."

She smiles up at me as I return to my normal height. Move on? Can I move on? It's not like I can forget what's happened to me. That... I can never forget.

"Comrade, I love you so much that I eventually started loving you more than my mum. I realise now that she was never my mum and Damon was definitely never my dad. I love you like a brother, Comrade. You're the reason I forgot, you're the reason why I decided to forget everything and move on because that's the only way we can make it through the trauma we've been through," Kate says quietly, shining tears brimming in her eyes. I never knew she could be so deep, even for a 13-year-old.

"I love you too, Kate!" I whisper, wrapping my arms around her tiny frame. I love Kate like a brother would love a sister and no more, but also so much more.

A feral growl suddenly rips through the air, cutting short the emotional turmoil of Kate and mine. I freeze and tighten my arms around Kate. I'm going to be getting an earful for this, but it'll be worth it.

I slowly turn around, sending Kate a message with my eyes to be quiet and still, and come face to face with the person I've been wanting all morning to see. Although now... not so much.

"What the-" Alex starts to scream, taking big steps towards us. I hold up a finger, though, stopping her in her tracks.

"Now, Alex, listen to me," I say cautiously, pushing Kate towards the backyard door. Unfortunately, Alex sees the small movement and growls again.

"So when you said you loved me, you didn't really mean it? Huh? Is that the deal?" Alex screams. She throws her hands up in the air as a fire ignites in her eyes that scares me. As soon as her words click, though, my eyes widen.

"What?" I question quietly, completely forgetting about Kate and only focusing on the raging girl in front of me.

"You say you love me and then go say it to another! You sick bastard!" she screeches, slapping me across the face. My head whips to the side, only for my dark eyes to catch a pair of gold ones.

"Comrade? Alex? What's going on?" Celina asks as she steps into the kitchen. She's wearing the outfit I randomly picked out for her, and she's looking as beautiful as ever.

I am about to open my mouth to explain everything, but Alex beats me to it.

"Well, Comrade dearest just admitted his love for another girl. Does it need more explanation?" Alex seethes, sending Kate a glare that would bury her a lot more than six feet under.

"Alex, you need to calm down and listen to Comrade's side of the story," Celina speaks softly, walking up to Alex without an ounce of fear in her eyes.

"His side of the story?" she spits, now sending me the same glare she sent to Kate. Celina just nods as Alex continues to glare at me.

"Well?" she asks irritably. I blink and blink again, then blink a third time before it actually registers that she's gonna let me talk. Better do this quick...

"This is Kate. She was Damon's adopted daughter. When you guys came to rescue me, she was there too, but somebody found her, and she's been healing for who knows how long and now she's ok. We were just catching up, and she's only thirteen, and I'm not in love with her, and I'll only love you Alex. Promise!" I breathe out in a rush, not letting Alex object as I take her into my arms.

"See, now that wasn't so bad, was it?" Celina asks with a smile on her face as she walks up to Kate and leads her outside.

"Celina!" I call a little worried. I don't want Kate being around anyone without me at the moment. Plus, Celina had somewhere to be.

"I know, Comrade, but I only want to talk," Celina tells me softly as she places a hand on Kate's shoulder and makes her way to the backyard. The backyard seems to be the safe haven for everyone at the moment.

Alex pushes me away softly and looks up at me with guilty blue eyes.

"So... you're not in love with another girl?" she asks with a high pitched voice. It's usually the voice she uses when she wants the answer to a question to be something it's not.

"No, Alex, I'm not in love with another girl. Only you," I assure her, kissing her on the nose lightly.

"So, I just completely embarrassed myself and went all possessive?" she asks, her cheeks turning a light shade of pink. I chuckle and nod my head.

"You've got to be kidding me..." I hear her mutter harshly to herself. I laugh at her face as it screws up into one of embarrassment and disbelief.

Alex continues to talk to herself as I just stare down at her. I must look like a stalker or a very happy mate right now.

"Why are you staring at me? Do I have something on my face?" Alex asks in a rush, her eyes going wide as she pats all over her face. I chuckle once more and grip her hands in mine, bringing them between us.

"No, your face is perfect," I whisper. I place a soft kiss on her lips as I wrap my arms around her waist. Before I can even think to go any further, Alex pulls away with a stern face. What did I do now?

"Don't think this changes anything from yesterday. You owe me big time for doing that," she scolds, a scowl on her face. I purse my lips to conceal my laughter. That was the best prank in the history of pranks. No question about it.

"Oh come on, Alex. It was only a joke," I bargain. The scoff that comes from her tells me otherwise.

"I don't want to talk about it. Who was that girl?" she questions suspiciously, quickly changing the subject. I sigh and rub my face. I motion for Alex to sit down as I take a seat opposite her.

"The girl's name is Kate," I begin, but don't continue. Memories of her smile and laughter fill my mind, making me smile. Then memories of the countless nights of Damon torturing her and the bruises that covered her body. Who would ever, in their right mind, do that to an innocent little girl? I guess Damon hasn't been in his right mind for a while, though.

"Comrade!"

I blink and snap out of my little flashbacks. I turn my eyes to Alex's worried ones and smile.

"Sorry, uhm, how do I say this? To put it simply, Kate was Damon and his mate's adopted daughter. After Damon's mate, Phyre, found out that she couldn't have pups, she convinced Damon to adopt. Kate had lost her parents in the war, I'm pretty sure, so Damon took her in," I explain. Alex nods along as she motions for me to continue.

"They played a happy family for a while, two years in fact. For those two years, though, Kate came down to see me nearly every day. Her face was the only kind one I saw, her smile was the only one that didn't hold hatred and disgust. She was like a safe haven for me, the only thing that kept me going. During the first year, I had lost all hope, but Kate made me find that hope again. She made me... well, me again," I say softly, remembering the first time I saw Kate.

She had stumbled down the steps and landed square on her ass. I looked up at the sound, expecting to see a guard or Damon, only to come across a dark blonde haired beauty. When she saw me, she didn't gasp or look away; she smiled. A beaming, toothy smile she did. I'll never forget the first few words she said to me and I quote, "If you don't smile then your face will be stuck like that forever." It was at that moment that I chuckled or actually cracked a smile in a whole year. Kate was an angel, the Moon Goddess in human form. She was my Kate, and she still is.

"So Kate's pretty important in your life then, uh?" Alex asks, bringing me out of the happy memory.

176

"Yeah, she is," I whisper. I don't really know what else to say. What do you say?

"Does that mean she knows what happened to you during those three years? Does she know what made you the Comrade you are now?" Alex questions, her head tilted ever so slightly to the side.

I furrow my eyebrows and mutter, "What do you mean?"

"I mean that all I ever heard about the 'amazing' Comrade was that he was so full of life and laughter and fun. Sure, you're that Comrade now, but not to the extent you used to be. That's made pretty obvious through Celina every time she sees you," Alex admits, averting her eyes to a crack on the table.

Full of life. Laughter. Fun. That's true, I was like that. I still am, after a few long months. I'm not the same as I was, though. I don't think I'll ever be.

"Well, everyone has to grow up sometime. My time just came early," I grumble, not really in the mood to talk anymore. Alex always seems to bring up this subject of me not being the same as I used to be. If you ask me, it's none of her business really.

"Your time came early? What about Celina? She pretty much had to grow up straight away. What about me? Huh? After my mum had died, I had no one! My dad couldn't, wouldn't, and doesn't look me in the eye! He's completely shut me out, and I can't do a thing about it! I've had to deal with no mum for the last three years! She couldn't wait for my wedding day, the day when I'd finally meet my mate, the day that she would see her first grandchild. She lost that opportunity during that bloody war. So don't go telling me you're the way you are because you had a minor bump in your life. There are people

177

out there who are having a worse life than you at the moment. For goodness sakes, Comrade! Open your eyes and live! You can't live in the past!" she screams at me.

I stay frozen in place, her words running through my head over and over again. I learnt three things from what Alex just said.

One. Her mum died. She's never told me that, and I don't think she meant to. She's had to go through pain by herself, hiding it all inside. At least when I lost my parents and was shunned from my pack, I had the Nightfall Pack to help me through it.

Two. Alex's dad is an emotionless man who can't even look at his own daughter.

Three. Both Alex and Kate have the same idea... I can't live in the past, I need to move on. I need to pick up the pieces of my life and get my shit together because a miracle isn't gonna happen anytime soon. I gotta get back on my feet and go on with my life, but first... I need to tell Alex the whole story.

"Well Comrade, what's it gonna be? Are you gonna tell me why your life is so messed up, or are you gonna walk away from me with a blank look on your face like you always do? Pick wisely because I will not be coming back to you when you choose the wrong one," Alex warns, pointing a thin finger at me with a look in her stormy eyes that says, 'Don't mess with me.'

"Alex, if I tell you what happened to me, you can't repeat a word of it. Not. One. Word," I say, accenting every word. Alex's eyes widen. She slowly sits down on a chair and nods her head, her mouth sealed tightly.

"I guess I should start from the capture..."

Comrade's story...

"The war was pretty much over, but I saw one of Damon's wolves run into the forest, so I followed them. I caught them easily and killed them, but I wasn't expecting what came next. There was so many of them...all at once. They all just jumped on me and grabbed me by their jaws. I had no way of escaping. They knocked me out not soon after. I woke up in that terrible cell...

"Nothing happened for the first three days, or what I'm assuming it was. I had no clue what was going on and I had no clue where I was. Shit, I didn't even remember what had happened for a while. The war and the capture and the triplets were erased from my mind like they never existed. When the memories came back, it scared me half to death that I could forget all of that. I was so scared, Alex, so scared. I'd never been so scared in my life...

"Then one day, or night, the door separating me from the world opened. I thought it was Celina and Axel coming to rescue me. My hopes were crushed though when none other than Damon himself walked through that door. That's when everything started to happen. All the pain and the grief. All the suffering and hatred. All the worst emotions imaginable, but the one that hit me the most was hopelessness. I had given up without even allowing a week to pass. I was so weak. I honestly thought I had given up on all hope before you guys came to the rescue.

"Before you, though... that was torture. I never knew there were so many ways to hurt a man until I first stepped foot in Damon's torture room. Knives. Belts. Hammers. Clamps. Shackles. Silver Chains. Handcuffs. The list is endless. There was just so much evil in that one room, I honestly couldn't believe my eyes. One thing I do believe, though was that Damon was, and is, a sick man.

"I don't want to tell you every hostile thing he did to me, but I will say this: he broke me. He broke me in more than one sense of the word. He broke my bones, he broke my heart, he broke my strength, and he broke my hope. I had nothing left to hold onto. Then, Kate came into the picture.

"Kate made me smile and laugh and forget about everything for a brief moment. She made everything disappear. I learned to love her. She was my dark-blonde-haired, 13-year-old girl. Damon and his mate didn't deserve her. Kate deserves parents who will love her like her own parents did. Kate was my shining star, and she will always be.

"When everything went wrong with Kate, though, the foundation we built up started to break. Damon found out about her visits to me over the last two years, and he was unforgiving. Instead of torturing me, he tortured Kate. He hurt her and made her cry. If he did that to his own so-called daughter, I wouldn't want to see what he would do to his mate and pack. Pretty much, all my hope was crushed and burnt without a second thought.

"When that guard opened the door that day, though, I knew something was happening. Something that would help Kate and me. You found me, you saved me, and you loved me. I love you beyond all imagination for that, Alex. Thank you.

"When I woke up and Celina and Axel were talking to me, though... I don't know... Everything just seemed forced and unnatural. I hated it, but I couldn't do anything about it. I lost the ability to open up to people. I shattered Celina's heart by doing that. I caused her so much pain, I felt it. That's the thing when you're a royal's guardian, though. You feel all of their strongest emotions. You wanna know what Celina's strongest emotion was? Sadness. She was so sad, it was unfathomable. I didn't want to be the cause of her pain, but I knew I was.

"Over the months, though, I've been better. I've had talks with Celina, small ones, but they're talks. I've been spending time with Axel and Callum. I've been joking and smiling and having fun, and you know what? It's all because of you, Alex. It was all your doing.

"So, eventually, I ended up here with you," I finish, my head still resting on Alex's shoulder. We had made our way to Axel's office so that we could speak privately.

"Comrade... I-I don't know what to say," Alex whispers. She lets out a breath and relaxes back into the couch. I look into her stormy eyes to see an internal battle raging through them.

"You don't have to say anything. I answered your question, and that's that. No explanations or comments needed," I whisper back, picking myself up so I can plant a kiss on her cheek.

We stay like that for a while, no disturbances or mishaps. Just the two of us, together.

"Comrade?" Alex asks in a tired voice. I look under my arm to see her eyes only half open.

"Yes, my little mate?" I question back in a cheeky tone as I nip her ear. She releases a breathy chuckle, closing her eyes completely.

"I love you,"

I smile at her soft and gentle voice.

"I love you more," I say back before Alex falls into a deep sleep.

20

COMRADE

"Comrade! Comrade, wake up!" a frantic voice screams softly in my ear if you can scream softly. My eyes shoot open, and I sit up like a bolt. My head connects with something hard, causing me to groan.

"Ow, that hurt. Note to self, never wake Comrade up so close to his face," the voice says again. I avert my eyes to see Celina rubbing her head.

"Celina! I'm so sorry!" I exclaim, quickly getting up off the couch and going to her aid. Before I can get there, though, another groan fills the room. I look back over at the couch to see Alex rubbing the back of her head. I groan loudly. Great, I've managed to head butt Celina and drop my mate's head onto a sofa. Fantastic.

"Alex, I'm sorry," I say quietly as I kiss the back of her head. She waves me off with a grunt and a small 'I'm ok'.

"Comrade, this is serious. We have news," Celina cuts in. I look over to her to see the gold in her eyes swirling with anxiety. I quickly nod and help Alex up.

"Let's go," I announce, motioning for Celina to lead the way. Alex stands beside me and gives me a worried look. I don't know what to say so I just send her a small smile in return.

Celina leads Alex and me to the backyard where most of the pack have been gathered. I furrow my eyebrows as I see all the confused faces and Axel standing in front of them all.

"Comrade, what's going on?" Alex whispers to me. I honestly don't know, so I just shrug my shoulders and make my way to the front of the crowd, towing Alex behind me.

"Now that we have everyone here, I would like your attention please!" Axel's loud voice booms over the quiet chatter. It instantly falls silent as everyone looks at their alpha.

"As most of you know, the war that happened three years ago was not one that was won, but one that had just begun. Damon, the leader of the pack who attacked us, has risen again. Just this morning, we got a snippet of his scent and traced it back to a camp not too far from the border. As I said before, the war had only begun, and now it's time to end it. I need as many volunteers as possible. Although they won't be as big as they were last time, they still are trained killers. Anyone who wishes to fight, stay. Anyone who doesn't wish to fight, you may go. Thank you," Axel finishes, stepping down from the stage.

A few people move off, mainly the couples with younger children. I snap my eyes to Celina and Axel. Why didn't they tell me? I start to march up to them as I see Celina whisper something in Axel's ear. He looks a bit unsure about it, but he nods his head.

"One final announcement!" he yells over the now loud crowd. "No females under the age of 21 are allowed to take part."

"Oh hell no!" a voice I can only describe as my mate's, yells.

ALEX

"Oh hell no!" I yell once I've heard Axel's announcement. All eyes seem to snap to me as I march up to Axel in utter fury. No females, huh? No females! Stuff that shit! I'm getting into this war if it's the last thing I do!

"Alex, now is not the time," Axel hisses to me, his fists clenching.

"I don't give a damn!" I hiss back. Before I can take another step, though, Comrade's hand lands on my shoulder. I look at him with wide eyes.

"Alex, you're not going to this battle, and that's final," he states sternly. My mouth drops open, and my eyebrows shoot up. He's agreeing? He can't be serious!

"You know what? Stuff you all! I'm outta here!" I say annoyed, storming out of the yard with all of the pack's eyes on me.

I do not have to deal with this crap. My mum died fighting with that son-of-a-bitch, and I'm gonna die fighting, too, if I have to. I will not sit back on the sidelines and watch as my mate, and my pack throws themselves into a war that can't be tamed. I will not allow it.

Whether Axel likes it or not, I will be fighting in this war. One way or another.

COMRADE

"How are we gonna do this?" I ask, getting straight to the point as we stare at a map of the surrounding territory.

"We go in three waves. Wave one will be our best fighters, including me. The second wave will be like a distraction wave. The third wave will be the wave that will wipe everything out. Their numbers are small, but their fighting is good, and we need to beat that," Axel explains. I nod my head along with the other pack fighters and Callum. I haven't seen Callum for a while, but now's not the time to catch up.

"When do we move out?" I question, noticing that the sun is just starting to go down.

"Tonight at midnight. There's no moon tonight so it will be pitch black. Those wolves who have a lighter coat, roll in some mud. I do not want any of my pack mates dying tonight. Nobody will touch Damon, he's mine." As Axel says the last sentence, his eyes lock with mine. I grit my teeth but nod my head. I don't like the idea, in fact, I hate it. I am not in the position to argue with him, though, not after the stunt that Alex pulled. I'm just gonna have to go along with it. For now.

"Right, get everyone ready. Callum, you're in charge of the dispute of the waves. Comrade, you're in charge of putting the rest of the pack into the safe houses. Also, make sure Celina and Alex get in there. I will not be leaving this land until they are locked inside a safe house. Understand?" he asks with hard eyes. I give a stiff nod then make my way out of the door.

Alex is not gonna be happy about this one... I know for a fact that she is pissed about not being able to come along to a gruesome fight that she may not come out of alive. Why wouldn't somebody be pissed?

"Alex!" I call as loud as I possibly can. I stand down the bottom of the stairs waiting for an answer but get nothing.

"Alex!" I yell louder.

"What!"

I block my ears at the loudness of Alex's voice. I turn around to see her standing behind me with her hands on her hips, one hip cocked out, and a pissed off expression on her face. See, told ya.

"What are you doing down here? You're supposed to be in our room," I say suspiciously. If I've learnt anything about Alex, it's that she's an eavesdropper. She's always listening in on other people's conversations.

Alex rolls her eyes and snaps, "Can't a girl get something to eat?"

I sigh and shake my head, running a hand through my hair.

"Whatever. Where's Celina?" I question. I'm not really in the mood for Alex's attitude at the moment. She can go and complain to somebody else. Jeez, I sound like a dad talking about his child.

"Right here. I heard the yelling," I hear Celina's voice behind me say. I spin around to see her walking down the stairs. I smile at her and reach out my hand to help her down the last few steps.

"M'lady," I say politely in a horrible British accent. I hear Alex scoff while Celina bursts out laughing. I look at her with a raised eyebrow.

"D-do you remember that time when you and C-Callum tried to make me laugh for the first time? That was hilarious! You both had horrible British accents!" she exclaims as she lets out another laugh. As the memory comes back, I also burst out laughing.

"You totally freaked out about your hair! That was hysterical!" I scream, holding my stomach to try and stop the laughing.

"What the hell are you two talking about?" I hear Alex ask through our laughter. I must admit, this is not the best time to be laughing at old memories, but technically, Celina started it.

"Nothing, nothing!" I chuckle out, taking a deep breath as Celina does the same. We look at each other as grins split out faces.

"That was funny," Celina whispers, another chuckle escaping. I clear my throat to stop another chuckle from escaping me when I see Alex give me an annoyed look.

"Ok, ok, we'll get back to the matter at hand," I say defensively, putting my hands up in the air. Alex rolls her eyes and motions for me to say something. Before I do, though, I realise something. This is me, this is the jokester Comrade playing around in a serious situation. I'm me again. I'm Comrade.

"I am under strict instructions to have you two put into a safe house before one wolf leaves this territory," I say with a distant voice, still coming to my new realisation.

"You've got to be kidding me..." I hear Alex whisper as she groans. I shake my head and snap my eyes to her. I can see the gears turning in her head for a compromise, but nothing is changing Axel's or my mind.

"Sorry, Alex, but you're coming with me," I say before picking her up and throwing her over my shoulder. She protests with lots of screams and punches on my back, but I just look at Celina to make sure she's coming. To my surprise, Celina also looks quite pissed off.

"Celina, it's for your own safety. You know that!" I tell her as I turn my body fully to face her straight on.

"I know, Comrade, but this is Damon we're talking about," she says quietly, running a hand through her pitch black hair. I give her a half smile and grab her hand.

"Exactly. This is Damon we're talking about," I repeat, making her realise the seriousness of this situation. In my opinion, I think Celina would be a massive help in this since she's got her royal power. She could literally blow the rest of Damon's pack away and beyond. I'm true to my word, though: I'm locking Celina and Alex up so that they're both safe and stay out of trouble.

In less than five minutes, I have Celina, Alex and any teenagers under the age of 18 who aren't fighting in a safe house.

"Where's everyone else?" Celina asks, her eyes filling with worry.

"Hey, it's ok. Families with small children are in another safe house and then everyone else is in another. Everyone will be locked up and safe. I promise," I tell her softly, giving her a kiss on the forehead. She lets her shoulders sag and a big sigh to escape her mouth.

"Ok, I'm trusting you, Comrade," she says as she points a finger at me. I smile and nod. It's my job to make sure everyone's safe so everyone will be safe. I've also made sure that Kate is in the safe house with all the families. There are children her age and all the parents are great, so she should be amazing.

I avert my eyes to Alex, who's cuddled up in a corner with her head leaning against the wall. I walk up to her and crouch down to her level.

"I love you?" I bargain, making it sound like a question. The smile I love seeing splits across Alex's face as she shakes her head at me.

"I love you too," she says back, faking reluctance. I chuckle at her before grabbing the back of her head and leading her into a long kiss. We break apart for air, resting our foreheads together.

"See you soon," I whisper. Not waiting for a reply, I get up and quickly shut the door behind me, sealing it so that nothing can get in or out.

I take a deep breath and lean against the door. Alex is going to murder me for leaving like that.

I shut and lock all the other doors, doing a quick look over to make sure everyone who isn't fighting is safe inside the safe houses. The safe houses are stocked up with food and water, so they should be ok. We don't know how long they're gonna be in there, but Celina has the password, so she can get out with no problem and get everyone else out.

I make my way back up to the house and head straight to Axel's office. I stop at the door, just staring at the intricate carvings that got us to where we are today. Just think, if Celina had never run through our territory and if she had never touched the carvings on this door, what would our lives be like now? Celina could still be a rogue...

I place my hand on the door and give a half- smile. This is where the journey began... and this is where it's gonna end.

189

21

ALEX

If I chose one time in my life to say the unmistakable 'f' word, now would be that moment. That, insert 'f' word here, bastard.

If he thinks he's gonna get away with bolting out of here after a measly little kiss, he thought wrong. If he thinks I'm gonna stay cooped in this safe house, then he has another thing coming along with a kick to the balls. If he thinks for one second that he's gonna get away with anything he's done to me in the last few hours, he's not gonna live very long.

"I can't believe him. I'm gonna murder him when he comes back," I mutter to myself as Celina comes to take a seat next to me. She gives me a small smile.

"Alex, you can't blame him for trying to keep you safe," she tries to argue, placing a hand on my shoulder. I shrug it off and put my head in my hands.

"That's the thing, Celina! I'm gonna blame him anyway. I'm the best female fighter, if not the best fighter we've got, and they're not even gonna let me fight! I feel restrained and useless, and I never wanna feel like that again," I whisper, my mum's dead body flashing through my mind. I couldn't help her, no matter what I did.

"Alex, you can't dwell in the past. What happened to your mother is a terrible thing, and I know how much it hurts, but you have to try and move on. Yes, she'll always be your mother, but she wouldn't want you to be drowning in self-pity!" Celina tells me, replacing her hand on my shoulder. I sigh and rest my head against the wall behind me, closing my eyes.

"Why does the world hate me?" I groan. Celina gives a breathy laugh through her nose.

"The world doesn't hate you, but Axel seems not to favour you either," she admits. I chuckle at that and nod my head in agreement.

"Come on, Celina! You don't just want to sit here and do nothing, do you? What would you do if Axel told you not to take part in the war?" I question incredulously. Celina sighs and glances at her three triplets who are running around keeping people entertained. Comrade must've got them in here when I wasn't paying attention.

"He did tell me that I wasn't to take part. I had just given birth to the pups, and I died. I physically died. It was a miracle that I woke up, but I have a destiny and so do you. If Comrade says you can't go to this battle, then don't. If your heart's telling you to, though, follow your heart," Celina tells me, still staring at her triplets as some teenagers play around with them.

Die? She died? That's new information...

"Celina... I don't know what to do," I sigh as I feel a lump form in my throat. My heart's telling me to go, but Comrade's voice is still ringing in my ears telling me not to. How do you choose between your heart and your mate?

"What do you want to do, Alex?" Celina asks me, her golden eyes turning into my blue ones. I take a deep breath through my nose and let it out through my mouth.

"I want to fight. I want to defend my pack. I want to help. Most of all, though, I want closure," I whisper. I feel a new determination build up within me. I'm gonna fight, and nothing's gonna stop me. Except maybe the door that's impenetrable. The determination that is building up inside me slowly dies down as I realise this fact.

"Jett! Dylan! Clarissa! Come here please!" Celina calls softly to her three children. Three sets of silver eyes swirling with gold snap to Celina before their little feet are scampering to get to her.

"Yes, mummy?" Jett asks. I have to hold back in awe at the future alpha, laughing inside at the pure innocence of him.

"Mummy's gonna go with Alex and help Daddy. You need to be good, understand me? Jett and Dylan, you don't let Clarissa out of your sight. Clarissa, be good, baby. Now, not a word to daddy, yeah?" Celina whispers, dragging all three of them into a hug. Dylan and Clarissa giggle while Jett frowns.

"But Mummy, Daddy wants you to stay." Jett pouts, gripping his mum's shirt. Celina looks down at him with a smile before bending to whisper something in his ear. His eyes widen as a grin splits his face. He nods his head viciously, making Celina chuckle.

"Good boy. Now, shall we, Alex?" Celina asks. I look at her in confusion. We? I don't think Axel will be too happy about that.

I open my mouth to say something, but Celina beats me to it, "I know that Axel won't be happy about it, but I'm not letting you go out there alone. Either come or stay, because I'm going either way."

"Ok!" I mumble, standing to my feet. Celina follows my actions and walks straight to the door. Curious eyes follow us, but Celina pays no mind to them.

"Luna, I don't think it's a good idea to be going out there," a feminine voice says, speaking up. I turn around with a frown on my face. A woman with blonde hair and blue eyes is staring at Celina in worry.

Celina also turns around and smiles at the woman. The woman keeps the frown on her face, but you can see in her eyes that she's going to agree to whatever Celina's going to say.

"Nancy, it'll be fine. I promise. By the way, next time Chloe calls, say hi for me," Celina says. She then turns gracefully around and punches in a code. I furrow my eyebrows as she continues to hit the lock pad with her small finger. There has to be at least twenty numbers so far. Celina's eye then gets scanned, and the door opens the tiniest bit. I would've missed it if I wasn't looking.

"Right, shall we?" Celina asks, motioning with her hand to the door. I step forward and give it a slight push. I only open it enough for both Celina and me to slip out, but it's enough. As soon as we step out, Celina shuts the door again, it locking automatically.

I glance around only to find that no one's here. They must've already gone.

"Now, Alex, we can't just go charging into this battle like Axel is dumbly doing. I'm gonna fly there, and I'm gonna fly you there. When we get there, though, shift. Please, I know you're strong in human form, but you're stronger in wolf form.

Just... be safe," Celina mutters worriedly as she draws me into a hug. I blink in shock, but gently wrap my arms around her.

"Don't worry, I will. I promise," I whisper back, burying my head in her shoulder. I swear, Celina is the best Luna a pack could ever ask for, and I love her for that.

Celina breaks the hug and smiles at me. She turns around and motions for me to get on her back. I purse my lips unsurely, but after a little encouragement, as gently as I can, I hop onto Celina's back. Not wasting a second, she lurches up into the air. I actually gasp at the shock and speed of it.

Holy crap, I'm flying.

"Don't forget what I said, Alex. I meant it," Celina warns me. I nod obediently before she takes off into the sky again.

I can already hear the growls and snapping of jaws as I ease my way through the forest. Coming up to a clearing, I crouch down behind a bush and observe.

Axel underestimated Damon's numbers. That's the first thing I notice. Although Axel's got a lot of wolves fighting for him, he has a limited amount. If he had just let females fight, he wouldn't be having this problem...

The second thing I notice is that a sandy-coloured wolf is barreling his way through wolf after wolf and heading straight for a dark brown one. I instantly recognise the wolf as Comrade.

The third thing I notice is more of a surprise than anything. I don't know how I noticed her, but I did. Hovering up high in the sky is Celina, squinting down at the fight with a frown. She suddenly raises her hand and roots begin to grow out of the ground. Wolves from Damon's pack start to be pulled down to the earth and wolves from Axel's pack take advantage of it.

I glance over the mass of wolves, searching for one wolf in particular. I finally spot his black coat. Axel's large wolf is looking up towards the sky and growling, his silver eyes narrowing. I roll my eyes. He honestly didn't think she'd stay away, did he?

I take the distraction of the roots and choose that time to shift into my blonde wolf. I shake my head a little and then slowly stalk out into the clearing. I don't get very far before I'm tackled by another blonde wolf. I growl and buck the wolf off me, sending it spiraling into a tree. The wolf whimpers, shrinking away into the fight again. I huff. What a wimp.

A feral growl rips through the air, capturing my attention. My eyes widen to the size of saucers when I see Comrade lunging for Damon's neck. I howl and sprint to where he is. I don't pay any attention to anything else around me as I continue to run towards Comrade.

My eyes stay locked on the two wolves as Comrade's teeth barely graze Damon's neck. Damon obviously saw it coming and moved out of the way at the last minute. After that, everything just went in slow motion.

Damon whirls around and narrows his eyes into slits at Comrade. Comrade growls at the action and goes to lunge again. Damon's jaw opens wide as Comrade lunges for his back, but before Comrade can get a good hold, Damon's teeth latch onto his back and sink in.

Deep.

Everything happens at once.

I let out a heartbroken howl.

Celina screams from above me.

Axel goes barreling through the crowd of wolves.

The most awful, painful, and heart-shattering thing that happens, though, is when Damon rips his jaws from Comrade's back. He tears out a big chunk, leaving Comrade to collapse onto the floor with blood freely flowing out of him.

I pump my legs to go faster as I desperately try to get to Comrade. Thoughts rush through my head at what my life will be like without him. I planned to have a kid and get married and be happy. I can't do anything like that without Comrade. I'll be so heartbroken that I'll kill myself.

I unknowingly shift as I collapse beside Comrade's wolf and throw my body over him. I release a strangled cry as his dark, almost black eyes, look into my watering blue eyes.

"Comrade... Please don't go. I have so much planned. We were going to mate and have a kid and get married and be wonderful. You can't go," I whisper as I ball my hands up in his fur.

"You have to be alive to be here for Celina's wedding. You have to be alive so that I can punch you repeatedly for being so stupid. Comrade, you have to stay alive," I whisper even quieter as tears continuously fall down my cheeks.

"Comrade? Oh my Goddess, Comrade!" a strangled cry calls from above. I look up slightly from Comrade's blood soaked fur to see Celina swooping down in a rush.

I bury my head back in his fur, not caring that a war is going on behind me or that Damon is probably standing over us with a smirk on his wolf's face or that I'm most likely gonna kill myself after this. The only thing my mind can concentrate on is the fact that in mere minutes, my mate is going to die.

196

I swoop down from the sky with only one thought in mind. Comrade.

I fall to my knees beside him, not caring that I'm getting his blood all over my legs. I reach a shaky hand out to his head, softly rubbing up and down his snout. He whines and tries lifting his head, only to have it crash back down onto the grass. I suck my lips into my mouth to keep myself from crying. This is my guardian, the one who started it all. If Comrade didn't convince me not to run, then I wouldn't be here today. Most likely, I would be dead. Comrade is my guardian, best friend, and protector. I'll be damned if he dies today.

"Please, Comrade, please. Just a little longer... Think about everything we're gonna do with our lives. Please, Comrade..." I hear Alex whisper as she continues to cry. I swallow hard at the sight of the two. This must've been how Axel felt when I died... The only difference is, once Comrade dies, he's gone forever. I, along with so many others, won't be able to deal with that.

A bark from beside me makes my head whip around so fast that I may have gotten whiplash.

Damon. Looking down at Comrade with disgust in his eyes.

I don't know what emotion overtakes me at that moment. Maybe anger, I don't know. What I do know is that I completely lose control over my actions, all common sense being thrown out the window.

I growl the loudest and most ferocious growl I've ever growled, making Damon's attention snap to me. His eyes widen before they narrow and he growls back.

Wind starts to whip around me, blowing my hair in all different directions. Damon growls again and takes a step closer to me.

"I would be walking away if I were you, Damon!" I say menacingly as the wind picks up. Damon's wolf stumbles to the side slightly as the wind starts to take its toll on him.

"All you've done is hurt people in your life. You hurt me, Comrade, Kate, your mate, and you've hurt your pack members by putting them through war after war. When will you see that it's enough?" I desperately ask as the ground starts to shake.

"Celina? Celina, calm down," a soothing voice says from behind me. I slightly turn my head to see Callum looking at me cautiously. He glances between Comrade's bleeding body, a pain-filled expression crossing his face and I, before settling on me.

"Callum, get Comrade out of here. I can deal with Damon," I mutter as thick roots start to appear around Damon's feet. He releases a surprised yelp as he tries to maneuver his way out. Of course, he doesn't succeed.

"Celina!" I hear once again from none other than Axel. I do something I've never really done before that. I growl at him.

"Axel, just get Alex and Comrade out of here. Now!" I scream at him, feeling my eyes shine with a new intensity.

"Celina..." My name's said for the third time by Callum. I look at him and motion to Axel with my eyes, silently sending a message with my eyes to help him.

I turn back to Damon to see him slightly cowering in fear. I narrow my eyes at him and pinch my lips together. The winds that are swirling around us pick up, even more, the ground moving with such an intensity that it knocks Damon off his feet.

"Celina?" a small voice whispers. I look behind me to the source of the voice to see Alex staring at me with tear-stained cheeks and quivering lips.

"Make him pay."

I nod my head at her as Axel picks up Comrade's human form and takes off running. Callum cradles Alex to his body, holding her bridal style, before taking off in the same direction as Axel.

I take a brief moment to glance around. The remains of Damon's pack are dead, leaving a bloody mess of human bodies.

"Have a look around, Damon. You're finished," I say while turning. My eyes widen as I see Damon's fist heading straight for my face. I quickly dodge and stand behind him.

I take a deep breath as I feel power course through me, slowly building up.

"You can't beat me, Celina. You're worthless, pathetic. Axel's only put up with you because you're his mate. Nobody wants you, you are nothing!" Damon spits.

Anger bubbles up inside me as I feel another wave of power engulf me. This time, it's stronger. Just like all those years ago in the medic station, a shining gold dress starts to appear on my body, my hair starts to whip around me, and my eyes start to become all golden. I don't know why this happens, but I'm almost positive it has something to do with me being the next Moon Goddess.

Damon's eyes widen as he starts to see what's happening. He stumbles back, going to make a run for it. I raise my hand and in a flash, roots shoot out of the ground and take him up into the air, holding him there.

He lets out a scream, thrashing around as he tries to escape my hold.

"Why are you doing this?! I helped you, Celina! I made you the person you are today!" he screams at me. I tighten the roots.

"You did nothing for me." My voice comes out light and melodic, a major contrast to what I'm truly feeling.

"I hope you enjoy hell!" I say strongly then tighten the roots so much so that Damon's bones crack and crush under the pressure. I watch on with a calm composure as the life slowly leaves the eyes of the man who has tortured me for nearly my whole life.

22

ALEX

Stupid Aileen...

Stupid Damon...

Stupid Comrade...

Stupid everything!

Everything is so freaking stupid!

First, Comrade has to go and attack Damon, then Damon has to go and attack Comrade and then Aileen won't let me into the medic room, and everything is just stupid!

"Far out..." I sigh angrily as I pace back and forth outside the medic room while running a hand through my hair. Aileen even locked -- yes locked -- the door just to make sure I wouldn't come barging in there. Seriously! Stupid!

"Alex, you need to calm down!" Axel's voice rings through my ears. I stop my pacing long enough to shoot him a glare.

I point my finger at him as I say, "No! You need to calm down."

I go back to my pacing.

Ok, come on, Alex! Think of anything other than the fact that Comrade is lying on a hospital bed bleeding to death.

Chocolate.

Bunnies.

Super glue.

Christmas.

Easter.

Blue.

Red.

Ahh! This isn't working!

I stop my pacing and lean against the wall, my hands gripping my hair so tight that I think I'm damaging my scalp. I slide down the wall and curl myself into a ball, releasing a small whimper. I rock back and forth trying to calm down. This is all wrong -- so, so wrong.

Next thing I know, somebody's pulling me into a hug. I don't take notice of who it is as I wrap my arms around their waist and let the flood gates open. I just cry and cry and cry into this person's chest, letting all my emotions out at once.

Comrade's dying in the room right behind me, and I can't do a thing about it. I'm stuck outside in the arms of somebody who I wish was Comrade. He's everything to me, he's my rock. I love him.

He's made me laugh and smile and just have fun. I've made him laugh and smile and have fun. Where's that all gonna go if he goes? What I am going to do? I won't be able to live without him. I won't be able to be happy.

"I-I d-don't wa-want him to-to die!" I wail, gripping the person's shirt tight. They try to shush me and rub my back in a soothing way.

"It's ok. It's all gonna be ok!" the voice whispers. But it's not gonna be ok. Everything's falling apart and crashing down on me like a ton of bricks.

My stomach starts to twist and turn as thought after thought races through my head about what not being able to see Comrade's smile when I wake up is going to do to me. Or the way his hair sits on top of his head throughout the day. Or the way his eyes twinkle when they land on me. Or the way he walks, speaks and laughs. What's gonna kill me the most, though, is not gonna be able to hear him say I love you ever again. I will never be able to hear those three beautiful words glide out of his mouth like the wings of a bird gliding through the air ever again.

He'll be gone, and I'll be alone.

"Alex?" a tired voice says from behind me. I take the moment to remove my face from the person's chest and look at the person the voice belongs to. Aileen.

She's covered in blood from head to toe. Her mask thing is down around her neck, and she's holding deep red gloves in her hand. Except, I don't think they were that colour to begin with.

I rip myself out of the person's hold and rush over to her, nearly tripping over my own feet.

"Please Aileen, tell me he's okay," I whisper, my voice croaky and hoarse. I swear, if she says anything but that he's okay, I'll go and dive straight off a cliff.

"Alex, I have to be truthful," Aileen starts, putting a hand on my shoulder. More tears well up in my eyes as they start to fall down my already soaked cheeks.

"Is he okay?" I repeat, my lips trembling with every word. I sound weak and vulnerable, exactly what I'm feeling.

Aileen sighs before saying, "He's alive, barely. We've managed to comatose him. We don't know if he's gonna wake up, but we'll do everything in our power to try."

I feel ecstatic and devastated at the same time, not really sure what emotion is stronger. I'm ecstatic that he's okay but absolutely devastated that he may never wake up.

"Can I see him?" I whisper again. Aileen gives me a sad smile and nods, opening the door wider for me to step through.

I take a deep breath and get ready to step into the room before a deep voice stops me, "Alex, just remember that you're strong."

I look behind me to see Axel staring at me with a big wet spot on his shirt. It clicks in my head that he must've been the one I was crying on. I would feel embarrassed if I wasn't feeling miserable.

I nod at Axel as I see Celina burst through the door. I only catch a glimpse of a retreating gold dress before Aileen closes the door of the medic station behind me.

"Follow me, Alex," she tells me, motioning with her hand. I obediently follow, taking notice of the amount of blood on the floor. I have to bite my tongue to keep a sob from escaping.

Aileen stops at a door that I've become all too familiar with. This was the door that I came to every day for at least three weeks. This was Comrade's room, and it is again.

"I thought it would help if you were in somewhere familiar," Aileen murmurs. She delicately places her hand on the door handle and pushes down, the door opening with a small click.

"Stay as long as you like," she says again, leaving me as soon as the last word leaves her mouth.

I stare at the open door. What do I do? Do I go in? Will I be able to handle it? What if I walk in and see something different from what I expected? Ugh! What do I do? I don't know what to do!

I close my eyes, purse my lips and push the door fully open. I don't open my eyes for a long time, not really having the courage.

"Come on, Alex, just open your eyes," I encourage myself. I finally work up the strength to open my eyes, but I instantly regret it.

There, lying limply on the bed is Comrade. The covers of the bed are pulled up to his waist, allowing the bandage covering his whole upper body to be on full view. His face looks peaceful, apart from the busted lip. His arms lie still by his side, not even twitching. All in all, he looks a lot better than what I thought he would look like. I was expecting him to look like he just got out of a brawl. Still, the sight of him is horrible.

A sob pushes its way through my lips as I notice the tiniest amount of blood seeping through the bandage. Since he's lying on his back, I can't see the whole wound, yet the blood still seems to make an appearance.

I hurriedly shut the door behind me and bolt to his bed. I don't think twice about gripping his hand in my own two, feeling the amazing sparks shoot throughout my body.

"Comrade... My poor Comrade," I mumble to myself as I brush away some of his dark hair. I can't hold it in any longer as I burst into hysterics.

"P-please wake up! I-I don't kn-now what I'm g-gonna d-do with-without you!" I cry as I bury my head in his bandage covered chest. I cry and cry and cry some more, not caring what I would look like right now.

I came straight here after I was carried away by someone, I don't know who. I was too focused on the fact that Comrade was losing blood. A lot of it. I didn't care that I still had his blood on me when I showed up, all I cared about was him. I must look like a mess with his blood, my matted hair, and my most likely blotchy face, but that's ok. The only thing I'm worried about right now is Comrade and if he's ever gonna wake up. For the love of the Moon Goddess, I hope he does...

Two months later...

"...and then Ally and Taylor just jumped on me! I couldn't believe it! They got me good," I say as I sit by Comrade's bed.

Light from the open blinds of the window shines into the room, making Comrade's body glow. His dark hair is a lot longer now. It hangs over his ears and over his eyes, so much so that I have to move it out of the way every few minutes.

Comrade himself hasn't changed much. He's still in a coma, but his wound is fully healed. He had to get an operation done on his back since Damon damaged it pretty bad. I couldn't understand why Comrade hadn't woken up after his wound healed, but Aileen tried to explain it to me. She said that just because his wounds healed, doesn't mean that his body has. He was injured in wolf form, so it's taking its toll on him. Honestly, I was pissed about the news.

Another thing I discovered was that not only did I nearly lose Comrade, but I lost my dad. Apparently he threw himself into the fight without a second thought and was killed soon after. His funeral was the day after the semi-war. I'm not surprised, but a little disappointed. I understand why he did it, though, he was dying without mum. However, he still left me all by myself with a half dead mate and a broken heart. His death only piled onto the weight that's pushing down on my chest.

"So, that's all that's happened so far. Nothing exciting," I mutter, staring at Comrade's closed eyelids. The amount of times his dark eyes have haunted my dreams is unbearable. I don't want them to haunt me. I want them to look at me with that sparkle they use to have.

I brush the hair away that's fallen over his eyes for the tenth time today. I always come and visit Comrade after breakfast. I don't leave for lunch. I eat in here when Aileen brings it to me. As for dinner, I don't eat it unless my stomach is like a bear growling. So, pretty much I'm here first thing in the morning and then stay here until I'm so tired I feel like I'm gonna collapse.

It's just gone past breakfast. I was actually late today because I've been feeling sick lately. I've been getting headaches and stomach aches, I've even gained some weight! I think I may have a stomach bug or something...

"So, I was thinking... When you wake up, maybe we can go away for a while. You know, like a holiday? We could go anywhere you like. I mean, it's just a thought, but it could be fun," I mumble, playing with Comrade's fingers and picking out the dirt underneath his nails. I don't get a response, but I didn't expect one.

I sigh and rest my head on his chest, tracing small lines onto his stomach.

"I miss you," I whisper, tears pricking behind my eyes. Comrade's all I have left. I can't lose him, too.

A soft knock at the door captures my attention, but I don't bother to look up. It's probably Celina or Aileen.

"Alex?" True to my word, Celina's soft voice drifts around the room. I sigh through my nose and stop my hand to lay it flat against Comrade's chest. His chest lifts slowly up and down as he takes slow and even breaths, his heart beating steadily.

"How's he doing?" Celina asks, taking a seat on the other side of the bed. I shrug, mumbling a small 'ok.' Celina nods as she looks back at Comrade. A small frown overtakes her face as she notices his hair.

"He needs a haircut," she mutters. I chuckle and nod my head, running my fingers through his long messy hair.

"Yeah, he does," I agree. It goes silent after that, neither of us really knowing what to say. I don't really mind. I'm happy just to be absorbed in thoughts.

I suddenly get a pain in my stomach, making me gasp loudly and double over. I groan as I fall to the floor and grip my stomach tightly, feeling the bile rise in my throat. Not again...

"Alex! Are you ok?" Celina's worried voice asks quickly. I nod as I try to breathe pain, gripping my stomach tighter. The pain passes after a few minutes, making me release a breath I didn't know I was holding. I put a hand to my head as a headache hits me hard. I groan again as a pair of arms lift me up.

"Ugh, my head!" I grunt. Celina places me back in my chair as the headache continues to pound against my head. I take deep breaths to try and calm my racing heart down.

"Alex, are you sure you're alright?" Celina asks again. I just wave her off with my free hand, giving her a grunt.

"This has been happening to me for the past month. I'm fine," I mutter, trying to keep my voice down. I really don't feel like hearing anything loud at the moment.

Celina frowns at me and crouches down so that she's at my height. I furrow my eyebrows and ask her what she's doing, but she holds up her finger.

"Alex, answer me truthfully. Have you been feeling pains in your stomach, headaches, tiredness, and cravings of random stuff?" she asks, her eyes as serious as I've never seen them before. I blink a few times before slowly nodding my head.

"Let me guess, you've also gained weight?" she asks again, her eyes never leaving mine. A frown overtakes my face as I nod again. How does she know all this?

"Yeah, but I've just got a stomach bug. That's all. It's nothing major," I mutter to her. I feel my head loosen up a little bit as my headache slowly starts to disappear.

Once it's fully gone, I look at Celina again. Something's sparkling in her eyes as she shoots her gold eyes between me and my stomach. I think I need to start worrying about her...

"You need to come with me, Alex. Right now," Celina says with what sounds like... excitement? A look of utter confusion takes over my face as she yanks me out of my chair. I release a small yelp at the sudden force.

"What about Comrade?" I ask frantically, glancing back at my comatose mate. I don't want to leave him...

Celina doesn't answer me as she continues to drag me behind her. All I'm thinking while she's doing this is, what the hell is going on?

Celina stops once she sees Aileen. Aileen stops whatever she was doing and looks at Celina with the same confused expression as me. Celina just beams at her. She points to me before saying, "We need an ultrasound."

23

ALEX

Say what now?

Ultrasound? I think I would know if I'm pregnant.

"An ultrasound, Luna?" Aileen questions incredulously. Celina nods her head furiously as she practically throws me on the bed where everything is barely set up.

"Celina, I don't think-" I begin, but I'm cut off by Celina holding up a hand. I raise my eyebrows and fall back on the bed with a huff. Fine, if she wants to see an imaginable pup, so be it.

Aileen quickly gets everything set up, scurrying around me in haste. I look at Celina with an annoyed expression while she just beams at me.

"Aileen, if you don't want to-" I start to say, but I'm cut off again! This time, Celina's hand actually covers my mouth as the grin remains stuck to her face.

"Mmhpphm!" I try to exclaim, but it doesn't really work.

"Be quiet and don't argue," Celina tries to say sternly, but the grin that's stuck on her face makes her lose the effect. I huff stubbornly and reluctantly nod my head. Celina cautiously removes her hand from my face as Aileen makes her way over to me.

"Lift up your shirt and we can get started," she tells me as she flicks on the machine. I sigh and pull my shirt up to my bra line. This is ridiculous! I'm sure I would know if I'm pregnant.

Aileen squeezes the cold gel onto my stomach, making me wince slightly from the coldness. She doesn't hesitate to place the wand on my stomach and start moving it around. After a while, nothing shows up on the screen. I glance at Celina to see her frowning, the grin that was on her face long gone. I must admit, I do feel a tad disappointed. I've always wanted a nice, little family, but I'd rather have it at a different time when Comrade is actually awake.

"See, Celina, there's nothing there! I'm not pregnant," I tell her as I motion my hand to the screen.

"Just wait, something might come up," she mumbles. She leans forward in her seat as Aileen continues to move the wand around my stomach. I groan and throw my head back on the pillow behind me. This is a waste of my time...

Just as I'm about to get up and declare that everything was just a big misunderstanding, Aileen stops moving the wand. My breath hitches in my throat as I avert my eyes to the screen. I don't see anything, just something really, really small...

"Alex, do you know what this is?" Aileen asks, pointing to the really small thing. I shake my head, internally thinking that it's my stomach or something. For the love of everything, I really hope it is my stomach.

"Alex, that's your pup," Aileen whispers. She enlarges the screen so that I can get a closer look at it. My mouth opens slightly as I sit straight up, not caring if the gel gets all over my shirt. I reach my hand forward and touch the screen towards what Aileen claims is my pup. I bring my hand down and touch my stomach covered by my shirt.

I'm gonna be a mum. Oh, dang...

"B-but, I can't be a mum! I-I can't do that!" I exclaim, pointing at the screen. My breathing starts to quicken as I feel my chest tighten. A million thoughts race through my head as I think of Comrade and what his reaction would be right now. Would he be happy? Thrilled even? Or would he be disappointed and sad? After all, he's the dad. Then my thoughts travel to my own mum. She was only 20 when she had me, but still, she has three years on me. I can't have a pup while I'm 17! How the hell am I supposed to do that?

"No, I refuse to believe it," I say, shaking my head vigorously. No way in hell am I pregnant. Comrade and I did it ages ago! It was at least two months ago! I can't deal with this! Not by myself...

"Alex, you're having a baby. You have the proof, you have to believe it," Celina whispers, wrapping her arms around my shoulders. I shake my head as I grip her arms around me. This can't be happening... Not now...

"I'm not ready for a pup, Celina. I won't know what to do with it," I whisper, shutting my eyes tightly.

Celina's soft chuckle fills the air before she starts talking, "First of all, a baby is not an 'it'. Second of all, you won't be by yourself. You'll have Comrade to help you through most of your pregnancy. Third of all, of course, you're ready. I

213

wouldn't have been able to take care of the triplets if it wasn't for you. You're gonna make an amazing mother and have an amazing time with your little angel."

I draw in a shaky breath and nod my head, deciding to just come to an agreement with her words. I can't put this off. I just need to treat this like a wound. I need to discover it, tend to it -- which I've officially started -- and then just wait for it to heal. Another seven months and all will be well. Hopefully...

Jeez! Why do werewolves always have pups so early?

I'm currently sitting in Comrade's room. After a trip to get some calming food, aka ice cream, I came straight here. I'm trying to figure out how I'm gonna break the news to him. I know it sounds ridiculous, but I have this feeling that he can hear what I'm saying to him, but does not do anything about it. Weird, right?

So, here I am, pacing up and down the room and running my hands through my hair. How do you tell your comatose mate that you're pregnant with his pup? You just can't do it!

I sigh as I fall back onto the chair I've started to call mine. I sit in it enough...

I look at Comrade's face, imagining the toothy smile that I love seeing and the sparkle in his eyes when he's up to no good. It seems like whenever something big happens in my life, Comrade always does something to himself. Like, seriously. When my mum died, he got captured. Yes, he didn't know me, but still. Then when I found out he was my mate, he was stabbed in the back. Then he has to go and almost die of blood loss and here I am pregnant! Luck is just not on Comrade's side.

"Ok, so... Uh... How do I say this? Well, you see Comrade, I..." I try to say it, but it all just comes out as unfinished sentences. I groan and facepalm myself. I can't even imagine what this would be like if Comrade were actually awake... Actually, I can. I would be a stressed out mess, probably hide it from him as long as I can, have him find out, burst out crying because of the stupid hormones, have him calm me and say everything's ok, then live happily ever after with a healthy pup. So why does it seem so hard when he isn't awake?

"Comrade, I'm just gonna come out and say it. I'm pregnant," I rush out. I look at Comrade's closed eyes expecting, wishing, that he would do something. Anything. He doesn't though, not even a twitch of his finger or a change in the beeping of the heart monitor. I fall back into my chair with a sigh.

I place my hand on my stomach, closing my eyes. I'm carrying a being inside of me, and my mate doesn't even know it. How in the world is someone supposed to deal with this?

"What am I going to do?" I groan aloud to myself.

A soft knock on the door brings me out of my self-pity. I look up just to see a small head shyly peeks past the door frame.

"Um, hi!" the girl mutters, fully stepping into the room. I instantly recognise her as Kate. I bite my lip as I remember when I accused Comrade of loving her. Geez, that was so long ago...

"It's Kate, right?" I ask, standing up from my chair. Kate nods timidly, her blonde her bouncing with her head. It's funny really. She looks exactly like I did when I was her age, except the hazel eyes, of course.

215

"Hey, I'm sorry about the other day when I accused you of loving Comrade. I was in a bad mood and hearing him say that, just sort of set me off," I explain, scratching the back of my neck in embarrassment.

To my surprise, a fairy-like giggle travels throughout the room. I look at Kate to see her with her hand over her mouth.

"That's okay. My dad used to act like that with my mum whenever he heard somebody saying they liked her," she tells me. A smile graces her face, but her eyes show sadness.

"Yeah, my dad used to act like that, too." I chuckle. I run a hand through my hair as I remember one of the times when Dad heard the TV say 'I love you.' He came barging into the room only to discover that Mum and I were watching Disney. It was really funny actually. He got a pink tinge on his cheeks and scratched the back of his neck in embarrassment. Mum couldn't stop laughing and neither could I. Those were fun and less complicated times.

"Well, uh... Do you want to speak to Comrade? I'm sure he's been dying to hear from you," I say, sending her a cheeky smile. Kate beams at me and furiously nods her head, blonde hair bouncing everywhere.

"I'll leave you to it then," I tell her. I sidestep her as I make my way out of the door and close it behind me. Kate seems like a nice kid, she's got that nice personality in her. Plus, she was there with Comrade when he had nobody else. I thank her for that.

I slowly walk through the halls of the medic station with my head down. I wonder when Comrade will actually wake up... I mean, he's been out of it for two months. Two whole months. The only thing keeping me from not joining him is the fact that he might actually wake up. I mean, if he had

216

died in that surgery two months ago... I don't think my heart would've been able to take it. That's the downside about having a mate, you can't live without them. They can be a blessing and a curse.

Aileen told me a while back that if he doesn't wake up in six months, she's gotta cut the life support. When she first told me, I practically lunged at her in anger. I eventually calmed down with the help of Axel and Celina, but the news is still infuriating. I went on a total rampage in Comrade's room. I vented everything out of me, including my dad's death. He was the only one I could talk to, but he was the only one who wouldn't say anything back.

Celina's come to visit him a few times. She looks like a mess, probably like me. After all, she's been juggling the triplets, her Luna duties, and coming to see Comrade. Who knows, she probably has to keep Axel from going on a few rampages at one point. I don't know. Celina's an amazing Luna, though, and I know why Comrade became instant friends with her. I'm still a bit confused on the whole guardian thing, but I don't think I'll ever have to get used to that.

I haven't seen Ally or Taylor in what feels like forever. The other day was the first time I had actually seen them in what must have been a month!

"Oi! Where do you think you're going?" I hear an all too familiar voice call from behind me. My hands are frozen on the door handle of Comrade's and my room. Comrade...

"Hello! Earth to Alex!" the voice calls again before a hand starts waving in front of my face. I blink and take a step back, spinning around to find the culprit. I'm met with chocolate brown eyes. Taylor.

"I haven't seen you in ages!" I exclaim, practically jumping on her as I wrap my arms around her. Taylor laughs and wraps her arms around me as I bury my face in her shoulder.

"Jeez, I missed you," I mumble, pulling my head back with a smile. With everything that's been going on, I completely forgot about Taylor and Ally. Speaking of Ally...

I'm suddenly tackled to the ground from the side. I squeal as the vision of an afro enters my sight. Think of the afro queen and she shall appear.

"Holy hell, Ally! You couldn't have said hello normally?" I wheeze. I try to push her off me as she chuckles. She obliges with my wishes, sitting Indian style across from me with a big grin across her face.

"So?" she questions eagerly. I raise an eyebrow at her as Taylor takes a seat next to her. We must look really weird sitting in the middle of the hallway, but I could care less right now. This is the most human contact I've had in a long time. I'm glad it's with my two girls.

"So what?" I question back, my eyes darting between Taylor's chocolate brown eyes and Ally's nearly black ones.

"So, was it good?" Ally questions again, both her eyebrows rising at the question. My confusion must have shown on my face because they both rolled their eyes at me.

"I swear this girl is oblivious," I hear Taylor mumbles under her breath. I smirk at her, totally knowing that she's right. I'm oblivious to a lot of things, and this seems like one of them.

"What was it like to mate!" Ally yells, her eyes going wide. My eyes also widen as I slap my hand over her mouth. Taylor laughs at my shocked face, rolling onto her back as she *laughs. I glance around the hallway to make sure nobody heard Ally say what I think she just said.*

"I do not believe you just asked that," I grumble. I slam my free hand onto my forehead as I feel a headache coming. I swear these two are special in the head.

"Wef, ohelwhuffhuppund!" Ally tries to say through my hand, but it comes out muffled. I groan and stand from the floor, Taylor and Ally's eyes following me with caution. I open my bedroom door and motion them in with my hand. They squeal like the school girls they are at heart, making me laugh.

This is gonna be an interesting conversation...

That conversation consisted of many, many things that made me blush and hide my face in my pillow. They wanted to know everything! When I say everything, I literally mean everything. I should really talk to them again sometime, I miss them. They didn't ask me anything about Comrade or how I'm feeling or anything of that. They just made me laugh and forget about everything else. I love those girls like sisters, and I hope I never lose them.

Through all my thinking, I didn't notice that I was in the kitchen until somebody cleared their throat. My eyes snap up to the person who is lazily leaning against the fridge with a half smirk on his face. Callum.

"Alex, haven't seen you in a while," he says, sounding genuinely interested in me. I shrug and walk past him to the pantry.

"I could say the same for you, Beta," I mumble back. I honestly can't remember the last time I saw Callum. Was it before the war? No... Maybe afterwards? Ugh, I don't know. Maybe he was there when Comrade was having surgery, and I didn't even notice.

Callum's chuckle rings through the kitchen before he tells me, "Alex, you don't have to call me 'beta.' You can call me Callum, like you call Celina, Celina."

I half grin, mainly for two reasons. The first reason being that I don't have to address my beta formally and the second reason is that I found a bag of honey and soy chicken chips.

"Well then, try getting the alpha to agree to me calling him Axel," I say with some humor as I grab the chip bag and rip it open, popping a chip into my mouth. Callum grins and shakes his head.

"I don't think that'll be possible," he tells me with a grin matching my own. We both let out a laugh, the happiness only lasting a few seconds.

"Callum?" I question, a sudden thought coming to my head. Callum raises his eyebrows and motions for me to continue. "Have you found your mate yet?"

I regret it as soon as the question leaves my mouth. The sadness that coats Callum's eyes is obvious. Callum clears his throat before saying, "Uh, no. I haven't found my mate yet."

"Oh!" is all I say, suddenly feeling very awkward. It stays silent for a long while, and I really have no clue what to do. Callum seems to be standing there with a far off look in his eye, most likely thinking about his wannabe mate.

"Callum, I'm sorry. That was way out of line," I mumble my apology, looking down with guilt consuming me. To my surprise, Callum chuckles. I peer at him curiously to see a smile on his face.

"It's no problem, Alex. It's a reasonable question. After all, I'm a beta at twenty-three who should have met his mate ages ago. I'm sure she'll pop up soon enough, though," he tells me with the same smile. I smile back at him. I step closer and hold up my fist. Callum laughs at me for a moment before bumping his fist to my own. He then tries to steal the packet of chips from me, but I quickly move away to the other side of the counter. I stick my tongue out at him as he rolls his eyes with a grin.

"I'm a ninja master, Callum. You'll never get my chips," I tell him in a fake sensei type voice as I pop a chip in my mouth.

He raises his eyebrow again – he seems to do that a lot – and mutters a 'whatever.'

With the tense atmosphere gone, I decide to go for a general topic. "So, I'm pregnant."

My eyes widen, and I slap the hand that's not holding my chips over my mouth. Great, Alex, well done! That was such a general topic! Why not go to the top of a freaking mountain and scream it to the world? Hey, world! I'm pregnant!

"W-what?" Callum asks astonished.

"I, uh... I said that I'm... an eggplant!" I exclaim. Callum's astonished look becomes one of confusion. He opens his mouth to say something, but I quickly beat him to it, "Anyway! Got to go! Bye!"

I rush out the kitchen faster than you can say bubblegum and head straight back to the medic station. I don't believe I just said all that! Eggplant? Really? That's the best thing I could come up with? I couldn't have said legend or something cool? For goodness sakes, Alex! Get your crap together! I'm blaming the pregnancy hormones.

24

ALEX

"Lilly! What do you think you're doing?" I scream as I see my five-year-old climbing a tree. I rush over to her as her glorious giggle fills the air.

"I wanna touch the clouds, mummy!" she screams back down at me. Her wild blonde hair sways around her as her dark eyes look down at me innocently.

"Lilly! Get down here right now!" I yell again. I'm beyond furious and beyond reason as I see my darling daughter wobble a little before balancing again.

"Lilly!" I scream again.

"Alex! What the hell are you yelling so loudly for? We'll get another complaint from the neighbors!" an all too familiar voice yells from the house. I spin around to see Comrade standing there with a pissed off look on his face. I glower at him.

"Well, Comrade dearest, why don't you look up in the tree and see why I'm yelling so loudly?" I say sweetly, a sickly sweet smile gracing my lips.

Comrade looks confused for a moment before he peers towards the tree, his face instantly going pale.

"Lilly! You get down the tree this instant, or you're going to have a very sore backside!" Comrade yells, his fury showing on his face.

"But daddy!" Lilly drawls out, a pout resting on her lips. "I wanna touch the clouds!"

"I don't give a rat's as- whisker if you wanna touch the clouds! You get yourself down here this instant!" he screams, his voice going much louder than mine. Lilly whimpers and pouts before slowly making her way towards the tree trunk.

"I just wanted to touch the clouds," I hear her grumble at which I roll my eyes. Five-year-olds these days.

The thought instantly leaves my mind though as I see Lilly's foot misses the branch underneath her. Her tiny body comes barreling down through the leaves and branches, her scream filling the air with mine.

"Lilly!"

I wake up with a start. Partly from the dream, but also from the pain in my stomach. I grip the side of Comrade's bed as I take a deep breath in and let it slowly out. Holy hell this hurts! The pain subsides after a while, and I let out a sigh.

I look towards the window to see the moon high in the sky and stars coating the darkness like tiny diamonds. I smile at the sight.

I place my hand on my stomach and think back to my dream. Lilly... I like that name. Her innocence really suits it. I

223

wonder if the dream was a sign? I mean, what if it's the future for Comrade and me? He'll be awake! I beam at the thought.

Of course, I don't allow my brain to believe my thoughts are false hope.

After staring at the sky for a while, I slowly fall back to sleep, my hand gripping Comrade's tightly.

"Alex? Alex, wake up," a small voice rings in my ear.

"Mmm, five more minutes," I mumble, turning my head away from the giggling now filling the room.

"Alex, get your lazy ass out of that chair before I make you," another voice says. I turn my head back around to see Taylor and Ally standing there looking at me with massive grins. I groan.

"Come on, guys, let the lady sleep," I mumble, burying my face in the bed sheets.

"How about no? We wanna know about some news..." Taylor trails off. I groan again. The baby. That's right, I'm pregnant.

"I really don't want to talk about it, guys..." I mutter, closing my eyes again. Next thing I know, my chair is being scraped away from Comrade's bed, and the two eager faces of Taylor and Ally fill my vision.

"Well, miss grumpy pants, we want info. So spill!" Ally squeals excitedly. I sigh, knowing I won't be able to dodge their pleas for very long.

"Fine, fine. I don't really know anything honestly. I'm two months along, I don't know if it's a boy or girl and I have no clue if Comrade's gonna wake up to see his baby," I explain,

224

giving them all the info that they need to know. A tense silence fills the room after that.

"You know, Alex, there's no point thinking that way. He will wake up, and when he does, he will be ecstatic to know that you're pregnant with his pup," Taylor tells me as she gives me a sideways hug, Ally joining in.

After that, Taylor, Ally and I just talk about everything and anything that comes to mind. It's actually really nice to just be able to talk to them like this again. I haven't done it for a while.

"Well, we better get going. You look like you're about to pass out! Get some sleep!" Ally scolds me with a grin. I laugh a bit at that and nod my head. I'll probably just fall asleep here anyway.

I say goodbye to Taylor and Ally as they both walk out of Comrade's door. I smile down at Comrade and brush his hair away from his eyes. He'll be happy about all this... Hopefully.

"Alex? Alex, come on, dear! It's time to get up now," a soft voice says lightly in my ear as they start to shake me. I hum for a moment before opening my eyes and looking up at Aileen.

"Come on, Alex! It's time for your check up," she tells me with a smile. I nod my head and yawn, my brain still half asleep.

"Mmm, ok," I mindlessly mumble back as an answer. Aileen chuckles lightly at me as she helps me up. In my tired state, I miss the way she frowns at my stomach and the slight worry that now shines in her eyes.

She directs me to the checkup table as I rub my eyes, releasing yet another yawn. Jeez, I'm so tired.

"Alex, you do realise that you're nearly two and half months along, don't you?" Aileen asks me as she comes and takes a seat beside the bed. I furrow my eyebrows. Has it really been that long?

"Uh... Yeah, I guess. Why?" I question strangely. Aileen doesn't answer but just continues to stare at me. She gestures for me to lie down, so I simply comply as I continue to give her a look.

"Alex, with you, only carrying one pup and with no royal or alpha blood in you, your pregnancy should be the same as any other wolf. Any other wolf would have their baby in three months, no more than maybe two weeks late. You, my dear, look like you're only one month pregnant," Alison explains, her eyes leaving mine as she allows me to digest this information.

I blink. Blink again. Then blink a third time. What is she saying? I know I should be having my pup in the next few weeks... Maybe it'll have a growth spurt? No, I'm pretty sure pups don't do that.

"Aileen, what are you saying?" I question, hoisting myself up on my elbows to stare at her with wide, stormy eyes.

Aileen sighs, dropping her eyes from my line of sight.

"Aileen?" I push, my voice firm.

"Alex..." she starts to say, only to pause and take a breath." You might have lost the pup."

I freeze. Lost the pup? How could I have...

"Oh my god..." I whisper, the news plummeting down on me like a bucket of ice. I cover my mouth with my hand, my eyes widening to the size of the sun.

"Oh my god!" I wail, the tears now falling, my heart now racing, my breathing now rapid and my brain thinking of how devastated Comrade is going to be when he wakes up.

"Alex, Alex, we don't know for sure yet. You never know, you might have been carrying twins without us knowing it." Aileen's distant voice echoes in my head. I latch onto that sound, her melodic voice being my life support. Everything's just falling apart...

"Just lay down and we'll check, ok?" Her voice sounds again, clearer this time. I numbly nod, lying back down on my back. It's little to no use, though, my heart's already broken. I know I've lost the only thing I have left if Comrade doesn't wake up. If Comrade doesn't wake up... If Comrade doesn't wake up...

"Have you been feeling pains at all? Maybe experiencing bleeding?"Aileen asks as she squeezes the gel onto my stomach.

"Pains," I whisper, my mouth feeling dry from the effort to say such an agonising word.

Aileen places the wand on my stomach and moves it around a little before my pup comes into sight. I suck my top lip into my mouth to keep myself from crying. Please be ok, please be ok...

"I'll just check for the heartbeat," Aileen tells me with a small, tight smile. I numbly nod my head and wait to hear the little sound of a heart beat fill the room.

It doesn't come.

"Are you going to check?" I whisper again, thinking Aileen just didn't check yet, and my life isn't about to come crashing down around me.

"Alex... I'm so sorry. Your pup-" Aileen starts to tell me, but I cut her off by raising my hand.

"Don't!" I say with a hard voice. Aileen nods her head and leaves the room, most likely to give me privacy.

The only way I can describe this feeling is like my heart is shattering into a million pieces of tiny icicles. I feel like my insides are being twisted and turned. I feel as though my whole life is falling apart and I don't have my mum, my dad, my mate, no one. I have no one. No one to help me through this pain. No one to help me through anything that's happening in my life.

All at once, I break down. Tears flow freely down my cheeks as uncontrollable sobs wrack through my body. My heart constricts in my chest, and my lungs shrink to the size of a jelly bean. Everything around me just falls apart. I curl up into a tiny ball as I just wallow in my self-pity.

I've lost the only thing that's been keeping me sane through these last few months. My pup was the only life source I had that could truly make me smile and feel content. Now it's gone. That's the worst part, it's gone.

I cry harder as the repeating thought of 'it's gone' plays in my head like a broken record. Then, something even worse than losing my pup fills my mind.

Comrade.

Comrade never had the chance to know about the pup, never had the chance to feel it, see it, believe it. I've taken that chance away from him, and I don't know if I can get it back.

"Why me?" I whisper through my sobs. "Why me?"

Sitting and staring out the window of Comrade's bed as the rain pelts down on the glass, seems to match my mood perfectly. I trace my fingers over the fabric of the bandages that now wrap themselves around my stomach. Aileen removed my pup, removed a once living thing from me and just took it away.

I can't say it hurt because I can't remember. I was asleep for about three hours because of the drugs that Aileen put on me. When I woke up, my stomach was stitched back together, and my pup was nowhere to be seen. Not even blood stained the sheets of the bed or even the smell of blood in the air told me that I had just been through an operation. The only reminders I have are these bandages and most likely the scar I'll now have to constantly remind of what I lost.

A tear rolls down my cheek at the thought once more. I've lost my pup, and now I have a constant reminder.

I duck my head and stand from my seat, intending to go to Comrade for comfort. He's still in a coma, but apparently, Aileen says that he's improving. I don't know how she can say that; maybe she's just giving me false hope.

I stand at the side of Comrade's bed, running my hands through his hair. It got cut a few days before my operation, but it already seems to be growing again. I like it long, though. It suits him better than the shorter hair he always wears.

"I don't know why you won't have your hair long all the time, Comrade. It suits you," I whisper with a small smile as I keep on running my hand slowly through his hair.

"I know this is selfish of me, but if you would only wake up, I could dump all of my problems on you and just grieve. I could soak in my sorrow until I was ready to accept and move on from the fact that I lost our pup. You aren't awake though, and you probably won't wake up. Please, though, Comrade, please, help me be strong. Help me survive through this. Please," I beg in a whisper as a single tear slide down my cheek. I just want him to wake up.

I duck my head and bite my lip, trying desperately to control my emotions. It's just so hard... Everything's so hard now.

What happens next, I don't think I can believe.

As I lay my head on Comrade's chest, seeking the comfort I so desperately need, the steady beat of the heart monitor speeds up, his fingers start to move ever so slightly, and his eyelids start to flutter.

I blink and step away, the chair falling over from the force. This can't be happening! He can't be waking up! It's not possible.

My emotions get the better of me as I do the only thing I can. I scream. I scream and scream until I can't scream no more. Then, as though the Goddess heard my screams, those beautiful dark eyes that I haven't seen for so long, peek back at me.

25

ALEX

My jaw stays slack, and my eyes stay open as those gorgeous dark eyes continue to stare at me. This can't be happening... This just can't be...

"Oh my god..." I whisper, barely audible. Comrade, my previously half dead mate who's supposed to be cut off from life support, is staring back at me with those dark eyes I've been wishing to see since the day he closed them.

"A-Alex?" his rough, scratchy voice whispers, the words sounding like they took a lot more effort than they were supposed to. Tears start slipping from my eyes. In over two months, that's the first time I've heard him say my name. The only person, who I've wished every night to say my name, has finally said it.

I nod my head while taking slow steps closer towards him.

"Yeah, that's me," I say with a weak smile. Before he can say anything else, my arms wrap around his torso and I bury my head in his chest. In return, he wraps his arms around my waist, but they sort of just rest there. I don't expect him to be jumping up and down after being out of it for months, and I also don't expect him to have enough strength to cuddle me. Here he is, though, barely doing it, but doing it nonetheless.

"I've missed you so much," I whisper into his chest. My tears leak onto his shirt as I just lie there with his arms resting on my waist.

"I've missed you too. So much more than you could ever imagine," he whispers, voice still rugged and rasped.

"Alex?! Alex! What's wro-" a frantic sounding Aileen screams, only for her voice to be cut short. I slightly turn my head and offer her a small smile.

"He's awake," I beam, turning my head once again to face Comrade, a smile gracing my face. "He's awake."

Aileen just sort of stands there for a moment, her eyes wide and mouth ajar.

"B-but, you weren't supposed to..." Her voice trails off disbelievingly, but her sentence catches my attention. Wasn't supposed to what?

"What do you mean, Aileen?" I grit through a locked jaw. Aileen averts her eyes to my own before smiling.

"Nothing. It's just a miracle he's woken up!" she exclaims with glee. My eyes narrow into a suspicious glare. Was there something Aileen wasn't telling me?

One second I'm glaring at Aileen, the next, Celina and Axel burst through the door in a frantic state.

"Who screamed?! I heard screaming! Oh Goddess, is everyone alright?" Celina's puffed voice rushes out in one breath. I chuckle and look into Comrade's dark eyes.

"Everything's perfect," I say, my smile growing each second. Celina's gasp echoes throughout the room as Comrade slowly moves his head to face her, a smile showing on his face.

"Hey, Snow," his voice whispers, the scratchiness not yet disappearing. Celina's hand covers her mouth as her eyes go large as the size of saucers.

"Comrade..." Her barely audible voice travels through the room. "Oh, Comrade!"

In less than a second, Celina's beside the bed with both her hands framing Comrade's face. I growl lowly at the contact. Another growl from across the room cuts my growl short, though. I twist my neck to see Axel giving me a look that pretty much says 'growl at my mate again, and it won't be pretty.' I take a deep breath in to calm myself down, reminding myself that Comrade is Celina's guardian, and she has a right to be near him. No one else does, though...

"Are you ok? How many eyes do I have? Do you feel dizzy? Oh my Goddess, Comrade! If you ever do this to me again I'll be the one to kill you, you hear me?!" Celina babbles on and on until, eventually, Axel has to step in.

"Sweetheart, I think you're overwhelming Comrade. Just give him time to breathe and please stop squishing his face," Axel's soft yet stern voice tells her. Celina stops her onslaught with furrowed eyebrows. She looks at Comrade, only to see him with a fish face caused by the force from her hands. It actually looks kinda funny.

"Oh, Comrade! I'm so sorry!" she explains, taking a few steps back into Axel's waiting arms.

Comrade chuckles a little before saying with a smile, "It's ok, Celina. I'd rather have a squished face than not have one at all."

I smile at his pathetic joke and brush some stray hair off his forehead. Comrade's eyes turn to mine. I can't help the smile that splits my face at the sight of those dark pools. Out of everything that I can possibly love about Comrade, his eyes would be my favourite. Those dark abysses that give you a peek straight into his soul are what I love most about this man.

"We'll leave you two alone for a while. It's good to see you awake, Comrade!" Axel says with a final nod before practically dragging Celina out of the room, Aileen following closely behind.

"So, what have I missed?" Comrade asks with yet another chuckle.

"This," I say quietly before softly planting my lips onto his. My eyes involuntarily close as sparks erupt from our lips and travel all the way down to my toes. Goddess this feels good.

I slowly pull back, my eyes still closed. The tingling feeling on my lips stays as I feel Comrade's fingers gingerly trace them.

"What a lovely wake up gift," Comrade says in a cheeky tone, making me open my eyes and give him another small kiss.

"You have no idea, Comrade, no idea," I whisper. His eyebrows knit together for a moment before gripping my waist in his hands gently.

"No idea of what, Alex?" he asks, those amazing dark eyes full of concern. I smile sadly as I think over everything that's happened in the past few months that Comrade has no clue about. Firstly, the fact that my dad died in the battle at the same time that Comrade was severely injured didn't really lighten my mood for a couple weeks. Secondly, Callum, the poor guy, not being able to find his mate has put most of the pack in a gloomy mood because they need an heir for the beta title. Then there's the fact that I was pregnant. There's also the fact that I lost our pup, all because I was too lost in my own self-pity and didn't take the time to even notice that I had another living thing inside of me growing.

"Hey, it's ok. You don't need to cry. I'm safe and awake now. It's ok," Comrade coos, pulling my head into his shoulder as the tears I didn't even know were present start to fall.

"I-it's not o-ok, Comrade! I-I've been a-all a-alone for t-two months-s! Y-you have n-no i-idea what I've be-been th-through!" I wail while sounding like a selfish bitch. You know what? I don't even care. I've been living without a mate for over two months, I've lost our pup, my dad died and who knows what's gonna happen within the next week. You never know, maybe there'll be a freaking earthquake!

"Alex, come on. Please don't cry. I hate seeing you cry," Comrade says with a pained voice in a failed attempt to comfort me. I just cry harder and harder, and wail louder and louder, until the only thing I can do is whimper and silently let the tears fall.

Comrade runs his hand through my hair, the movement slow and soft. I sniffle and breathe out through my mouth; my breath stirred some of Comrade's hair.

"Oh, my little mate, what's happened to you?" Comrade whispers into my ear. Being too exhausted to answer, I close my eyes and fall into a deep sleep.

26

COMRADE

I run my hand through my beautiful mate's hair while she sleeps soundly on my chest. Trust me, after being out of it for so long, sleeping is not on my priority list right now.

I sigh as my eyebrows furrow. Alex's tear stained face from hours ago is still imprinted in my mind, and it's killing me not knowing what has hurt my mate so badly. It couldn't have just been from me being in a coma. She looked so destroyed and just about ready to give up. It's tearing my heart out not knowing what to do.

I sigh again while my hand leaves her hair and travels down her back. It's comforting to know my mate is right by my side again. I have no doubt in my mind that she was by my side at any point in time while I was under coma, but having her here now, with me, is the best feeling in the world.

My feeling of contentment is cut short, however when I notice the slight bump on her lower back. My lips turn downwards into a frown and my eyes narrow slightly. I gently lift the bottom of her shirt upwards to see what's caused my curiosity.

My whole body goes rigid when I see the pristine white bandage wrapped around her torso, looking like it was put on just a few hours ago. How did I not see this before? Did something happen to her while I was unconscious? My heart breaks as I realise that I could've protected her, but instead I chose to go and get myself pretty much mauled.

Alex moves slightly in my arms before her eyes start to flutter. I look down at her with a pained look on my face. I always have to go and hurt people, haven't I?

Alex's stormy eyes half open as she stares up into my dark ones with a smile. Her smile quickly drops when she sees my face. She sits upright; her eyes wide open now, she cups my face in both her hands.

"Comrade? What's wrong? Are you in pain? Do you want me to get Aileen? Where does it hurt? Comrade, answer me!" Alex says hurriedly as she makes a move to stand up. I softly grab her hands that have now left my face and gently pull her back down.

"I'm fine, Alex. Really," I tell her with a small smile. She releases a long breath before running a hand through her hair.

"Don't do that! I thought- Never mind..." Her voice trails off into a whisper as her head bows slightly. I hook my finger under her chin and lift her head up.

"Will you do me a favour?" I ask quietly, only to have Alex nod her head furiously. "Why do you have a bandage wrapped around your torso?"

Just like me when I first discovered the pristine white bandage, Alex's whole body goes rigid. Her eyes widen slightly, and she sucks her lips into her mouth.

"It's, ah... I-it's nothing," she says in a voice that doesn't seem to belong to her.

"It doesn't look like nothing," I push. I lean forward slightly and rest my hands on her neck.

"You can tell me anything, you know that, right?" I ask her pained, both from the pain in my muscles and from the pain of thinking she doesn't think she can tell me.

Alex merely nods her head and looks down, but not quick enough as I see tears brimming in her eyes.

"Alex, please tell me. I'll do anything I can to make it better. Anything," I promise. Moving my hands from her shoulders to her face, I see the struggle behind her eyes. It's clear as day she doesn't want to tell me, but she can tell me anything and everything, so why is this any different?

"Alex?" I ask softly, feeling like I'm walking on eggshells. The last thing I expect her to do is burst out crying, but that's exactly what she does. Her whole face breaks down, and tears start rushing down her face as her shoulders sag in defeat. She grips my shirt so tight that her knuckles start to turn white.

"I'm sorry! I'm so so sorry!" she continues to wail, never letting go of my shirt. I wrap my arms around her waist and whisper sweet nothings in her ear. Whatever happened is obviously not a light subject for her.

"Alex, please tell me. I won't do anything. I just want to know what happened. Please!" I beg, my emotions getting the better of me as she continues to sob. Please Goddess, if you can hear me, do something. Anything!

Alex's hands leave my shirt as she wipes the tears still falling down her cheeks furiously.

"I-I can't... You'll hate me!" she whispers. She bows her head and starts to back away. I grasp her wrist before she can go any further, though.

"Hate you? I would never hate you. No matter what you've done or are going to do, I will never hate you. I promise," I tell her with so much sincerity that she has to believe me.

"You promise?" she asks, broken. I nod my head, tugging on her wrist to bring her closer again.

"I promise," I reply, never once letting go of my little mate who just looks about ready to go jump off a cliff.

It's silent for a moment. I try looking into Alex's eyes, but she's looking anywhere but me. I try to say something to get her to look at me, but her whisper stops me, "I lost it."

I furrow my eyebrows at her statement. Lost what? Did she lose a piece of jewellery? Maybe something of her mum's?

"What did you lose, Alex?" I ask softly, pushing my hand through her hair to comfort her in some way. She mumbles something ever so quietly that not even my werewolf ears can hear.

"Alex, you're gonna have to speak louder," I push, just wanting to know what's wrong. As ridiculous as this may sound at this moment, Alex is reminding me of the first time Axel made Celina cry. It was the first time I took her into my arms and tried to make her smile and just calm down. I remember that day clearly, sitting on the floor of Axel's office. Looking at Alex now, all I can see is the same broken expression as Celina that day. It makes my heart ache...

"Alex," I whisper again when she stays quiet.

For the first time since we started talking, Alex's stormy eyes connect with mine. Her eyes... Her eyes look so...

"Comrade, I lost our pup." Her voice travels through the air and into my ears; her sentence circling round and round my head before it finally seems to snap. She what?

"What?" I question, looking at her with wide eyes. Pup? She wasn't pregnant when we locked them in the safe houses! I mean, was she?

"Please don't make me say it again," she pleads in a whisper, but I need to hear her say it again. I need to make sure I wasn't just imagining.

"Just tell me that isn't true," I plead, my hands framing her face as she goes to look away again. "Please tell me you're just messing with me."

"I lost our pup!" she says slower, big fat tears sliding down her face as she bites her lip. My hands drop from her face and cover my own face instead. It's real... Alex lost our pup... I didn't even...

"Please don't hate me!" Alex sobs, backing away from me in a rush. Her hand rests over her bandaged covered stomach. My eyes zero in on the motion. Once again remembering when I figured out Celina was pregnant. Only that the difference from then and now, is that instead of discovering my mate is pregnant, I've discovered she's lost the pup.

"Please, Comrade! I'm so sorry! I had no idea I would lose the pup! I didn't even know I was pregnant! We had only just mated! I'm so sorry! Just please don't hate me!" Alex continues to wail on and on, falling to the floor and crying hysterically into her hands. My own eyes fill with tears from the fact of losing our pup and because of my heartbroken mate thinking that I hate her.

240

Gathering up all my strength, I push back the thin sheet covering me and move my body to the side. Look at me, I've been awake for less than twenty-four hours, and I'm up and at 'em. I'm probably gonna get a scolding of some sort for this, but I honestly don't care. I just want and need to get to Alex.

I slowly push myself off the bed, taking a deep breath. My knees instantly buckle from underneath me, but I tighten my lips and muster up my strength to push on. I eventually let go of the bed for support and nearly fall to the floor again, all the while Alex is still curled into herself crying and muttering sorry over and over again, that it makes my heart ache even more.

I practically stumble over to where Alex is curled up and very unmanly-like fall to the floor next to her. I hiss from the pain that it caused me, but suck it up. My mate is my first priority here, not my pain.

"Alex..." I say pained, mainly from the impact of falling to the floor, but also because of the state Alex is in. "Come on, look at me."

Upon my request, Alex lifts her head up from her hands and looks at me with so many emotions swirling in her beautiful eyes. Her bottom lip trembles as she opens her mouth to say something. I shake my head, silencing her.

I move a little closer so that we're only a breath away from each other and look into her eyes.

"I would never hate you," I say to her then crash my lips onto hers. She gasps as she wraps her arms around my neck, pulling me ever so closer.

So, that's how we stay, on the floor in each other's arms. This is gonna be something hard for both of us to get past, but we can do it together.

"I love you," I whisper in her ear. "So, so much."

"I love you, too," she whispers back as she falls asleep in my arms.

I sigh for the umpteenth time tonight when my eyes land on Alex's stomach. I gently pull her shirt up to just below her chest to the bandage fully covering her lower torso and stomach. A single tear escapes my eye from the sight. A beautiful pup was once growing inside of my equally stunning mate, and I didn't even get the chance to feel it, see it, experience it. At that moment, I make a promise to myself:

I'm never going to leave Alex alone ever again. No matter what the cost.

27

COMRADE

"Happy birthday, dear Alex! Happy birthday to you!" the very loud and very off pitch singing of entirely the whole population of eighteen to twenty-five-year-olds in the pack screams. My mate wrapped in my arms laughs with glee and merriment as she stares down at the enormous cake in front of her.

"Make a wish," I whisper in her ear, placing a soft kiss on her neck. Alex giggles a little before closing her eyes and blowing out her 18 candles.

Cheers are heard around us as Alex's laugh fills the night air. I also laugh, but more at her than with her. The fact of that just makes me laugh even more.

"What'd you wish for?" Ally and Taylor scream at once, their voices easily traveling over the loud music playing. Only members of the pack over 18 were allowed to attend this party since Alex's sole purpose is to get drunk. She doesn't really like alcohol, but tonight she is letting go and just enjoying it. So, obviously, Ally and Taylor just had to come and see their composed friend hit it off with some vodka.

Alex laughs a little before bringing a finger up to her lips and whispering loudly, "It's a secret."

Her giggles fill the air again as Ally and Taylor grab a hand of hers each and drag her off into the middle of the makeshift dance floor that we all set up in the backyard. By 'we,' I mean myself, Axel, Callum, and a few other pack members. Of course, Celina decorated the whole lot while Ally and Taylor took Alex out to a spa treatment. We set it all up in a few hours, so we're all pretty happy with the outcome.

I shake my head with a smile when I see my already drunk mate stumble onto the dance floor and start waving her hands around in the air. I chuckle at the sight. I walk over to the drinks and grab myself a beer.

"This is one hell of a party we set up, eh?" the all too familiar voice of Callum drifts through my ears. After I got out of recovery, Callum and I got close again like we used to be before everything went downhill. He still hasn't found his mate, but I don't think he's too fussed anymore. He has Celina to watch over now since I got handed the opportunity to look after the pups instead.

Yeah, after I got out of recovery, Celina walked up to me with this massive grin on her face and pretty much said, "Comrade, I trust you with my life so I can entrust my pups' lives to you."

Of course, I said yes! I tell ya what, though if Alex didn't help me when we needed to babysit, I would be in a coma again.

"Yeah! I think Alex is really enjoying herself. Not that she's gonna remember any of this in the morning, but you know." I shrug in answer to Callum's question. Callum laughs and pats me on the back. Even though there's a two to three-year age difference between us, we get on like brothers, including the mock fighting.

"Comrade, I can guarantee that she won't even remember her name or yours in the morning." Callum laughs. "Especially with the way she's doing it on the dance floor."

My eyes instantly snap to see Alex no longer doing that stupid dance I saw her doing before. Oh no, she's swaying her hips in the most seductive way possible while running her hands down the sides of her body. I growl loudly and stomp over to her, hearing Callum's laughter in the background the whole time.

Getting to the dance floor, I grip her hips with my hands and spin her around to face me. I growl lowly and pull her further into me. Alex looks up at me innocently and giggles. My annoyed expression drops instantly as soon as her eyes connect with mine. For the life of me, I could not look away from those stormy depths.

"Comrade! What are you doing here?" Alex shouts over the music as more and more of her giggles fill the air. I laugh at her while shaking my head. So drunk, so, so drunk.

"I'm here to stop my very sexy mate from doing any more of those very alluring moves. You may be mated to me, but there are plenty of guys here checking you out," I growl, annoyed again. Alex just giggles though like she doesn't have a care in the world.

"Comrade!" she groans, her head flopping onto my shoulder. "I'm thirsty!"

Again, just like that, my annoyance evaporates into thin air and is replaced by amusement. I lead her over to the drinks and just let her run free about what she wants. Probably not the wisest decision, but it's her eighteenth, and this is probably gonna be the only time in my life that I see Alex get drunk. I want to savour the moment!

Alex giggles as she picks up two Jell-O shots. She bounces her way over to me and hands me the blue one.

"Come on, Comrade! All I've seen you drink is beer! Bleh! Have something exciting!" she exclaims to me, screaming to make sure I hear it over the music. I laugh and shrug. Why not?

We clink our glasses together and get ready to down the shots before Alex's hand on my wrist stops me.

"Wait! I want the blue one!" she says quickly, snatching the blue Jell-O shot out of my hand and replacing it with the red one she had. I shake my head and down the shot, the jelly-like substance sliding down my throat with ease.

"See! Wasn't that fun?!" she exclaims as giggle after giggle leaves her lips. I chuckle and nod my head. She squeals before taking another two shots, giving me an evil grin. I narrow my eyes at her in suspicion before she darts away in the direction of what I believe is Celina and Axel. One of the younger pack members volunteered to babysit the triplets so they could come. A nice gesture, but also one she'll regret. Those three are little devils! I swear!

"Celina! I've been looking for you everywhere!" I hear Alex in the distance. I chuckle again, shaking my head and moving towards the food.

ALEX

"Celina! I've been looking for you everywhere!" I exclaim as I finally stumble upon Celina and Axel, Jell-O shots still in hand.

246

You have no idea how amazing I feel! I feel like I could fly and go to the moon! I feel like I could go surfing even though I've never tried before! I feel like a million dollars! I look like it, too! A giggle leaves my mouth at that thought.

I love Comrade so, so, so, so much for throwing me this party! It's amazing! It's like we're all on cloud nine! Maybe even ten!

"Alex! You look drunk," Celina says worriedly, taking a step closer. I shove the Jell-O shot in her face as I vigorously nod my head.

"Yep! I'm as drunk as a 70's rock band and loving every minute of it!" I exclaim, throwing my hands in the air and giving a big whoop, followed by a bunch of other people whooping.

Celina laughs at me, before Axel steps in, "You won't be saying that in the morning."

I giggle at him and shove my other Jell-O shot into his hand, giggling again at the widening of his eyes.

"Wait one second!" I tell them, holding up one finger so that they understand.

I stumble back over to the drinks table and grab myself a yellow Jell-O shot before quickly scurrying back over to Celina and Axel.

I giggle before screaming loudly, "Cheers!"

I down my shot as Axel downs his, also downing Celina's. Oh yeah! Celina doesn't drink! I forgot about that! I giggle at my stupidity and happily skip away to where my bestest friends in the whole wide world are.

"Ally! Taylor!" I squeal with excitement. They both squeal, equally as excited before dragging me into a hug. We giggle and jump around for a while, probably looking like drunken idiots. On the other hand, we are drunken idiots!

I giggle over and over again as we continue jumping. I pull away with a gasp as I suddenly realise something. I love Comrade... I love Comrade!

"Comrade!" I scream as I run away from Ally and Taylor in search of my mate. I love him, I love him, I love him!

"Alex? Alex, what's wrong? Are you hurt?" Comrade's frantic voice fills my ears as two strong hands clamp onto my waist and spins me around to face a pair of dark eyes.

I giggle, swaying a little, before screaming again, "I love you!"

Comrade visibly relaxes, and I giggle. Again! What's with all this giggling? It's even starting to annoy me, and I'm drunk! I giggle at that thought.

"I know you love me, Alex!" Comrade murmurs before placing a soft kiss on my lips. I shake my head and point my finger into his chest, ignoring the eruption of sparks down my spine.

"No no no! You're supposed to say 'I love you, too, my amazing and perfect mate that I would never trade for a strawberry'!" I say in a low, manly tone, trying to impersonate Comrade. I remember way, way, way back, like way back, that Comrade and I fought about chocolate and strawberries and which one was better. Of course, chocolate is, but Comrade doesn't think so.

I giggle gleefully as I see Comrade's face turn into a scowl.

"I do not sound like that," he grumbles. I giggle again and nod my head furiously, making myself a little dizzy.

"No, you do! You really, really do!" I say with a giggle again. Comrade rolls his eyes before picking me up and throwing me over his shoulder. I squeal in both excitement and outrage, thumping my fists on his back.

"Comrade! Put me down!" I tell with a laugh. Tears start falling from my eyes from the amount of laughter I'm doing. Good Goddess, I'm so drunk, it's laughable.

"Thanks for coming, everyone! It's getting close to one so hightail it back to your own houses!" Comrade exclaims and in return gets a round of laughter. One o'clock! My birthday was over an hour ago! That's hilarious!

"Three cheers for the birthday girl!" the familiar voices of Ally and Taylor scream above both the music and the laughter.

"Hip hip! Hooray! Hip hip! Hooray! Hip hip! Hooray!" everyone cheers at the same time. I release a whoop that makes everyone laugh as Comrade turns around to take me inside.

I giggle the whole time as he takes me up the stairs to our room. I sigh dreamily – our room. That sounds so nice. I giggle again, and I can just feel Comrade roll his eyes at me.

"You are gonna have the worst hangover tomorrow," I hear Comrade grumble. "So guess who's gonna be looking after ya? Me! You know why? I'm a good mate."

At this point, it sort of just sounds like he's talking to himself. I giggle, how funny's that? Talking to yourself! You know, they say that talking to yourself is the first sign of crazy. True fact!

All of a sudden, I leave Comrade's shoulder and land face first into the bed, our bed. I sigh again. Our bed.

I start squealing and kicking my legs as I feel Comrade start taking my shirt off. It tickles!

"C-Comrade! Stop! That t-tickles!" I squeal out between laughs. Comrade's hair falls over his eyes as he shakes his head with a chuckle. Upon my request, Comrade agreed to keep his hair long, but not surfer-long, more like the long I wanted. I giggle again for the umpteenth time that night. That makes no sense...

"Well, Alex, unless you want to sleep in jeans and a shirt instead of a comfy and very sexy nightgown, I would highly recommend you stop moving." Comrade's husky voice travels through my ears. I instantly stop moving, becoming as still as a board with my lips sucked into my mouth to keep myself from laughing.

Comrade continues to undress me, and I suddenly feel all my energy start to drain.

COMRADE

As I finally get Alex's arms through the nightgown she bought a few days ago with Taylor, I see that her eyes are starting to droop. I half smile at the sight of her hair all messed up and her droopy eyes as well as the pout that's on her lips. I slowly lean in and give her a small peck on her pouting lips, making an airy giggle filter through the air.

I've honestly never heard Alex giggle so much in one night. It's both adorable and annoying, but more adorable.

"Comrade, come lay with me," Alex mumbles as she falls without any grace at all onto the bed. I chuckle and undress down to my boxers.

It's silent for a while as I just hold Alex's back to my chest. Her breathing hasn't evened out yet, so I know she's still awake. I unconsciously draw circles onto her hips until she turns around fully to face me.

I stared into her sleepy eyes, wondering what's hidden behind those stormy blue depths.

"Comrade?" Alex's quiet voice asks as it drifts through the air.

"Yes, Alex?" I ask back, equally quiet.

"You wanna know what I wished for? I wished that we could still be able to have a pup. That's what I wished for," her sad voice trails off as she falls asleep with her head on my chest. My heart constricts as her words start to sink in.

After her miscarriage and my recovery, we went to see Aileen about having another pup. She pretty much told us that Alex's body wasn't fit to hold a pup and that the odds of us having one naturally is 17%. We haven't spoken about it since that day and having Alex bring it up, drunk or not, makes my heart shatter into a thousand pieces.

I don't deserve Alex. I don't deserve her strength or kindness or the way she makes people laugh. I deserve none of that, but I have her anyway, and she has me.

I pull Alex closer towards me as she sleeps soundly. I bury my face in her hair as I fall into a dreamful sleep. After all, the dream of yesterday is the hope of today and the reality of tomorrow.

28

15 years later...

COMRADE

"Alex! Hurry up! We need to get going!" I tell my mate. I check my watch in an annoyed fashion as I push my hand through my long hair. Alex still likes my hair long, even after fifteen years.

"You know, Comrade dearest, you could get your lazy ass up here and help me!" Alex's sharp reply is screamed as I see her standing up at the top of the stairs with her hands planted on her hips.

Ten minutes later and I've helped Alex bring down twelve bags compared to my three.

"Jeez, Alex, where the hell did all this stuff come from?" I question as I wipe the perspiration from my forehead. Of course, our room had to be on the second floor at the end of the hallway.

Alex gives me a cheeky grin before saying in an equally cheeky voice, "Girls gotta pack what girls gotta pack."

I roll my eyes at her answer and go to say a snarky remark back, but I'm stopped when another scream travels through the house.

"Comrade!" Celina's frantic voice travels through the air. I'm instantly looking everywhere for her until I see her burst out of the kitchen door and come barreling towards me. Callum suddenly appears also, but at the top of the stairs. He must've heard Celina's scream.

"Celina? What's wrong?" I rush out as I grab her upper arms and stare into her golden eyes. Even though she's thirty-four, her eyes look as though they're still those innocent sixteen-year-old I met so long ago.

"The boys are chasing me!" she exclaims in fright before two massive figures burst through the kitchen door, almost getting stuck in the process. I roll my eyes when I realise that she's talking about Jett and Dylan. I see Callum relax his stance at the bottom of the stairs as he leans against the rail.

"Celina, the worst they're gonna do is tickle you," I say with a grin. Celina squeals and hides behind me when she sees Jett and Dylan start to advance.

"Comrade!" Celina whimpers behind my back. I take a glance at my watch and sigh. We're late anyway, may as well make us a little later.

I hold up my hand to Jett and Dylan, who instantly stop walking.

"As your guardian and your mother's former guardian, I tell you to stop whatever you're about to do to your mother until I have left pack grounds. You have free reign to her then," I tell them seriously, but a grin breaks out on the last part.

253

Celina whacks my back from behind but steps out into the open nonetheless.

"Thanks, Uncle Comrade! We'll be sure to keep that in mind," Jett says in that deep voice of his with a grin similar to his dad's.

A clearing of a throat suddenly grabs my attention. I turn around to look at Alex as she impatiently taps her foot on the floor.

"Well, thanks to that little occurrence, we are now late! We need to get going!" Alex screams, looking a little frantic. I chuckle at her, deciding to keep my remark about her having a million bags to myself.

Jett and Dylan suddenly grab both Alex and me, then crush us in a hug. We both hug back. I see Alex close her eyes, and a small smile grows on her face. Even though we can't have our own pups, the triplets are pretty close.

"We're gonna miss you, Auntie Alex," Dylan whispers, placing a soft kiss on top of her head.

"Feeling the love over here, boys," I mutter to myself. Since they have both alpha and royal blood in them, though, they hear and say they're gonna miss me too.

We say goodbye to Celina, Callum, and also Axel since he showed up just in time to see us off.

"Okay, everyone, see you in around a year!" I yell as I put the last of our bags in the boot of the car.

Just as I'm about to get into the driver's seat to take Alex and me away, a soft voice from the doorway stops me, "Wait!"

I freeze in my tracks and snap my head towards the door to see a mass of white hair and tears come barreling towards me. Clarissa.

I open my arms and just wait until she launches herself in my waiting arms and buries her head in my chest. She wraps her arms around my waist as I wrap my arms around her shoulders.

"I'm gonna miss you," I tell her, wrapping my arms around her tighter.

I see Alex standing in front of us with a sad smile on her face. She places a hand on Clarissa's shoulder and quietly says, "We'll be back soon. I promise."

Clarissa nods her head and pulls away. I gently wipe the tears from her face and kiss her forehead.

"Can you promise me something? Promise me that no matter what, no matter what is thrown your way, promise me that you'll fight and never give up. Promise me that and I'll leave here happy," I whisper to her, cupping her face with my hands.

Clarissa nods her head while whispering in her beautifully soft voice, "I promise."

CELINA

I wave goodbye to Comrade and Alex as they finally disembark on the way to their worldwide cruise for a year. I sigh as I wrap my arms around Axel's waist and rest my head on his shoulder. I watch as all three of the triplets sag with sadness. I used to have that feeling when everything wrong is happening in my life.

"You know what? We won't even notice they're gone. This year will fly by in no time, and your favourite auntie and uncle will be right back home," I tell the three of them, looking into their beautifully unique eyes. It's unbelievable how strikingly similar we all look, but I wouldn't have it any other way.

"They're our only auntie and uncle," Dylan mutters, making me laugh.

"Come on, guys, cheer up. School starts up soon," Axel tries to cheer them up, but he knows he's torturing them. I slap his chest lightly as Jett and Dylan groan and stomp back inside. Axel laughs loudly as he follows his very annoyed sons into the house. I breathe a happy sigh as I watch Axel continue to torment them. Boys will be boys, I guess. I came to those terms many, many years ago.

I turn around to face Clarissa, only to see her still staring off into the distance where Alex and Comrade left. I place my hands on her shoulders.

"Have I ever told about the story when I first met your uncle Comrade?" I ask her quietly, recalling the day when he came running across the border to stop me. I smile at the memory.

Clarissa nods and says quietly, "Yeah, dad made you cry, and he came and calmed you down then stayed with you."

I chuckle and shake my head.

"No, not that story. That's the second time I had spoken to your uncle. I'm talking about the first," I tell her. I wrap my arm around her shoulder and steer her away from the door.

"It all started when I ran through a certain alpha's territory..."

The End

Can't get enough of Comrade and Alex?
Make sure you sign up for the author's blog
to find out more about them!

Get these two bonus chapters and
more freebies when you sign up at
violet-samuels.awesomeauthors.org!

Here is a sample from another story you may enjoy:

AN IRREVOCABLE DESTINY
A FATE YET TO BE DETERMINED

UNIQUE
DIFFERENT
FOUND

VIOLET SAMUELS

1

CELINA

Have you ever felt like you can never escape? Have you ever felt like there is no one there for you? Have you ever felt like the whole world is against you and you just want to get away and be free? Have you ever felt that you can never be loved or cherished?

That's my life.

I feel all of these things. You can't change what fate has in store for you. But sometimes, I wish I could just be free and live my own life. I haven't been able to do that for a total of nine years.

My mother and father died when I was seven. I was abandoned and left with my godforsaken pack. I had no regrets when my mother and father died. I spent every second of every day with them, and they never argued. We didn't have any major fights, and we all loved each other so much. I didn't think my parents had any regrets either. I think they made the mistake of leaving me alone, though.

You're probably wondering why I'm blaming it on them, aren't you? Well, I don't. I blame my pack for being worthless, unfair, stupid and plain right mean. Childish I know, but true, down to the last detail. Every beating, every bruise, every broken bone and every possible evidence of them abusing me supports that horrid theory.

Ever since my parents died, I've been like a slave to the people I call my pack. I cook, wash, clean, organize and pretty much do everything for them. They throw away money like it's no big deal, and they don't spare a second glance to anyone who's 'lower' than them.

Someone like me.

All the wolves in my pack are gorgeous with either brown or blonde fur and have a mix of either blue, green, brown, or almost black eyes. Having plain blue or green eyes is rare. They have slim or muscular bodies and have the perfect height just to be much taller than humans. Unfortunately, that beauty is tainted by their bitter egos and cold hearts.

My parents were like the pack looks wise, but not personality wise. My parents were kind and thoughtful, always putting others before themselves. They never should've been in this pack in the first place.

The funny thing is, I look nothing like my parents or anyone in the pack for that matter.

Instead of blonde or brown hair, mine is pitch black, pin straight and comes down to just below my shoulders. My eyes are a shining gold that lost its shine many years ago, so now it looks like a light shade of mud. My lips are almost red and, strangely, my skin is pale. I'm not sure why... Werewolves usually have beautifully tanned skin. I'm also a bit shorter than everyone else, but I still have that slim body that anyone would die for. In my parents' opinion, being different is what makes you special. What makes you special, is what makes you unique.

I've never believed it, though. All it has ever done was got me teased, and pushed around for being 'different' and 'unique'. It has always been like that. Even with my parents, they always said the pack was just jealous of my obvious beauty, one that I am oblivious to.

Another thing. When I turned sixteen, I made sure I was far away from the pack house, almost on the borders of our territory. The reason? I was shifting. I didn't want to give everyone the satisfaction of seeing me in pain, and watching my every bone break after the other. I can honestly say that it is the most painful thing you will ever experience in your life.

When I shifted, I discovered that my wolf was snow white. Not one trace of color other than white covered me. I was astounded. I had never seen a white wolf. Even my mother's and my father's wolves were brown and blonde, respectively. They told me that when I shifted never to show to anyone my wolf unless they have my full trust. Nobody has.

I don't know what it means to have a pure white wolf, but I know that I'm different yet again. This time, in a way, I thought I could somehow fit into my pack. I thought wrong. When I came back, I got a beating because I was gone for most of the day, and everyone missed lunch and breakfast. That night, I had to make a three-course meal instead of the usual one, and I had to clean the house until it was spotless. Let's just say I stayed up way past midnight...

I haven't been for a run since. That was three weeks ago. My wolf has been howling in my head, and it feels like she's scratching my insides apart. I badly want to let her out, but I'm too scared. I don't want to get beaten up again.

My wolf has told me multiple times to get away, and I've been considering it for months now. Tonight's the night. I'm leaving. I'm ditching this stupid place and leaving for good. When I told my wolf, she was practically jumping with joy.

I'm making the dinner right now. Although this pack has treated me like nothing, I'm gonna give them something to remember me by, and if that means food, then so be it.

I decide to make one of my favorite courses. For entree, bruschetta with mini prawn cocktails. For main, lasagna with garlic bread. Then for dessert, my personal favorite, chocolate mud cake with whipped cream, ice cream and chocolate covered strawberries on top. If it were me, I would just skip the entree and main and go straight for the dessert.

I set the table for the pack, and as soon as I finish placing the last of the entrees on the table, they walk in through the door. As soon as they get a whiff, they come barging into the dining room, taking a seat and digging in. No 'thank you' or 'this is nice', just like the usual.

I always keep a spare bit of dessert for myself after I finish cooking, so while the rest of the pack eats, I tuck into my mud cake. At least they let me eat, I guess.

When I hear the bell, I walk back out and collect the empty plates, taking them back into the kitchen. To let them digest a bit, I wash it all up and place it on the drying rack.

I come back out with the last of the mains and am about to walk out when Tina, the pack slut, calls my name.

"Celina!"

I slowly turn around, keeping my hands behind my back, and my head bowed. I'm wearing the correct uniform for serving dinner, and my hair is neatly pulled back into a high ponytail, so I'm not sure what she wants. Whenever someone in the pack calls my name, it's usually because I'm in trouble.

"Why the whole 'fancy-fancy' food? Is it a special occasion? Let me guess... Is it for Damon's birthday? A little present from you?" She snickers at me. I feel all eyes turn to me, but I obediently keep my head down. Damon is the soon to be the alpha of our pack and is turning eighteen in about four days. It's a big thing, and I'm supposed to cook for it...

"I guess you could consider it that. If the alpha is kind enough to accept my gift, of course," I answer in a small voice. I was told from the beginning to address Damon as alpha and nothing else, unlike the rest of the pack.

The room falls silent as every eye turns to Damon, who's sitting at the head of the very large dining table. I look through my long, black lashes to see his face. I'm met with a considering expression.

He nods his head once. "I accept your gift. I will expect a grander and more appropriate gift on my actual birthday, though. Do you understand?" His tone's filled with power and authority.

"Yes, Alpha, I understand," I say, returning to my former position with my head down.

"Good. Now, off you go." He shoos me off, and as soon as I enter the kitchen, I hear their laughs and snickers. I will myself not to cry. I've shed too many tears over these heartless people.

They soon finish their meals, and it's time for dessert. I've finished mine by now, so I place theirs on the table with a blank face. They eat up and by the time everyone has finished and has stayed around talking, I've cleared the large table and washed up.

I enter back into the dining room and wait in my usual spot by the door of the kitchen. Every night before I go to bed, I either get hit or nothing for the meals I've cooked. It's the same with breakfast, lunch, and any other meals they eat. As each one walks out of the room, I either get shoved or ignored. Which means they liked my cooking. Tina, on the other hand, slaps me across the face. You probably think that's harsh, but that's equivalent to someone else's shove. So just imagine what someone else's slap is to her. It's not a pretty sight.

Damon is the last to leave, and he stops in front of me. I cautiously lift my head and stare into his beautiful blue-green eyes. He has a blank face, as do I. We stare at each other for a moment before he walks out and leaves me alone in the dining room to fix up.

Damon has been my crush since I was about ten, even though he treats me like the worthless thing I am. His brown hair and blue-green eyes are the main aspects that draw many other female wolves in and me. He hasn't found his mate yet either, which means he's available. He wouldn't go for me, though. Not in a million years. I'm too different.

I head to bed in the early hours of the night. The pack no longer requires me after about 7:30 pm, so I am ordered to bed, which I quickly oblige, so as not to get beaten. I still have bruises from the worst ones.

The sad thing is, I believe everything my pack had said since my parents died. That I'm not beautiful, but ugly. That I'm not unique, but different. That I'm not a part of their family, but their slave.

I sigh as I enter my makeshift room. It's bare, except for a large window that lets the moonlight from the full moon flood into my room. My bed is pretty much a sheet on the hard, splintered, wooden floor, and my pillow is a pillow cover stuffed with newspaper.

I won't be sleeping there tonight, though. Not anymore. Not ever again.

I pack what little belongings I have inside a sack. A pair of worn out jeans, an oversized shirt with holes in it, a skirt, one other shirt that appears to be clean, and a pair of socks. I don't own any shoes.

I grab the only piece of jewelry I have, my mother's silver necklace, with her and my father's names engraved into the heart-shaped pendant. The pendant has a yin and yang symbol in it, but it's made with little black and white crystals. I slip it into my shirt and proceed to the window.

I open it wide, and without a glance back, or second thought, I jump. I jump to my freedom and my new life.

I shift into my snow white wolf and take off with my sac in my mouth. I don't know where I'm going. I don't know if I can survive. I am only a newly shifted wolf at the age of sixteen.

What I do know? I'll never have to see my 'pack' again. That is enough to make me smile slightly in my wolf form. As I cross the border of the territory, my wolf lets out a howl, filled with happiness and joy.

We're free. I'm free.

Never again will we have to face the Moonlight pack.

If you enjoyed this sample then look for **Unique, Different, Found** on Amazon!

Other books you might enjoy:

Break Me, Mate
Nique Joaquin

Available on Amazon!

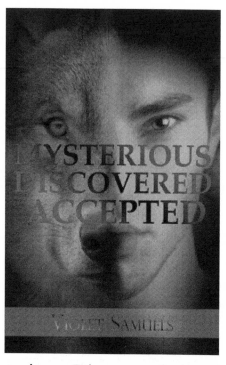

Mysterious, Discovered, Accepted
Violet Samuels

Available on Amazon!

Introducing the Characters Magazine App

Download the app to get the free issues of interviews from famous fiction characters and find your next favorite book!

iTunes: bit.ly/CharactersApple
Google Play: bit.ly/CharactersAndroid

Acknowledgements

This story is a work of fiction. Everything from the plot to the characters have all been created by my imagination and solely that. I thought one day, why not write down one of the stories going through my head? So I did and look where that got me.

Firstly, I would like to thank my friends. They were there for me when I first started writing this book and they were there when I finished it. They have been my rock and I'll be forever grateful to them for it. They never gave up on me and when I gave up on myself, they hauled me back up and pushed me to go on.

I would like to thank my parents and older brother. They supported me every step of the way with enthusiasm and happiness. I'm glad they were with me on the journey that I didn't even know I was walking down. They halted their plans to encourage me and motivate me to get this book published and I will always love them with all my heart for that. So, to my parents and brother, thank you so so much because without you, I wouldn't be here.

I would also like to thank my dedicated and amazing readers on Wattpad. If it wasn't for them, my book never would've hit one million reads and it probably would've never been published. They helped me to continue writing and not give up when writers block got in the way. They were always there with their amazing encouragements and awesome attitudes. Thanks Wattpad and I hope you guys continue to achieve the max.

One of the most important people in the process of publishing this story though, was my agent Le-an Lacaba. She's been a wonderful agent, always being there to help me through the process and actually giving me the unimaginable opportunity to have my story published. She helped me overcome fears and uncertainties along the way. I will always hold her close to my heart for everything she's done for me. Thank you Le-an and

I wish for you to have unmeasurable success in the future.

Everyone in my life has helped me write, create and publish this story and I couldn't be happier. It makes me cry knowing that all these people have given me the opportunity to do something I never believed I could do.

So, I don't have one specific person to thank for everything, but I have an immense amount of wonderful, inspiring and thoughtful people to thank because without all the people involved, I never would've achieved what I have today.

I love you all and you will always be close to my heart. Thank you so much and please, never forget the amazing fortune you have given me to be able to publish. For everything everyone has done, I am eternally grateful.

Thank you and I love you,
Violet

Author's Note

Hey there!

Thank you so much for reading Forgotten, Saved, Loved! I can't express how grateful I am for reading something that was once just a thought inside my head.

I'd love to hear from you! Please feel free to email me at violet_samuels@awesomeauthors.org and sign up at violet-samuels.awesomeauthors.org for freebies!

One last thing: I'd love to hear your thoughts on the book. Please leave a review on Amazon or Goodreads because I just love reading your comments and getting to know YOU!

Whether that review is good or bad, I'd still love to hear it!

Can't wait to hear from you!

Violet Samuels

About the Author

Violet Samuels lives in Australia, being half Australian and half Portuguese, and is a young girl/woman that is still in her youth. Even for being young, she's never lived in one place for more than two years.

However, the favourite place she has lived was on the Whitsunday's.Violet loved the Whitsunday's because it's where Unique Different Found all began and it's where her friends convinced her to go for it and have a go. Look at where that's brought her.

Violet Samuels is a bubbly and energetic girl/woman who is kind, caring and has a big heart. She loves to dance, sing and act and can't wait for so many people to read her book to let them escape from the rest of the world, even just for a little while.

Sign up to her blog for more freebies and updates!

violet-samuels.awesomeauthors.org

Made in the USA
Middletown, DE
30 March 2018